The Beirut Pipeline

THE BEIRUT

Farrar Straus Giroux   New York

PIPELINE

A NOVEL BY Ray Alan

Copyright © 1980 by Ray Alan
All rights reserved
Printed in the United States of America
Published simultaneously in Canada
by McGraw-Hill Ryerson Ltd., Toronto
Designed by Karen Watt
First edition, 1980

Library of Congress Cataloging in Publication Data
Alan, Ray. The Beirut Pipeline.
1. Title.
PZ4.A322Be   1980   [PR6051.L2]   823'.9'14   79-23972
ISBN 0-374-11018-2

To Mike Kolatch and *The New Leader*

Secrets with girls, like loaded guns with boys,
Are never valued till they make a noise.

—George Crabbe (1754–1832)

We'll leave it alone. It's the only secret service that earns any money.

—Clement R. Attlee
(British Prime Minister, 1945–51)

The police forces of the Syrian and Lebanese republics are divided into two bodies, the civil police and the gendarmery . . . The weakness of the two forces is the tendency to abuse of power and neglect of duties.

—*Naval Intelligence Handbook BR 513*
(The Admiralty, London)

The Beirut Pipeline

1

The first time I read Arnold's letter I thought one of us had lost his memory. I read it again and it began, disquietingly, to make sense. I typed another sentence of the article I was working on, crossed it out, and returned to the letter. I decided to show it to O'Neill.

"You'll be popular!" O'Neill's secretary said. "It's half-past twelve." Through her window I could hear the hungry snarl of a lunchtime traffic jam. She stood up and began locking away her trays and carbons, wiggling a bit in case I hadn't noticed her almost luminous yellow stretch pants.

She was a lissome Scots girl named Heather. Three months before, on her arrival from London, she had seemed Britain's answer to the Japanese cuddly-toy invasion. Her long, fair hair and silken complexion made everyone want to stroke her. Now, after twelve weeks of Cyprus sun, she looked like a smoked salmon. She was hooked on the sun. She walked on the sunny side of the street, sunbathed in the parched garden of the villa in which we had our offices, and grew a new skin every other week.

O'Neill was putting his jacket on and wearing that determined man-of-action look he had when he was thinking of a brandy sour.

I said: "You know Arnold Amery, don't you?"

"Not very well. I've met him at one or two parties, and in that club they have in Beirut." He screwed in his monocle and scowled at the letter. When he had read it he opened his eyes wide and caught the monocle in his left hand. "Are you really thinking of leaving us?"

"This is the first I've heard of it."

He sat behind his desk, waved me to an armchair, and reinserted his monocle. He read the letter again. Then he looked at his watch and said: "I suppose we'd better talk about this now. I'm going to Limassol after lunch; and most of tomorrow, as you know, I'll be leaning over the rails of the U.S.S. *Franklin D. Roosevelt.*"

"Don't even try," I said. "It hasn't got any."

He sighed. "There's still time for you to volunteer to do this feature on the Sixth Fleet. You know how you love boats and helicopter rides; and you can swim."

"The admiral would be offended. You're the bureau chief. They're still fighting the class war at sea. Besides, I'm up to my gills in the Arab League donnybrook."

"Don't be too hard on the Arab League. Remember we invented it."

"That's ancient history."

"For us, maybe. We've outgrown imperialism and moved on. We don't need accessories like the Arab League any more. But the Arabs are stuck with it." He tickled his squawk box. "A spot of lubricant? I'm parched . . . Heather, are you still with us? Be a doll and rustle up a couple of brandy sours."

The squawk box said something about lemons.

"Again!" O'Neill exclaimed. "God help us! Is this Cyprus or Siberia? . . . Of course they keep! . . . Well, tell Nikko to plant a lemon tree, then. In the meantime, bring us a cool siphon."

In his youth, O'Neill had lived in Bonn, and his appearance and manners had Germanic as well as Anglo-Irish facets. He had short hair of the color you would get if you mixed sand and cigar ash. His face was square and smooth, and—unless he was very relaxed—about as expressive as a stone wall. His eyes were gray. He dressed neatly and—overlooking the monocle, if possible—inconspicuously.

Before joining our organization he worked at Leconfield House, headquarters of the British Security Service.* He was

* What the British press calls "MI5" or "DI5." (Neither abbreviation

glad to come to us because, as he put it, "an Irishman in the Security Service feels at times like a security man in Ireland: there are too many memories." Our head office liked him because he somehow combined the instincts of a security man with the flair of a journalist. London thought him a splendid example to neophytes like me.

He gave me a one-man security show now. First, he unplugged his telephone. Then, he switched on a portable air-conditioning unit London had recently supplied—not in order to keep us cool, but because it incorporated a powerful bug-jamming device. Finally, he lowered the wooden shutter outside his office window—in case the old lady across the street was listening to our conversation with the aid of a laser beam sensitive to vibrations in the pane.

When Heather, tight-faced and even redder than usual, brought us the siphon, O'Neill took a bottle and glasses out of his old carved corner cupboard. He liked furniture with a history or at least an anecdote behind it. His desk had belonged to a German general and his chair to a murdered Syrian dictator; he had acquired the cupboard from a Cypriot priest in exchange for a Smith & Wesson revolver.

"Brandy, Heather?" he asked, knowing what her reply would be.

"No, thank you."

"I'm serious about that lemon tree, you know. Tell Nikko to plant it just outside this window." He pursed his lips slightly, to warn us that a legpull was coming, and added: "You'll be able to sit in its shade in your free moments instead of sweltering in the sun."

Her face relaxed. "I love the sun."

"It's a dangerous love. The local girls stay in the shade."

"They weren't brought up in Kilmarnock."

She gave us a quick smile and went to her lunch.

---

means anything: the service is not under military control.) Leconfield House is on Curzon Street, London W1.

5

O'Neill poured two tall brandy-and-sodas. He said: "A citrus tree can make a good screen against laser eavesdropping and long-range mikes. But let's talk about Amery. You know him pretty well, don't you?"

"I used to, when I worked in Beirut."

"He was working for the Sisters,* too, wasn't he?"

"Not as a hired hand."

O'Neill looked doubtful. "Are you sure?"

"I saw his mife once." (A mife or microfiche is a condensed personal file.) "There was no accounts-code entry. Anyway, he didn't need the Sisters' money. His income from Levant Mining & Chemicals was four times that of the SIS area officer, even on the new scale."

"But he was given assignments?"

"He helped me with a few inquiries. What else he did, I don't know."

"When you left the Sisters, did you discuss with Amery your reasons for leaving?"

"No. I might have if I'd seen him, but Beirut was no longer my base and we'd been out of touch for nearly a year."

"Is he still in touch with the Sisters?"

"I can't say. It's possible."

"He was never afflicted with your moral collywobbles?"

"Not really," I said. O'Neill waited, looking into his glass, so I went on: "He was a lot more experienced than I, and I doubt if he's ever been as naïve as I was in those days. The things that steadily disillusioned me—things like the waste of resources, the petty corruption, the feuding and incomp—"

"I know, I know. Don't get worked up."

"Well, all that irritated him from time to time, but the way a Catholic is irritated by a corrupt priest—without losing his faith. His confidence in Broadway† never seemed to waver."

* Our term for the British Secret Intelligence Service (SIS).
† Broadway Buildings, in southwest London: then the headquarters of the SIS.

O'Neill chuckled. "We'd better recruit him fast before he takes holy orders. He sounds the type the service relied on in the thirties: the ex-officer-businessman who did his stuff for kicks . . . and, sometimes, a sense of duty. I thought the species was extinct. But you'd better take me through this now." He pushed Arnold's letter across the desk.

I read it again:

> You'll remember my telling you, the last time you were in Beirut, that I was thinking of recruiting someone to handle our public (and other) relations and act as my private trouble-shooter. I gathered you were tired of routine journalism and might be interested in a job of this kind.
>
> I now feel I must take a decision as soon as possible and I'd be very grateful if you could come to Beirut within the next ten days to talk about it. Don't resign from *Outlook*—I don't want O'Neill after my blood. Might they release you (unpaid leave?) for a few weeks so that you can make a study of our problems and needs before committing yourself?
>
> We're passing through a critical period. Good teamwork and your and O'Neill's special knowledge of these things could make a vital difference.
>
> See you soon?

"The first paragraph," I said, "had me worried. Then I remembered that 'You'll' at the beginning of a personal letter used to be what we called a traffic sign. It meant that an important subject was being raised. The first paragraph would be camouflage—it might be fiction—though it would contain some indication of what the writer wanted. The rest was to be taken seriously."

"So what's bothering Amery?"

"He's run into trouble—something too big for him to handle alone, something he thinks will interest us. He wants me to go to Beirut as soon as poss, get the facts, and report to you with a view to calling the Team in."

"The Team" was our term for Tossteam, the service we

worked for. The name Tossteam—an acronym—originated the day Prime Minister Clement Attlee described it as "the only secret service that earns any money." Tossteam owned the weeklies *Outlook* and *Insight* and other publishing, television, and advertising interests.

O'Neill took back the letter. "I'm not happy about his using the word 'teamwork.' "

"He's been in the intelligence community long enough to be able to guess I'm probably working for the Team."

"And long enough to know that he shouldn't drop heavy allusions like that in a letter. It's bad security—and a little too flip for my taste. It was enough to mention my name twice to let you know where he hoped you'd go for reinforcements. Which brings us to the big question: Why is he asking for our assistance? Why hasn't he approached the Sisters?"

"Maybe he has, and his problem's outside their repertoire."

"Ask him about that if you go to see him."

"If?"

O'Neill drained his glass. "This is a personal letter. Let's keep Amery's problem on that level until we know more. We can't bring the Team into play every time an old pal gets a parking ticket or discovers his girlfriend's bugged. If this thing is so important, why didn't Amery come to Cyprus and talk to us?"

"Levant Mining & Chemicals is a family firm and Arnold runs it as his father did. Perhaps he just couldn't get away. Or maybe the problem itself is pinning him down. I've a feeling it's something serious. He's not a scaremonger."

"I'm not saying he is. But I'd like to know more about his relations with the Sisters. You know the directives we've had about not interfering with each other's maidens." He snapped his mouth shut for a moment and glared up at the ceiling. "Take that grin off your face, Sigmund." He looked at me again. "I was intending to say 'middens,' I swear. To come back to Amery: If, say, he's quarreled with the Sisters and they're causing a bit of unpleasantness for him, we can't intervene. I don't want to lose my pension."

"So you don't want me to go to Beirut?"

He sighed. "I didn't say that. I don't see any immediate need for you to go to Beirut on official business. But I wouldn't object if you asked for three or four days' leave and flew there to discuss with your old friend the possibility of his giving you a PR job. If you met any other acquaintances in Beirut and told them that was why you were there—fine! If you found that Amery had got onto something of real interest to us, with no sisterly complications, I would tear up your leave application, open a file, and give you an assignment."

"Will you pay my fare and expenses?"

"Of course—if your trip becomes an assignment."

"I can't take the risk. Anyway, I haven't the fare in my bank account. I told you about the boat I'm buying."

He shook his head. "Dangerous things! Remember that CIA chap who was drowned."

"He did have a little help."

"Perhaps. It was never proved."

"Pity. About Beirut, I mean. It might have been interesting to know . . . But I mustn't delay your lunch." I stood up.

O'Neill got up, too, and tucked his monocle into an inside pocket, looking at me thoughtfully. After a pause, he said: "All right, MacScrooge. Lock the door. I'll give you the fare. But you pay your own expenses."

I bolted the door. He opened his safe, took out a cashbox, and gave me the fare plus five pounds.

"Buy the ticket yourself," he said, "not through the office. Book for next Tuesday's flight. I'll have recovered from the Sixth Fleet by then. Ask Sam to take over the Arab League. Cable Amery this afternoon to tell him you're coming. Word it as if you're taking his job offer seriously." He locked the cashbox and returned it to his safe. "Amery's not married, is he?"

"No."

"Yet he's well off, sociable, reasonably good-looking . . ."

"Lots of people consider marriage a declining industry."

"I once heard it suggested—only suggested—that he might be—"

"I've stayed with him twice and I'm still undeflowered. Is the extra fiver danger money?"

"No. It's an entertainment allowance. I'd like you to buy a couple of drinks on the Beirut plane. One for you and one for that Russian geologist you got on so well with at the mining congress."

"Strogonov?"

"He's leaving Cyprus on Tuesday—for Beirut. I learned yesterday that a seat had been booked for him. I hadn't intended to do anything about it, but as you're keen to go to Beirut it seems a good idea for you to travel on the same plane." Now I knew why he was paying my fare. He added: "I've a hunch Strogonov's more important than we think. So resume your chitchat, try to meet him for drinks or a meal in Beirut—"

"So long as the Kremlin pays."

"You won't guzzle the whole fiver on the plane. Anyway, remember your orientation course. Russian official contacts should always be cultivated; one never knows when they may pay off. Now that the Russians are in the market for Western credits and technology, they're more approachable."

On the orientation course they also told you that "adequate resources" would always be available for the cultivation of Russian contacts. The only resources I could flash in front of Strogonov were five pounds and Heather's telephone number.

I said: "Cast thy bread upon the waters."

"Quite." He liked biblical quotations.

"But all I've got is breadcrumbs."

"Breadcrumbs are fine. You mustn't appear too affluent."

"Should I wear shoes or my old beach sandals?"

"If you'd prefer to stay here and write about the Sixth Flee—"

10

"I'll see Polydora after lunch," I said quickly. "If the comrade's traveling alone, she'll get me the seat next to his."

"Good."

"It's too hot for chocolates so I'll have to slip her a bottle of eau de cologne. The trouble is, she likes the expensive stuff."

"That's all right." He smiled generously. "Buy it out of the fiver."

2

Strogonov was a stocky, sociable man with a young face and graying hair. He seemed to be traveling alone. Our contact at Cyprus Airways had given me the seat adjoining his, but I walked slowly past it, as if looking for another, until I saw he had recognized me. We shook hands and I pointed to the seat and said: "May I?"

"Of course. It seems to be free." He spoke English correctly but hesitantly and appeared eager to practice it.

We got along fine. I nodded politely when he said the Labour Party was the petit bourgeois wing of British conservatism. He nodded politely when I said Soviet "socialism" was essentially state capitalism. We talked about the Mideast cabaret circuit and I explained how naïve working-class girls are ensnared in it by wicked bourgeois impresarios. We agreed to have dinner together and, perhaps, do a little research.

When I told him the Stanhope Club would take telephone messages for me, he asked: "What does that mean— Stanhope?"

"It's the name of an eccentric Englishwoman who lived in south Lebanon a century and a half ago."

"Everywhere," he said, "I hear of eccentric Englishwomen. The Arabs say to me: 'What kind of men are these English that they let their women roam around, provoking scandals, instead of keeping them at home to cook and have babies?' "

We reached Beirut soon after sunset. Lights were flashing on and the city glittered like a jeweler's display along the base of its gray mountain. Strogonov did not have diplomatic status and walked with me through the passport control and customs. Two dour-looking men were waiting for him at the far end of the customs hall. I took care not to show any interest in them or their car in case he had an escort on the plane who might be keeping me under observation.

I cashed a traveler's check and bought an evening paper with big banner headlines. Then I asked a taxi driver to take me to the Stanhope Club.

The headlines proclaimed that the paper's star commentator had been murdered the night before and recalled that he had been running a campaign against corruption. The last time a journalist had been murdered in Lebanon the United States Sixth Fleet had had to intervene to glue the country together again. I asked the taxi driver if there was going to be another civil war.

"Not unless the cabaret girls start something," he said. He spoke English with the singsong Lebanese-American accent of the returned emigrant. "Everybody knows it was Lili who had it done."

I asked who Lili might be.

I saw him looking at me, pityingly, in his mirror. "The cabaret singer. She was his girlfriend. They quarreled. Everybody knows that. And his boss—the owner of the paper—took her over. Everybody knows that, too. So the boss pretends it's a political murder to cover Lili. He probably helped her hire the killers. Everybody says so."

The street lights flashed by too fast for me to read the details, and Arabic small print gets in my hair at the best of times, so I asked him how it had happened. He told me the columnist had, as usual, left his car at about 3 a.m. in an all-night garage two or three hundred yards from where he lived and gone on home on foot. He had an apartment on one of those quiet narrow streets that crawl obliquely uphill from the waterfront district. Their seaward side is precipitous in places; where no building can be perched there is a low parapet and, beyond it, the sort of drop down which many an awkward problem has been discarded. The columnist had been found in a scrapyard beneath one such gap with a dent in his head.

13

"It was bound to happen," the taxi driver went on, "after he made that scene outside her dressing room. Everybody says so." He braked outside the Stanhope Club. "It's a big affair. All the top Western newspapermen will be pouring in soon." As I paid him he peered at me. "Are you a newspaperman?"

"Yes."

"I knew it. I've driven every important Western newshound there is. Smell 'em a mile off. Are you an important one?"

"No."

"Ah, well . . . We all have to make a start. But here's your big break! Be the first to interview Lili! Western papers love stories like this one. They don't waste space on politics like ours do. But ours are learning. Take this affair: they're giving it as much space as the best Western papers would."

The Olde English Taverne in the basement of the Stanhope Club was the creation of an Armenian decorator whose knowledge of Olde England came from Hollywood. Its bar was a monument of oak and dark-red leather that had been studded with brass nailheads and expertly kicked about to give it a patina of age and rusticity. There were barstools to match, and two brass spittoons whose use would have provoked an emergency general meeting. A thatch canopy over the bar added a Congolese touch. In a big gilt-framed painting, huntsmen, horses, hounds, and fox alike gaped in bewilderment at the thatch, the arak, the Cyprus brandy, and the sleek olive-skinned barman: some evening, after the right amount of pink gin, someone would be sure to transfer them to the library, to the more congenial company of *Country Life* and *News of the World.*

The inmates were at work on the columnist's death as I walked in. "Frightful," an auburn-haired woman was saying. "The parapet's exactly fifteen inches high. No railing or anything."

The barman, who remembered me, grinned and served me

14

an arak and a saucer of olives. Gently, I added water to the arak, watched the two clear liquids meet to weave their usual white magic, and waited a moment to enjoy the cool aniseed fragrance and see what it did to the foxhounds in the painting. It was a club rule that if ever they snarled at you, you must leave the bar.

On my right, an oldish professorial type was lecturing a pale young woman on the formalities to be observed when you pushed someone over a cliff in these parts. "If some tactless policeman does ask an embarrassing question too many, his officer's price will generally be reasonable. And senior officials and politicians offer the resourceful man a second line of defense. It's rarely necessary for the private citizen to strain after ministerial favors—except as an investment."

His audience said something. I caught the word "Levantine."

"Levantine . . ." echoed the lecturer. "Isn't that a matter of perspective? I imagine our House of Lords and Honors Lists look pretty Levantine to most outsiders."

I looked around the room in search of a familiar face. My head felt suddenly as if something inside it had short-circuited. I found myself staring at a goddess: a vision in blue and gold, radiant on a dark-red throne.

I inspected my arak. Half of it was still there and the foxhounds were still ignoring me. I took a deep breath and looked again. This time I saw a blonde in a club chair. A blonde who had picked the perfect dress to counterpoint the melody of her hair and eyes, and the right setting for her masterpiece.

Her hair splashed over her shoulders in a golden cascade. Her face might have been Nordic or Mediterranean—southern in its smoothly rounded outline, with a hint of the north in the cheeks and eyes. They were large eyes, thoughtful and alert, and their blue was the blue of cornflowers in an Alpine meadow. Her eyebrows were long, widely spaced, unusually straight. A firm nose and chin suggested determination but not brashness. Her mouth was small, almost coy. Her tanned arms

15

and legs looked as if they had been designed by Michelangelo—and from the attitude of the acolytes around her I guessed that the rest of her matched.

The goddess said: "I'm afraid I sympathize with Lili . . . if Lili is really guilty, and if she did it herself: I trust she did—there are certain intimate things that one ought never to do by proxy." It was a cool voice, unhurried and mellifluous—honey with a slight Central European tang. The vowels were just a little too pure, the consonants too precise.

I stayed tuned to her frequency. A little later she said: "If Lili is arrested we must form a committee to defend her. She is an artist. To dump an obsolescent admirer in a scrapyard—what integrity!"

"I say! You'd better look out, Denbor!" an acolyte exclaimed hopefully.

"Denny is safe enough," the goddess said. "The worst he has ever done is bring me here." She smiled at an impassive rabbit-faced man perched stiffly on a straight-backed chair beside her. He had sandy hair, careful blue-gray eyes, and a thin-lipped, rather priggish, mouth. He looked as if he had the embassy laundrymark tattooed on his chest.

"The club's not that bad," he said primly.

I took to my arak and olives. Blondes always seem to throw themselves away on some jerk. I tried not to listen as the conversation meandered off to Lili's relations with the dead columnist's employer. The hell with Lili. She was probably a blonde, too. Soon they were talking in more general terms about superfluous newsmen.

An oilman said: "One journalist who ought to be consigned to a scrapyard is this Ray Alan who writes about the Mideast in—"

I swallowed the wrong way and made a noise like an asthmatic hippo. The barman coughed.

"I'm inclined to agree," Denbor said. "The trouble with so many foreign correspondents is that . . ."

16

The goddess looked bored. She would have heard Denbor's views on the press before. She uncrossed her legs slowly and tugged at her skirt, the way a woman wearing a short skirt always does, as if it had suddenly shrunk on her.

I heard someone cross the floor behind me, pause, and gasp. A hand like a tennis racquet patted me on the shoulder. A French voice exclaimed: "Ray Alan! Since 'ow long are you in town? You should 'ave let me know."

The people nearest us gaped. The barman mopped his brow. I beamed at the newcomer. He was a big man with rugged friendly features and a chin so broad his face was a rectangle. The brown eyes and smile would have charmed a boa constrictor. He didn't have hair—just black sisal matting.

"*Salud,*" I said. "You are Comrade Abruti of the French delegation, *no es verdad?* I am the delegate from Venezuela: José Antonio López-Pérez Pérez-López y Fulano de Tal."

"B-b-but . . ."

I asked him why the Soviet envoy had not yet arrived. The embassy boys froze like gun dogs. "But this is the Levant Labor Club, no?"

The goddess leaned forward and her gaze held mine for a moment. The glow of an orange lantern gleamed in her hair like a passionate promise. It was time for me to go. I was seeing things. The hounds would be after me next.

The Frenchman twigged at last, took my arm and led me from the bar, explaining that this was not the Labor Club. In the corridor outside we shook hands. Then we went upstairs to the big loggia adjoining the lounge and asked a waiter to bring us arak. The loggia was lit only by the glow of the lounge and we had it to ourselves. We sat in wicker armchairs in its farthest corner, overlooking the black-and-silver bay.

I said: "Julien, you brute, it's good to see you, but you might have had me disemboweled. There's a man down there comes out in a rash at the mere mention of my name."

He shook his head. "*Ah! Les Anglais!* Always at each

other's throat. Even so, this is paradise compared with the French club."

"What's happened there? Is the toilet still out of order?"

"It's overrun with locals. French-Lebanese friendship and all that. The place looks like a bazaar. One gets enough of that in daily life 'ere. One's club should be a replica of 'ome, to which one can retire to avoid becoming levantinized. The English 'ave the right idea about that."

"I wonder. Mental inbreeding is as dangerous as the physical kind. It's the heterogeneous cultures that are the most dynamic. Look at America."

He snorted. "Look at America! Dope in every school, mugging in every back street. That's not dynamism, it's delirium . . . *Merde!* Forgive me. I was forgetting you are 'alf American. You should wear a gun to remind your friends of your antecedents. It is not fair just to sit there and look normal."

A man in his late forties wearing a dark suit came out of the lounge, looked around the loggia as if he was thinking of buying the place, noticed us, nodded, and withdrew. He was lean and broad-shouldered, with fair hair, brown eyes, and a short mustache. I knew his face but couldn't label it.

"Colonel Blane," Julien said.

"I thought his face was familiar. I've met him in Cyprus."

Julien looked at me suspiciously. "This town is crawling with British Intelligence officers."

The waiter served our drinks. I said: "It's well known that French diplomats in the Levant blame the British and American secret services every time their embassy cat has kittens; but you're not a diplomat—you know the facts of life. Anyway, Blane was a transport officer. He's probably come here to drive a truck for one of the oil companies. They pay well enough."

"Your friend Arnold Amery was in Intelligence."

I groaned. "He worked for the British Mideast Office, an offshoot of the Foreign Office, in his youth, but only for a couple of years. He found its social life too alcoholic and its policies too pro-Communist for his tastes."

18

"Pro-Communist? Ah! You mean Philby and 'is friends*
. . ."

"And a few other dogmatists and deadbeats whose bungling favored Soviet interests."

"So now Arnold is just another inoffensive apolitical British businessman . . ."

"Come off it, Julien! You're in business here, too. I'm sure Arnold isn't running around insinuating that you're working for the Sdec." (The Sdec is the principal French external secret service: Service de documentation éxtérieure et de contre-espionnage.)

He grinned. *"Touché!"*

"Confidentially, the main reason I'm here now is that Arnold would like me to make Beirut my base and help him with his firm's public relations—in particular, press relations. He's never got used to the idea that when a local journalist makes hostile noises all he usually wants is an office job for a semiliterate relative."

"Or just straight baksheesh," Julien said bitterly. "That happened to my firm two months ago. I paid, of course. What else can one do? The locals 'ave used independence not to liberate themselves but to elevate baksheesh to the dignity of an institution. Beirut 'as become a pipeline for every kind of rottenness the region produces. I settled 'ere because I really wanted to 'elp these people. Now all I want is to make a packet and get out."

"How's your little bucket shop doing?"

"Booming. I 'ave a new showroom. You must come and see it tomorrow." He looked at his watch. "But let us talk of more serious things. My wife is spending the summer in Brummana. I go there Saturday and Sunday. The rest of the week I am a

---

* H. A. R. Philby, a senior officer of the British Secret Intelligence Service who turned out to be a Soviet agent. He and his friends played an important part in orientating British Intelligence and propaganda activities in the Near East in the late 1940s and early 1950s.

monk. So, since monks generally do themselves well, let us 'ave dinner at the Lucullus and—"

"It's a kind thought, but Arnold proposes to take me to some waterfront dive he's discovered. La Sirène. Do you know it?"

"I've 'eard of it." He looked surprised. "But are you going there with 'im tonight?"

"All being well."

"*Pardon,* but when did you arrange this?"

"I cabled him last week to say I'd be arriving this evening. He sent me a telex message the next day saying he'd meet me here and take me to La Sirène. Why?"

"Because I 'eard 'e 'ad gone to Alep."

"When did he leave?"

"About four days ago, by car. It is a fatiguing journey at this season, so I assumed that 'e will stay there a week or two."

"Arnold doesn't mind a long drive; and he's got his new Rover to play with."

Julien shuddered. "It is red. Like the *camion des pompiers.* I thought Rover—and Arnold—were sober people."

"If you break down on the Syrian steppe, it's better to be in something as bright as a fire truck than—"

"Wise people don't gallivant around the Syrian steppe nowadays." He finished his arak and stood up. "Well, since you refuse to dine with me, I abandon you. But we must 'ave lunch tomorrow. Come to the office at twelve for an aperitif and I'll give you some real *zahlawi.** Bring Arnold if he's free." He held out a massive paw. *"A demain!"*

In the lounge, loudspeakers began to throb with a treacly Turkish tango, and soon, through the open french window, I could see two couples dancing. There was a muffled explosion out in the bay. Lanterns were moving over the water. It was illegal to

* Arak from the Lebanese town of Zahle.

fish with explosives—so you crossed the right palm with a gold pound and everyone agreed your engine had backfired.

A woman's heels pecked at the floor of the loggia. It was the goddess. She walked slowly to the end wall and leaned over it, gazing at the starlit bay, lightly tapping the top of the wall in time with the tango beat.

Laughter rippled out from the lounge. The goddess turned, took a few steps, and halted. Blane, the former transport officer, was talking to another man just inside the french window. The goddess stood there, staring at Blane, her face and the front of her body aglow in the lights of the lounge. I saw her in profile, and it was a profile I could have gazed at all night. She seemed to be appraising Blane—or trying to identify him. Her eyes studied his face and build, followed his hand as he made a gesture, and went to his face again.

Blane noticed her and moved aside to let her pass, barely glancing at her as she walked by. The other man stared after her ravenously.

The club receptionist, a neat, brisk Armenian girl, came into view just beyond Blane. I went to the french window. Her fine dark eyes smiled when they saw me.

"Ah, Mr. Alan! I was afraid you had gone. There is a telephone call for you. From Mr. Amery."

Blane looked surprised, as if he thought the goddess and I had been canoodling out there. I followed the receptionist across the lounge and downstairs to the ground floor.

"The phone booth is out of order," she said. "Please take the call in my office."

She shut the office door behind me and stayed out in the lobby, but it was only a formality: the broad reception hatch beside her desk, which gave onto the lobby, was wide open. I picked up the unhooked telephone receiver.

"Ray?" Arnold's voice said. "Sorry to be so late getting in touch. I had trouble with the car. I had to leave it in Aleppo and come back by air, and I couldn't get a plane until this evening.

21

"What act?"

"Ondine's. When she— But I was forgetting you haven't seen her. I mustn't give away the surprise ending."

I looked at him. He was a big man—my height but beefier than I and about fifteen years older. His age was beginning to show. His back and shoulders drooped slightly, and his hair was thinner than I remembered. His broad face, normally a robust face that smiled easily, looked in the starlight, not only pale, but anxious.

He went on: "Before we go in, I want to thank you for responding so promptly to my SOS. You must have thought me frightfully presumptuous, or panicky, urging you to drop everything and dash to Beirut. But I'm in a vise. I've very little room for maneuver. How did O'Neill react?"

"He didn't like your using the word 'teamwork.' "

"I ought to have known that would get his back up; but I wanted to stress that I needed more than your personal help."

"And he wondered why you approached us rather than the Firm.* O'Neill's very scrupulous about—"

"The Firm's not involved. Unofficially, it knows about the situation that's troubling me; officially, it neither knows nor cares. I can understand its reticence. It's burned its fingers enough in the Middle East; and it has an official status in the eyes of governments and police services that O'Neill and his friends aren't encumbered with. If someone connected with O'Neill set off a bomb—forgive the extreme example—only the culprit would suffer if he were caught. When someone connected with the Firm behaves rashly, we risk a diplomatic incident and economic reprisals."

"Which is one reason why O'Neill's in business, I suppose. You mentioned a bomb. Is the action you're hoping for in that category?"

"Not really. But—"

A taxi emerged from the alley and deposited three men far-

* Members (and ex-members) of the British Secret Intelligence Service refer to it, among themselves, as "the Firm."

24

ther along the quayside. They stared at us and went into La Sirène. The taxi sped away.

Arnold picked up his bag. "People will think we're waiting for a boat. We'd better move before the port police take an interest in us."

"Can we talk in there?"

"I don't think it's bugged. The diplomats and politicians haven't discovered it yet."

The arched doorway was open, and as we went through it a small sallow man came toward us, rubbing his hands. He said: "*Ahlan wa sahlan!* Welcome!"

"This is the owner of La Sirène," Arnold told me. He continued in Arabic: "*Salaam alekum.* My friend has come all the way from Cyprus to see La Sirène . . . and Ondine. Are you expecting her?"

The little man smiled and shrugged. "The night seems auspicious. Is your friend a journalist?"

I asked Arnold: "What's the Arabic for 'psychic'?"

The little man heard his reply and chuckled. He told me: "You do not dress like a diplomat or a businessman, and your face is too frank for either profession; and you travel much." He pointed to the abrasions and tattered labels on my suitcase. "There are no oilmen in Cyprus. So I think you are a journalist."

He clapped his hands, told a waiter to put our bags in his office, and led us into the restaurant. It was a big L-shaped room, occupying the whole seaward end of the house and the side that looked onto the quay. At the joint of the L, a piano, a microphone, and a few chairs stood on a low triangular stage. The walls were white and decorated with strips of net, shells, starfish, sea urchins, twists of rope, small anchors, and copper lanterns. The lighting was discreet, not the neon smack in the eye Beirut usually inflicts. Dress was European. There were few women.

Arnold had reserved a table beside a big window overlooking the quay. "Arak and *mezze* to start?" the owner asked.

We said yes and he flounced off, rubbing his hands. Something moved above Arnold's head. It was an octopus in a big jar hanging from the ceiling. It danced up and down a few times, then sank to the bottom, scowling at me.

I asked Arnold: "About my face being frank—don't the Arabs use the same word to mean naïve?"

"Er—sometimes."

The *mezze* arrived by express delivery. There were about twenty small dishes of olives, anchovies, *lebna,* cubes of liver, *hummus,* stuffed eggs, strips of grilled octopus . . .* I looked at the octopus over Arnold's head: it scowled some more and started turning red. The waiter showed us the menu and we ordered a local version of bouillabaisse, to be followed by eggplant stuffed with lamb and pine nuts.

Arnold served the arak. We speared and nibbled our way through the *mezze,* gossiping desultorily for appearance's sake while we looked over the occupants of nearby tables and took in what we could of their conversation. They seemed and sounded harmless enough; and our problem was resolved when four musicians took possession of the little stage and, after the usual twanging and whining, launched into a lilting mountain tune. We both grinned, and Arnold's tense blue eyes relaxed. Eastern Mediterranean music is as nearly bugproof as anything known to man.

When the waiter had served our bouillabaisse, Arnold said: "You remember what I wrote in my letter about my need of a PR man and troubleshooter? That wasn't just dressing. Relations with politicians and pressure groups are trickier than ever. And there are security problems. If ever you do get tired of journalism—"

"How insecure are you?"

The owner of the place passed by our table, gave us a big

---

* *Mezze* are small dishes of appetizers served with drinks, like Spanish tapas. *Lebna* is a cheese made by straining salted yogurt. *Hummus* is a purée of chickpeas, to which crushed garlic, lemon juice, olive oil, and paprika are usually added.

smile, pointed through the window, and bustled off. The sky beyond the quay was glistening with an expectant sheen that dimmed the stars and silhouetted starkly the mountainous spine of Lebanon. A bright horn poked up from the black ridge; and, as we watched, a huge half-moon crept stealthily into view.

"About three weeks ago," Arnold said, "the company's offices were broken into. The thieves didn't take much: a few letters and reports, some maps of our concession areas in northern Syria, and an envelope marked CONFIDENTIAL, which a first secretary of the American embassy had sent me that afternoon."

He waited for me to ask what was in the envelope. I asked. He said: "Three cocktail recipes."

The stuffed eggplant arrived. The octopus above Arnold's head looked relieved and began hopping up and down. Arnold asked the waiter to bring something.

"All right," Arnold continued. "You're unimpressed. Office burglaries are banal. The police yawn when you report them. What happened next is closely linked with the big story. Do you know Dick Manning?"

I shook my head. "Who's he?"

"A rather good chemist, though his main interest is archaeology. You never met him when you worked in Beirut? He was with the company then. I don't think there's anyone in the Levant I trusted more in those days."

"Does he still work for you?"

"Only occasionally. He's gone into what he calls semiretirement. A few days after the raid on my office I received a visit from a local journalist—one who's acquired a reputation for muckraking and collecting baksheesh from people who prefer to keep their embarrassments private. It was obviously a softening-up call. But he told me enough to show that he'd got onto something rather startling that would land Dick—and, almost certainly, the company—in serious trouble if it was published."

27

"May I know what it is?"

"Of course. But not now—or here."

"So you'd like me to go and talk to this journalist, as one member of the world's oldest profession to another, and ask him what gives?"

"No; you can't. He's dead."

The waiter returned and handed Arnold a photo frame. Arnold thanked him and laid it face down on the table. He continued, when the waiter moved away: "He's the journalist who fell or was pushed into that scrapyard last night."

"You don't need me," I said. "Your security setup is perfect. Even I couldn't give you that kind of service."

"Oh, come, Ray! You don't think we go in for . . ." He served some more arak and said: "I'd planned to return from Aleppo yesterday. When I went to the hotel garage to get the car, its back wheels were missing. Wheels do get stolen in these parts, I know. But common sizes are chosen so that the tires can be sold easily. Mine are an uncommon size. They weren't taken for resale. They were taken to delay my return."

"Why should anyone want to keep you in Aleppo?"

"Possibly because the opposition didn't find what they were looking for when they searched the office and would like another go. Possibly because there's someone on my staff working for them who's looking through the confidential files while I'm away. That's why I don't want too many people to know I've returned: I'd like to barge into the office unexpectedly tomorrow morning."

"Who minds the stall while you're away? Pete McWhatnot?"

He nodded. "Pete McGlint."

"How reliable is he?"

He shrugged. "I used to have a lot of time for Pete. But then, up in Aleppo, something soured in him. He started hitting the arak. Loneliness, perhaps. One reason I brought him back to Beirut was to keep a friendly eye on him. He's better now—and certainly efficient. But he's not . . . not as human as he used to be."

"Is he completely in your confidence? Does he know all about your present worries?"

"No— Lord, no—and he mustn't. What I'm telling you is strictly between you, me, and the octopus."

The lights dimmed and the musicians swung into a rhythmic, rather mournful, piece that Levantine sailors sing. Conversation hushed.

Arnold said softly: "Read this."

He passed me the frame the waiter had given him. It contained a yellow page from a Paris weekly of eighty years ago: an extract from the memoirs of some forgotten French diplomat describing a storm in the bay of Beirut, one autumn evening in 1873, which caused the loss, close to the shore, of a French ship that was taking to Lebanon a beautiful Moroccan princess named Undina. She was on her way to marry a Lebanese emir. The body of the princess was never found; but, for years after, the diplomat noted, simple folk living near the waterfront reported hearing her singing and calling, especially on fine summer evenings when the moon was bright. Some even claimed to have seen her walking along the quay on which the emir's suite was to have met her, and superstitious Beirutis kept away from it at night.

"Here she comes," Arnold whispered. "Ondine!"

She was wearing a dark-blue abaya (a loose square-shouldered cloak), trimmed with gold cord, that glistened like the sea by starlight. Most of her black hair and the lower half of her face were veiled by a frothy headcloth of white silk. She was carrying a sprig of seaweed.

She sauntered slowly across the room toward the musicians, humming their sorrowful sea song. The room darkened. When she reached the stage a thin orange-gold spotlight probed up phalluswise from the floor to set her Moroccan jewelry ablaze. She sang.

Her face was handsome rather than pretty—the big eyes just a lash short of being too far apart, the mouth wide and

29

sensuous. It was her figure that had earned her the boat ride, and whenever she thought we'd been studying her face too long, she gave us the old one-two with her hips and let her cloak swish open briefly to show us what the emir had missed. But it was never overdone—the glow of a superb thigh, a ripple of light on gold-lamé tights, and the abaya curled back again. The discretion and showmanship were unusual for Beirut, where cabaret cheesecake normally comes as heavy as a cartload of clay.

The songs were standard Arabic pop. Their tone lightened progressively, and lanterns came on around the walls. Her last song but one was *"Um el-abaya* (Lady in the Cloak),"* which she sang with a North African accent. The audience clapped delightedly to the infectious rhythm, and she strolled around the room clicking her fingers and swaying voluptuously. Occasionally she paused at a table and joked or tickled someone with her seaweed—but without ever getting too close or dropping her veil, which she had let fall while she sang on the stage.

It was plain the boss had told her to say hello to us. Her big green eyes looked me over mischievously.

"You American?" she asked.

"Partly," I said. You can't tell everybody your life story.

So she pretended to chew gum, twitched, and quivered like a jukebox jerk, and flicked back her cloak to pull out an imaginary gun and pump me full of lead. From culture she turned to diplomacy. "Six Fleet!" she exclaimed, and stuck out her breasts and buttocks, swaggering briefly. "Vietnam!" she cried, and made a hissing noise like a punctured tire: the swagger was deflated to a nervous limp. The customers roared with delight.

"The New Statesman can use a girl like you," I said.

She looked at Arnold. "You English," she said. "You from the City in the Sea?"

I didn't get that—but Arnold obviously did. He was deathly pale, his eyes fixed on her in supplication. His hands were gripping the edge of the table. She was going to say more,

30

looked at him keenly, but then stepped back, whirled away from us, and took up the refrain of *"Um el-abaya"* again. Arnold just stared at her. I poured him an arak. He picked it up slowly. His hand was trembling.

When she got back to the stage, the lights went down again and a white spotlight came on this time, pencil-thin, picking out only her face. Her last song was a lament for shattered hope: a journey, a treacherous moon, a storm, disaster, eternal frustration—the sort of thing that reduces leathery Syrian sheiks to tears. She had her audience spellbound. Then, with barely a transition, it was the sea song again—insistent, repetitive, melancholy—and the spotlight went out. She was singing gently . . . then humming . . . then we heard her no more.

Two, four, six lanterns came on, in the corners of the room. She was gone.

People from around the corner of the L flocked to our side and stood gazing through the windows. The mountains behind Beirut were slumbering mammoths. The moon had soared free of them and its light floated in flakes on the lazy sea.

Ondine appeared on the deserted quay. Slowly, she walked to the head of the stone steps that led down to the water. There she waited, her head on one side, as if listening for a voice. Ten or fifteen seconds passed. Her figure drooped; there was a strange quick gesture of resignation; and her right hand clutched the front of her cloak. She moved forward.

The men and women clustered around our table were tense and hushed, pale in the reflected moonlight. In the shadows behind them, the musicians were still playing. It was the music Ondine had left us with, rippling and swirling and eddying, but always the same fatalistic rhythm, the same anguished theme, implacable as the sea.

The steps came down toward La Sirène, and Ondine faced us. She looked older now, older and shrunken, her eyes black pits in a face as white as a skull. Slowly, she moved down the steps. Halfway down, old and bent, and faceless suddenly in the shadow of the sea wall, she leaned on a handrail for sup-

31

port. Somewhere in the blackness beneath her a faint phosphorescence flickered. The music softened. She stepped into the water.

She took another step—ripples of silver danced out of the line of shadow—then another: deeper, deeper. The sea swirled around her waist. A woman standing beside me shuddered and crossed herself. Ondine went on down the steps. Soon her shoulders vanished beneath the water, and for a moment her head, enshrouded in white silk, rode grotesquely on the surface. Then her head disappeared, too, and sea and quay were void of life.

The music faded. The lighting returned to normal. People went back to their tables. Waiters began bustling around again.

"It's not possible," Arnold murmured.

A waiter brought us fruit. We ate it in silence. Arnold stared at the black water into which Ondine had vanished. Suddenly he said: "I've got to talk to the little man again—the owner. The sooner the better. Do you mind if we skip coffee?"

"I've stopped drinking it at night."

We found the owner in the entrance hall in conference with a big buffalo of a man dressed as a sailor. He fluttered excitedly when he saw us.

"Please come into my office," he said.

The office was cramped, and dominated by a big desk. Behind the desk a wide-eyed young man wearing a handlebar mustache and an Ottoman uniform peered at us from a huge framed photograph that age had clouded impressively with gunsmoke. The frame was tilted to one side, revealing a small safe in the wall.

The little man smiled apologetically, adjusted the picture to hide the safe, and said: "There is a taxi waiting outside with two men in it. The taxi driver has already seen four people leave without offering to pick them up. This is strange. It was my cousin, the man you saw me talking to in the hall, who warned me: he protects us from undesirable elements. This taxi driver may be harmless but . . . it would be wise to have another taxi come and drive you home. You may use my telephone."

Arnold thanked him and dialed a number. After ordering the taxi he said: "I am already indebted to you for this warning. Now I wish to ask you to do something which will put me even more deeply in your debt. Could you please arrange for me to meet Ondine—if possible tonight?"

The little man smiled sadly. It was a question he'd often been asked. "Did you not witness her return to the sea? Now, until tomorrow evening or the night after, it is not possible to see her."

"It would be a great privilege, I realize," Arnold said carefully. "I should be willing to compensate you for any inconvenience you might suffer."

A sigh. "If only I could help you—believe me . . . But it is quite impossible."

"My compensation would not be ungenerous," Arnold said in a strained voice. "And my friend would make a great effort to give La Sirène wide publicity."

The little man shrugged. "Only last week I had the same request from a high officer of the Jordanian Army. He offered me a Cadillac and a royal decoration, and he promised to have Amman radio broadcast a program about La Sirène; but still I could not grant his request."

We couldn't bat that kind of ball: we were still in the junior league. He went on: "However, I do not wish you to consider me inhospitable. On the evenings when Ondine does not come, we have two other girls to sing and dance. They are very sweet. If—"

Arnold smiled wearily. "You are very kind. But it is Ondine I wish to see. And I wish to speak to her for only five minutes."

Another sigh. "Ah, yes: five minutes with one woman can yield more delight than five years with another. But it is not possible. I am deeply sad." A car hooted. "There is your taxi. Thank you for your visit. *Ma as-salaamë.*"*

He opened the door. The bouncer in the sailor suit looked in expectantly. We picked up our baggage and left.

Our taxi was a gray Renault. Arnold gave the driver his office address. When we moved off a dark-blue Opel followed us.

On the avenue the Opel fell back a little. Arnold leaned forward and said something to our driver. We turned sharply into a side street, raced through a maze of deserted bazaars, and came out in the maelstrom of Martyrs' Square. From there we drove to the quiet business quarter where Levant Mining & Chemicals had its offices.

Arnold told the driver to cruise slowly around the block. There was no sign of the Opel. We looked up at Arnold's office windows. The driver sang softly, tapping his steering wheel. He was used to crazy foreigners.

"All seems to be in order," Arnold said. "Our burglar alarm telephones the police and switches on a light outside the building. And now—home, and a large brandy."

The taxi left us on a corner fifty yards from Arnold's apartment. As it drove off the Opel flashed by.

"It's not that I'm scared," I said. "The knocking noise my knees are making is just exuberance. But why was that Opel tailing us? And what did that crack of Ondine's mean?"

"Be patient. You'll feel better in my study with a brandy glass in your hand."

"What's the drill if the opposition break in? Do I throw the brandy glass at them?"

"If my place interests the opposition, they'll have visited it already."

"Have you a safe in the apartment?"

"No. But I've something intended to intrigue an uninvited visitor just as much: a solid, well-locked cupboard in my study. It contains nothing but a rather vicious booby trap—a kind of

* Go in peace.

34

chemical bomb which makes a noise, puts its victim to sleep for a few minutes, and scars his face temporarily with a weak acid. Our insurance people recommend them."

"I knew a man in England who caught a thief with a gadget like that. He had to pay the thief damages."

Arnold's apartment was on the ninth floor of a slender ten-story building with a mock-Gothic entrance that looked as if the architect's first idea had been to build a cathedral. The elevator appeared to be out of order, so we loosened our collars and set off on foot.

Every floor we came to seemed to add weight to my suitcase. It was a quiet, decorous building. For Beirut, unnaturally quiet, I was thinking. You couldn't even hear the neighbors' television sets . . . Then I heard what sounded like a magnum of champagne being opened—and a hoarse cry.

We froze.

Arnold smiled. A grim, cold smile. He snapped open his overnight bag and took out a small black revolver. He tucked the bag under his left arm and ran up the next few flights of stairs and along the corridor that led to the service door of his apartment. I liked it on the stairs. It was airy and calm and there were no angry men who had just had an acid bomb go off under their eyebrows. But I followed him. I noticed that the elevator was parked at his floor, its door wedged open.

He unlocked the door silently and we tiptoed into the dark kitchen and put our baggage down. Somewhere in the apartment a radio was pumping out a Shostakovich symphony. Cautiously, we walked across the kitchen, into the dining room, and through that to the hall that led in from the front door. There were two bedrooms and bathrooms on one side of the hall, and the drawing room, the study, and a big balcony on the other. The study door was a little way open and a bright sail of light streaked across the hall. Arnold peeped into the room, stiffened, then pushed the door open hard.

The man inside seemed harmless enough. He was coiled up on the floor, unconscious, in front of a small open cupboard immediately across the study from the door. The air was acrid.

Arnold strode into the room, looked quickly behind the door, and went down on one knee beside him. I stood in the doorway and looked around. The radio in the far corner, beside the recessed french windows that opened onto the balcony, subsided into a slow movement in which Shostakovich deplored violence and acid bombs. Lustrous brocade curtains were drawn across the window recess, and as I looked at them and wondered, I thought they trembled slightly.

I opened my mouth to say something, but at the same moment Arnold, still on his knee beside the unconscious man, yelled at me. I tried to spin around, but the jamb of the doorway caught my shoulder and something hit me behind the ear.

I was down on the carpet. Arnold was pointing his little revolver in my direction, and Shostakovich was getting worked up about the blackjacks and guns of twentieth-century civilization, too. Dimly, I heard a gun go off; and all of a sudden I didn't seem to be there.

4

A woman was cooing at me. I groaned.

I have no deep-rooted objection to women cooing at me. It's their right, if that's the way they feel. But I expect fair warning. I don't like them to surprise me with my head on the carpet.

"What a wonderful morning!" she cooed. "The birds are waking in the parks and avenues. The eastern sky is a great blade of steel. The air is clean and uplifting. This is the moment when man recognizes himself as master of the universe, the instant in which he realizes that nothing can stand against his collective will."

I groaned again.

She went on sharply: "What could be more futile than pessimism? We are on the threshold of paradise and all we have to do to enter is reach out and open the door."

So that's it, I told myself. Paradise. They've dumped you in an anteroom while they look through your file. My head felt as if a platoon of centipedes were practicing footdrill in it, but I plugged it into the space between my shoulders and sat up.

"Suddenly, the river is a flood of molten gold." Here she was again. "The Kremlin is inlaid with pearl, its battlements—"

"Wait a minute," I said; but she went prattling on. I shook my head. The centipedes fell over one another and their big army boots clattered about inside my skull. My eyes focused on a bookcase. I swiveled around in search of the speaker. "And now," she said, "Radio Moscow presents the Vladivostok naval choir singing 'Red Dawn.' "

The dial of Arnold's radio was still aglow. I was squatting in the middle of the study. My head was throbbing and I was thirsty. I remembered the other man who had been on the carpet—the victim of Arnold's chemical bomb. I turned my head slowly to see if he was still there. Yes, he was there, flat on his back now, head turned away. I crawled toward him.

Something was different. Someone had moved him and changed his clothes. I paused to let my breath catch up with me. My eyes watered for a moment and then everything grew clearer, as if a veil had been lifted. What I saw hurt me more than the bruise on my head and set me gasping for breath again.

It wasn't the intruder. It was Arnold. I lunged forward in quick panic to touch him. The big artery in his neck was quite still. His face had once been trying to warn me about the man in the hall who disliked my head, and it still had an anxious expression; but now there were the beginnings of a sneer on it, too. The little revolver lay beside him. I sniffed it. He had not had time to fire.

Still on my knees, I opened his jacket and shirt. One bullet had gone into the base of his neck and another into his lungs, both fired from his right. They had been small bullets and there was little blood. I shut my eyes to see him again as he had been during those last few seconds: down on one knee, half-facing the door, raising his gun to fire . . . The shots could only have come from the direction of the curtained french windows. There had been at least three intruders in the apartment: the one on the floor, the one who hit me, and another behind the curtains.

The radio began chattering about American colonization of Scotland. I stood up dizzily, walked toward it, and hesitated. The visitors had no doubt hit upon Radio Moscow at random to cover the noise of their attack on the cupboard; but they had probably twiddled the knobs first and they might have left prints. So I didn't touch any knobs: I went down on my knees again and gripped the cord and yanked the plug out of the baseboard.

The floor around the radio table and Arnold's desk was littered with files and a few loose letters and receipts. All the drawers of the big teak desk were open and most of what they contained had been thrown out. The top of the desk was bare except for a small rectangle of blue-and-white card with something printed on it in English and Greek: *Superfine Talcum Powder* and, in smaller letters, *Made in Cyprus.*

I walked on to the curtained french windows. There was enough space behind the curtains to hide a couple of cardinals. One of the windows was ajar. I pulled it open and stepped onto the balcony. The fresh morning air made me feel alive again. Above the foothills, dawn was surging up the sky like a pink-and-silver fountain.

Another french window led from the balcony into the hall. It was unfastened, too. I pushed it with my foot. As I did so, I heard a stealthy movement in the kitchen. I took a mashie out of a golf bag in the hall, tiptoed shakily across the dining room, flung open the kitchen door, and almost murdered the refrigerator. I drank some iced water and looked into the storeroom, bedrooms, and drawing room. None of them told me anything, so I went to Arnold's bathroom, washed my face and head, and took an aspirin tablet.

The bathroom cabinet smelled of ether. I found an empty bottle in it labeled ETHER. I sat on the bidet and tried to think. I would have been incapable of both standing and thinking.

After a minute or two I turned the bathroom stool upside down, examined it carefully, and tried unsuccessfully to unscrew its legs. Then I emptied the cabinet and unhooked it from the wall. When I worked for them, the Sisters had a fixation on bathroom equipment—especially cabinets, stools, and toilet seats, but not toilet tanks, which had been banned as hiding places since 1946, when C. read *The Lost Weekend.* * Arnold's bathroom cabinet had neither a false bottom nor a

* The head of the Secret Intelligence Service (the "Sisters") is traditionally referred to as "C." The hero of Charles Jackson's novel *The Lost Weekend* hid two bottles of whiskey in a toilet tank.

double back. The bottles and tubes seemed to contain what they were supposed to contain. But a blue-and-white carton attracted me. Printed on it, in English and Greek, were the words *Superfine Talcum Powder* and, in smaller letters, *Made in Cyprus*. The carton had a transparent plastic bag in it containing a white powder that looked like talc but didn't have the right smooth, slightly soapy, feel; this powder felt more like very fine salt. I tipped some into a plastic envelope and put it in my wallet.

I hung the cabinet on the wall, put the bottles and stuff back, examined the toilet seat, the mirror, and a few other things, and did the same in the guest bathroom. Then I returned to the study, pausing on the way to breathe in a refill of the cool clean air of the balcony. The air was stale in the study. I thought I could distinguish now, as a component of its staleness, a faint odor of ether.

I wrapped a handkerchief around my right hand and picked up the slip of blue-and-white card on Arnold's desk. Taped to the back of it was a visiting card announcing *Lieutenant-Colonel Henry Blane*. I returned it to the desk and looked around.

Arnold's booby trap had left stains on the carpet in front of the empty cupboard. Ten feet from the cupboard, beneath an armchair, I found a slim flashlight, the size of a fountain pen. It could have been dropped by the man who set off the booby trap—or by Arnold. I moved the armchair aside to look at it. Printed in white on the plastic body were the words JULIEN MONTRAND, MACHINES AGRICOLES, BEYROUTH.

A bell rang. I heard voices outside the front door. I looked at Arnold for inspiration but he had stopped caring about doorbells. I slid the armchair back into position and went into the hall.

The bell rang again.

I grabbed the mashie once more and sped through the apartment to the service door. I opened it and peeked down the corridor. Two men were arguing with the concierge. One of them carried a crowbar, the other drooped under the weight of a long gold-tipped cigarette and a pair of tinted glasses. The concierge was telling them in slangy Arabic that the Englishman was friendly with the Prime Minister and could make trouble for anyone who used his front door for firewood.

"*Márhaba*," I said. "Good morning. *Bonjour, messieurs.*" Trilingual Tony, the Levantine lounge lizard. My voice had a harsh strained sound.

They quivered. The concierge said: "He is not Mr. Amery."

The man with the cigarette stepped forward. He was a lean, aggressive-looking man of about thirty-five, fair and freckled. His pal was plumper and older, with coal-black eyes and crinkled hair. They both had the usual foot-and-neck disease: fussily patterned black-and-white shoes, and ties that looked like a cross-section of a *Guide Michelin* inspector's liver.

"*Qui êtes-vous?*" the lean man asked.

"Wait a minute," I said. "I'll open up the front."

I closed the service door and bolted it. As I did so, the playboys both shouted. I went back to the hall, put the mashie in Arnold's golf bag, and opened the front door.

The lean man with the cigarette asked again who I was.

"I was about to ask you the same question," I said.

"Sûreté," he snapped.

"Good. I was about to telephone you. Have you your police identification card?"

Angrily he flashed a card in front of my nose. It bore his photo and said his name was Inspector Bliss.

I stood aside. He strolled in slowly, looking around him a little arrogantly. The dark man gave the crowbar to the concierge and came in too, more impetuously. The concierge started to follow them but I shut the door. I led them into the drawing room.

"You were on the point of calling us?" Bliss asked.

"Yes."

"So it was not you who telephoned a short while ago?"

"No."

"Someone called our headquarters to say that an Englishman had been shot here." He crushed his cigarette in a clean copper ashtray and rubbed his hands. "So . . ."

I told them what had happened, showed them around, and pointed out the little flashlight. Bliss examined the back of my head. Then he lit a Jockey Club and his sidekick lit a Baffra and we went back to the drawing room to fumigate it.

Bliss sneered. "You arrived here about midnight?"

I nodded. My head bipped.

"You received two blows on the head and recovered consciousness not long before we got here—yes?"

"Yes."

"But you have no serious wound, nothing you might not have inflicted on yourself. You can't expect us to believe that two small blows on the head put you to sleep for so long."

I stared at them bleakly. A knock on the head always leaves me dull. I said: "I've told you all I know that— No, I haven't. Did you notice that the air in the study smelled of ether? Only slightly, but it's there."

Bliss shrugged. "No. Why?"

"It's possible that the men who killed my friend gave me a whiff of ether to immobilize me while they revived the man who set off the chemical bomb. There's an empty ether bottle in the bathroom. I imagine they wanted to keep me here—it would be one of them who telephoned you—so that you would find me."

"Why?"

"So as to waste your time and confuse the trail."

They grinned at me—smokily, contemptuously.

Bliss asked a few more questions but didn't seem to be listening to my answers. Carefully, he killed his cigarette in the same ashtray. Then he hitched up his pants. His right hand was suddenly holding a black automatic and pointing it at where my breakfast should have been.

He said in Arabic: "See if he has a gun, Jamid."

Jamid poked and pawed me and said: *"Mafeesh."*

"Show us your baggage," Bliss told me in French.

I led them into the kitchen and pointed to my suitcase. Bliss searched it, with the gun on the floor beside him. He opened my Leica case and said: "That is a fine camera. One of my ambitions is to have a camera like that."

I said nothing.

Tenderly, he fastened the Leica up again and put it back in the suitcase. He asked: "At which hotel are you staying?"

"I was going to stay here."

"Bien." He stood up. "You will now go to headquarters and make a formal statement. Then you will take a room at the Saint-George. Do not leave Beirut without our permission."

My head ached still; I needed a shower, a shave, and a lot of coffee; and my morale had last been seen trying to crawl under a rug. I nodded meekly and picked up my suitcase and followed the dark man out of the apartment. A Sûreté car was waiting in the street. The concierge and three bystanders watched us get into it.

"That's the murderer," someone said.

I asked my escort: "How do they know there's been a murder?"

He shrugged. "Everybody knows everything in Beirut."

He typed my statement himself and I was out of the Sûreté HQ within an hour. I went to the Saint-George, where I showered, shaved, and breakfasted. Then I took on the Beirut telephone system in single combat.

I concentrated on the doctors in the less-prosperous quarters of the city. I told them I was the *faits divers* reporter of *L'Orient:* I was trying to trace the whereabouts of a man who had been burned by acid in an accident in a garage.

After talking to eight doctors and getting nowhere, I telephoned our Beirut correspondent and asked him to lend a hand. Forty minutes later he called me back with the news that

43

he had traced a doctor who had treated a metalworker named Sami Hamam for mild acid burns during the early hours. I thanked him and noted Hamam's address. Then I put in my pocket a knockout aerosol that looked like a cigarette lighter. "Hamam" means "pigeon" in Arabic; but this one, I guessed, might not be the cooing kind.

5

It was a low yellow house wedged between taller neighbors in a quiet street near the waterfront, not far from La Sirène. Its façade was pockmarked where plaster had dropped away to reveal mud brickwork. Its door and closed shutters were the sun-scoured gray of age and apathy. The doorstep had worn as shallow as a diplomat's smile.

I walked the whole length of the street before turning back to pay my call. As I approached the house the second time, the door opened and a man came out—a stocky but nimble-looking man, smaller than I, wearing a loose-fitting brown suit. His head was muffled in a white *kufiya*. All I saw of his face was a brown beaked nose and the flash of an eye as he glanced along the street.

I was still over twenty yards away, but I paused at the end of a passageway as if waiting for someone. A little girl wearing a halo of flies came up to me hesitantly and held out a hand. The man in the brown suit pulled the door to and set off briskly toward the other end of the street.

I gave the girl a few piasters and strolled on slowly. By the time I reached the yellow house he was out of sight. I knocked on the paintless door. There was no answer. I knocked again, harder. Same again. I tried the doorknob. It worked. The door, unlocked, swung inward, creaking. I caressed the lump on the back of my head, reminded myself to buy a steel helmet sometime, and stepped inside.

The house was as gay as a catacomb and had something of the same smell. I shut and bolted the door and stood with my back to it. I was in a living room that ran right across the

45

house. Two low doors on the right, both open, led to a bedroom and the kitchen. The gloomy gray walls were hung with the sort of bogus tapestry work, showing improbable panoramas of domes and minarets, that Near Eastern bazaars import by the acre from Hong Kong. A low round table stood on a faded Turkish rug in the middle of the floor, and a row of straight-backed chairs lined the far wall.

The gentle bubbling of a *narghileh** came from the bedroom. I caught a whiff of its bittersweet smoke. As I listened, the bubbling stopped and a voice whispered something. I walked toward it.

A man in a gray shirt was sitting in a big bed, leaning on a pile of pillows. A patchwork quilt and a scuffle of Arabic newspapers covered his middle and legs. His forehead and right cheek were bandaged, but what I could see of his face was familiar. His left hand held the tube of a *narghileh* that stood on a bedside table. The walls of the bedroom were blue and decorated with three busty pinup girls and a calendar featuring the head office of Levant Mining & Chemicals.

He looked surprised, as if he was expecting someone else.

"Min ente?"† he asked hoarsely.

"English journalist," I said. "You speak English, don't you?"

"Speak English bloody good," he said. "I take lessons at the British Institute."

I nodded. "The director thought you'd like some books to read while you're in bed, and some conversation practice. Why are you studying English?" I asked, just to be asking something while I tried to decide whether he might have a gun within reach.

"Get me one big oil job in Kuwait. Get me outa this hole."

I pointed to the calendar. "Don't they pay well enough?"

"They bastards." He blinked bloodshot brown eyes at me.

---

* Water pipe, hookah.
† Who are you?

"And you one big lying bastard. How Mr. Marlow know me in bed?"

His right hand was bandaged, too. If he had a gun, it would be on his left side, then: my side. Under the bottom pillow. The drawer in the table was a little too far.

"Your pillows are slipping," I said. I stepped forward quickly and plunged my right hand under the bottom pillow. He yelped hoarsely and thrust his left hand there. We reached the gun simultaneously: I grabbed the butt and he had the barrel. I hit him on the side of the neck with the edge of my left hand. He let go. I pulled the gun out—it was a Colt .45 revolver—and stood back, thankful that so much of him was in bandages.

"Dirty bastard," he sneered. "Hitting one sick man. This all you English good for."

I went into the kitchen to check that the back door was locked. When I returned he was leaning over the bedside table clumsily serving himself an arak. His hand trembled. There was an earthenware waterpot on the table but he sipped the arak neat. He looked at me warily, his head tilted slightly, like a hen watching a centipede.

"What the hell you want?" he asked.

"I want to take your photo for the newspapers." I patted my Leica. "Soon you'll be a famous man. You'll be on trial for the murder of that Englishman who was shot last night."

He tapped his head. *"Ente majnoun."**

"It's you that's crazy if you think the man who hired you will protect you. He can't. The secret's out. It will be in all the papers tomorrow . . . with your photo. The man who actually pulled the trigger is more important than you, so your boss will try to protect him—at your expense. They'll persuade the Sûreté that you shot the Englishman. Your only hope is to tell me the full story. If I publish it, they'll find it difficult to put the blame on you."

* You're mad.

"What do it matter to you?"

"That Englishman was my friend. Who killed him?"

"How you find where I live?" he asked.

"I tailed you here. The Sûreté will be here soon. All the blame will be put on you unless you're smart. So—"

Someone knocked on the front door.

"That's the Sûreté," I said hopefully.

He thought about it, watching my face. "I think my friends come. They cut you in little bits."

I opened his gun. Only three of the cylinders were loaded. I turned the cylinders so that I could press the trigger three times without anything happening and snapped the gun shut. I pushed off the safety catch and pointed the gun at his left eye.

I said slowly: "I'm going to press the trigger every ten seconds until you tell me what I want to know. One, two . . ."

Whoever it was out there thumped on the door.

". . . six, seven, eight . . ."

He licked his lips.

I pulled the trigger. The hammer clicked down. He flinched. The next cylinder moved into position.

"One, two, three . . ."

The folks outside seemed to be kicking the door now, so it probably wasn't a social call. I stopped counting. I let him count himself, in his mind. As my finger tightened on the trigger again, a gurgle of fear burped out of him. He held up his left hand. I waited. His mouth tightened stubbornly. He said nothing. I pulled the trigger. He started violently. The next cylinder came around.

Two seconds, three seconds, four seconds . . .

The banging on the door stopped. There was a moment of silence. He was sweating. Flies buzzed.

A voice shouted in Arabic: "Sûreté! Open up!"

I smiled at him. A kindly, benevolent smile. The one used-car salesmen wear.

"Okay," he gasped. "I tell you. Then you help me if the Sûreté try to make one fix. Yes?"

"Yes." I lowered the gun. I didn't tell him I'd need someone to help me with the Sûreté when they found me there. "Who gave you your orders last night?"

He trembled sharply.

I raised the gun.

"He kill me if he know," he said at last. "But . . . It is one *Fransawi*. Julien Montrand."

A voice snarled in Arabic, from beyond the shutter of the bedroom window: "We can hear you. Open the door or we'll shoot our way in."

"*Tayyib,*" I said. "Okay."

I hid the gun under a cushion in the living room and unfastened the door. Bliss and his assistant, Jamid, were standing outside, guns in hand. They blinked when they saw me, and hurried into the bedroom as if they suspected me of cannibalism.

Bliss fired a brief barrage of questions at Hamam. Then he told Jamid to take a statement from him and returned to the living room to scowl at me.

"So this man was your accomplice," he said in his glacial French.

I said: "If he had been I wouldn't have told you about his acid burns. With that information it was easy to trace him. I'm surprised his employer didn't take him out of town."

"Or eliminate him."

"Quite."

"Perhaps we arrived too soon," he said nastily.

"Do you want to know how I traced him? Or don't the facts matter any more?"

He strode toward me, twitching his automatic the way a cat twitches the tip of its tail when it is getting angry. I thought he was going to hit me with it. The sound of a slap and a hoarse yelp came from the bedroom. Bliss grinned.

"*Bien.* Tell me your version of the facts."

I told him about my telephone calls to local doctors.

He shrugged. "You may have made these calls in the hope

of covering yourself. They mean nothing. Anyhow, you had no right to conduct a private inquiry."

"You forget that only I could identify Hamam. I couldn't give you his name before I saw him."

"You should have consulted me. What did he tell you?"

"He was just beginning to talk when you interrupted us. He said he got his orders from a Frenchman named Julien Montrand. Personally, I doubt it. I think——"

"You will allow me to do what thinking is necessary. Do you know anyone of that name?"

"Yes. He sells agricultural machines. His name was on that little flashlight we found on the floor of Mr. Amery's study."

"I remember. I shall go and see Montrand, of course. You will now discontinue your inquiries. When I call on Montrand I do not wish to find you there."

"You probably will. I'm having lunch with him."

He frowned. "I should prefer you not to——"

His assistant called from the bedroom that Hamam was ill. We heard an anguished whimpering.

We ran to Hamam's bedside. His neck was twisted and bent as if invisible hands were strangling him. The unbandaged half of his face, with its tortured mouth, was the face of a gargoyle. He had vomited on the shoulder of his gray shirt. Within seconds he was dead.

The liquid in his arak glass was white now. Bliss looked at me and sniffed it cautiously.

"Cyanide," he said. "His employer succeeded in getting rid of him, after all."

I pointed to Hamam's waterpot. It was the usual unglazed *brik* of the Levant coast, slightly porous, standing in a saucer to sweat and keep itself cool.

I said: "The poison may be in there. He drank neat arak when I was with him. Now his arak is white, so he must have added water."

Bliss snapped a question at Jamid.

"Yes," the dark man said uneasily. "His throat was bad. He

50

could hardly talk. So I let him pour a small drink. I added the water myself. I started rough; then I tried gentle tactics."

"Gentle tactics!" Bliss threw up his arms. He sniffed the water pot and blew his nose. "You see what gentle tactics achieve: the death of an important witness." He turned to me. "And you! You have a wonderful technique of showing and telling us things we are bound to discover for ourselves in due course. But you tell us nothing really important—such as who poisoned this *brik.*"

"It could have been a man wearing a brown suit and a white *kufiya.*" I told them about the man I had seen leaving the house.

Jamid began taking notes.

"No," Bliss said. "Take a statement from him while I talk to headquarters."

He went out, and his assistant and I sat at the low table in the living room. I dictated my statement and was signing it when Bliss returned.

Bliss said angrily in Arabic: "Mahmoud and his crew won't be able to get here for another hour."

Jamid swore.

Bliss read my statement and went into the bedroom.

I followed him and asked: "What did Hamam have on his record?"

"What makes you think he had a record?"

"I'm guessing you traced him by his fingerprints. You'd find them on that cupboard in my friend's study."

Bliss nodded. "A conviction for burglary."

"Was he the man who burgled Levant Mining & Chemicals?"

"It's possible. Two smudged prints were found that might have been his."

"How good a burglar and lockpicker was he?"

"Average. Above average, perhaps."

The musty air of the bedroom was aquiver with a hungry murmur. Flies were threshing and weaving above the bed.

51

Some were already exploring Hamam's tortured face. Bliss pulled back the quilt, scattering them.

He looked at me. "You may be quite innocent in this affair, Mr. Alan, but I doubt it. An innocent man would look sicker, more shocked, than you."

"I'm a journalist. I've seen worse than this."

"Anyway, you may go now. Think of us, poking about in dust and filth while you are lying on the beach. But we'll be seeing you again."

"Are you dying of thirst or can it wait a minute?"

"It can wait a little. He's engaged with Sheik Mansour."

She sniffed. "That old roué."

I pulled the shutter down over the little hatch and looked out of the office door. Julien was describing the finer points of a diesel pump to Sheik Mansour. I shut the door and gazed at the drawers of the handsome desk and tried not to listen to Hamam telling me his boss's name.

The typing stopped. A minute passed. Yvonne came in, put a tray on Julien's desk, and went out. More minutes crept by. At last Julien bustled in. He felt the carafe of water with the back of his hand.

"I need something to cool me," he said. "Last month, Sheik Mansour lost ten thousand dollars at the casino. Last week, 'e bought a necklace worth five thousand dollars for a cabaret girl. But 'e says that five thousand dollars is too much to pay for diesel pumps to give four of 'is villages water supplies."

He poured three drinks from a cut-glass decanter, added water, and passed one of them through the hatch to Yvonne.

"You forgot the olives," he told her.

"I remembered them after I prepared the tray," she said, passing him a saucer.

He set the olives on the corner of the desk between us and lowered the shutter. We drank. The arak was smoother than satin, but the way I felt, it might just as well have been sea water.

Julien said gravely: "I 'ad a Sûreté man to see me 'alf an hour ago. 'E gave me a shock. 'E told me that Arnold Amery 'as been shot. Early this morning, in 'is apartment."

"I know. I was with Arnold. I got a knock on the head. Didn't the Sûreté man mention me?"

"No. I was busy with Sheik Mansour, so 'e was very discreet and said 'e would come again this afternoon. I don't know why. Why didn't you tell me before? Did you see the assassin?"

"I've identified a man named Sami Hamam, but there were others in the apartment with him."

57

He frowned. "Sami 'Amam? I employed a Sami 'Amam two or three years ago. I fired 'im——'e was stealing tools. Tell me what 'appened."

I told my story again. I told him about the little flashlight. I didn't tell him of Hamam's accusation. When I'd finished he took a cardboard box from the bookcase and held it in front of me. It contained forty or fifty blue fountain-pen flashes.

"Over the last two months," he said, "I 'ave given away at least thirty of these. But I did not give one to Arnold. After lunch I will make a list of as many of the recipients as I can remember. I suppose that is what the Sûreté want. Take one."

I took one. "Thanks. Don't put me on your list."

The shutter rattled. He raised it.

Yvonne said: "I'm going now. There's nothing you need sign before this afternoon. *Bon appétit!*" She nodded in my direction. *"Au 'voir, monsieur."*

Julien closed and bolted the shutter. He said gloomily: "Let us go, too. Where would you like to 'ave lunch?"

"I'm not in the mood for one of your magnificent lunches. Let's go to the club. The news about Arnold will have reached there by now. I'd like to see how the customers are reacting."

Julien looked at me disapprovingly. "I don't like the sound of that. If you 'ave the idea of conducting a private inquiry into Arnold's death, drop it before it leads you into trouble. Remember 'Amam. In your place I should lead a very quiet life."

He had been toying with a pencil. Now, with a flick of his big fingers, he snapped it. It made a dry ugly sound, like a bone breaking.

The Stanhope Club was not known for its cuisine. The beef tasted like slices off an old football boot. The dessert ought by rights to have been dried in the sun and sold as a bathmat. After one sip, Julien pushed the coffee away. "They'll need it to wash the rest of the dishes," he said.

As we left our table, the goddess came into the dining room followed by Denbor and McGlint. She was wearing a short sleeveless dress printed with a kinky pattern of red and black blobs. She smiled at Julien but passed me over. Denbor nodded impartially. McGlint paused to exchange a few words with Julien—"A terrible blow!" I heard him say—and then strode importantly away to rejoin Denbor and the goddess.

Julien and I sat in leather armchairs in the lobby to catch a sea breeze.

"Tell me about that trio," I said.

"They are not usually a trio. Denbor does not like sharing Anna's company."

"Who's Anna?"

"Ah! I thought you 'ad a certain look in the eyes . . ."

Anna emerged from the dining room and crossed the lobby to the telephone booth. She read a notice taped to the glass door and went to the receptionist's office. She walked smoothly and decisively, with no hipcraft but still enough allure to stop a gold rush.

"What's the rest of her name?"

"Pjonzhak, approximately. Some evening we will get together over a bottle of cognac and I will try to spell it for you."

"Polish?"

"Yes. 'Er father was a diplomat. She works for a lawyer—Anis Salem."

"Secretary?"

"No. She does some kind of legal work. She 'as 'er specialty. I don't know what. I keep as far away from lawyers as I can."

"Are she and Denbor engaged?"

He laughed. "How delightfully old-fashioned that sounds! Do people still get engaged? I've 'eard that Denbor is waiting for a divorce; but 'is wife is a Catholic—she was 'ere until last summer—so it is complicated and expensive." He took out a battered packet of Gauloises. "Are you still off cigarettes?"

"Yes; but I've a weakness for Gauloises."

"Best cigarettes in the world." He passed me one that was shaped like a pig's tail.

59

Anna reappeared in the lobby and went back to the dining room, leaving a discreet hint of Arpège in the air.

I asked Julien: "Was Denbor on good terms with Arnold?"

He shrugged. *"Comme ça.* I think that they did not see much of each other. Arnold considered 'im a bit of a prig."

"And Pete McGlint?"

"Pete got on well with Arnold until two or three years ago. Then 'e started drinking too much. You know the Scots? They are extremists. Either reactionaries or Reds; either total abstainers or drunkards. Arnold brought 'im back from Alep because of the drinking. The transfer was arranged as a promotion, but Pete understood. After that, I believe, their relations—"

"Mr. Alan!" The receptionist was coming toward us. "Telephone."

When we got to her office she said: "I was just finishing my lunch. I'll take my coffee into the lobby."

"Please stay. I've no secrets."

The bright brown eyes examined my face carefully. "It is the Soviet embassy."

"I still have no secrets."

She smiled and sat at the small table by the window where she had eaten her lunch. I picked up the telephone.

"Mr. Ray Alan? This is Strogonov. You remember me?"

"Of course. How are you?"

"Well, thank you. I said I would telephone, and here I am. But not to arrange our dinner, unfortunately. The contrary. I must go to Syria for a few days for the inauguration of the new irrigation canal. May you be here still when I return?"

"I think so."

"Then I shall telephone again next week. Goodbye."

"Have a good trip."

The receptionist smiled over her coffee cup. I went back to Julien. He was relighting his Gauloise.

"Sûreté?" He asked.

"No. Soviet embassy."

He stared at me, and his match missed his target and singed the tip of his nose. He sneezed and coughed simultaneously, spitting out the cigarette, and burned his fingers while he was picking it up.

"Diable!" he exclaimed. "Will you never grow up?"

"I'm not pulling your leg. It was a pal of mine named Strogonov, a Soviet geologist. We had a dinner date but he's put it off for a few days. He has to go to Aleppo."

"Strogonov? To Alep?" He frowned. He stubbed the Gauloise in his ashtray until it looked like a pop singer's hairdo.

"Best cigarettes in the world," I said, "and you treat them like that."

"Merde!" He dropped it in the ashtray. "But 'ow do you know Strogonov?"

"We journalists get around. Not like you bazaar buzzards."

I heard the receptionist's voice again. She was standing in the doorway with a small towel in front of her mouth. She waved. I went over to her.

"Excuse me," she said. "I was cleaning my teeth. Telephone."

She hurried over to a small washbasin in the corner of the office. I answered the telephone.

A man's voice said in shaky English: "I speak on behalf of Mr. Edmond Assury. You have heard of him—yes?"

I had. One of the richest men in the country. Finger in a dozen pies—real estate, tourism, the press, banking, political appointments . . . A man to cultivate if your boy wanted to be president of the republic when he grew up. I said: "I think so."

"He would like to talk to you. Discuss one-two matters."

"What kind of matters?"

"Matters of mutual interest."

I waited and wondered. Over in the corner the receptionist splashed happily.

The voice added: "The death of your friend, for example."

61

"When?"

"This afternoon. I send one car for you. After half an hour?"

"That'll be fine."

"Good. Ah—Mr. Alan! This is private, your visit to Edmond Bey. You tell nobody—yes?"

"As you wish."

"Thank you."

I hung up. The receptionist was drying her hands. I asked her: "Could you give me Mr. Manning's address, please?"

"Is he a member?"

"I don't know. I thought he might be."

She shook her head and opened a drawer. She flicked through a card index and shook her head again. The head shaking surprised me. She ought to have tossed her head back and clicked her tongue.

I asked: "Did you go to an English school?"

"Yes. Why?"

"I wondered. You're very cool and efficient."

She smiled. "Madison, Masters, Montrand . . . We haven't a Manning, Mr. Alan." She shut her drawer. "Do you like women to be cool and efficient?"

"Provided they know when to warm up."

She turned to me. She had a grave oval face with a rather haughty nose and full lips.

"Two telephone calls," I said. "From men who've never called me before. At just the right time. One call would have been fine. But two? I don't like that much coincidence."

"I don't like coincidence, either. I like events to have a purpose and people to have a sense of purpose."

"Could it be that someone with a sense of purpose came in here not long ago and telephoned one of the men who called me, to let him know I was here?"

Her eyes, deep and unfathomable, held mine. What did the Armenians do to deserve such wonderful eyes? She said nothing.

62

"The blonde," I said. "Anna What's-her-name. She came to use the telephone. Did she talk to someone about me?"

"I can't answer a question like that, Mr. Alan. It would be . . ."

"I was brought up polite. I know how to say thank you." Her eyes sparkled angrily. "I am not an Arab."

"I wasn't thinking of offering you a bribe. You could forget my question and just gossip with me and let the information slip out unobtrusively; and I couldn't do a thing so long as that hatch is open, could I? So there'd be no question of bribery."

Her eyes seemed to be looking through mine into the back of my head. Slowly she smiled. She turned and strode briskly to the hatch that communicated with the lobby and closed it. She had a slim waist that accentuated agreeably her long, rather heavy, thighs. She came back to me with a sense of purpose that would have driven a turbine. I put my arms around her waist and the long, rather heavy thighs pressed against mine. Her full soft lips and mouth had a cool peppermint flavor.

In due course she said: "The lady you asked about didn't mention your name and at the time I didn't realize she was talking about you. She said: 'He is here now, but he has had lunch, so call back very soon.' That is all. I don't know to whom she spoke."

"How many calls did she make?"

"Just one. You should not offer me bribes like this."

"Why?"

"I'm married." But she still had an arm hooked onto my neck. "Didn't you see my ring?"

"I look at people's eyes, not their fingers."

"Then you will get into a lot of trouble."

"I'm in trouble already. Give me my bribe back."

Efficiently, if not coolly, she gave it back to me. It began to get very warm in there. Still clinging to me, she said: "My husband is a sort of journalist, too. His firm publishes magazines. He works all night Tuesdays and Wednesdays."

Gently, I disengaged. I leave restless wives for older or more desperate men. I said: "Night work is the big snag of journalism. But it must be a great consolation for your husband to know he's got such a wonderful wife back home."

"Yes," she said.

Julien said: "Why are you out of breath? You look as if you 'ad been for a climb."

"I got an invitation to go for one. More or less."

"Was that why she telephoned?"

"She? How did you guess?"

"A bit of 'er lipstick came over the wire. Telephones are a nuisance for that." I wiped my mouth with a handkerchief. Julien stood up, grinning. "Accept the invitation. It will take your mind off more dangerous things. As I said, let events take their course. I must go now and make my list for the Sûreté."

We shook hands, and I sat down and read an abandoned copy of the London *Times*. I looked for Mideast news. There was only one item:

DRUG THREAT IN ISRAEL

A sharp increase in penalties for drug trafficking was voted by the Knesset, Israel's parliament, today. Members had before them a Health Ministry report which declared bluntly that "the drug fad, cultivated by criminal elements in many Western countries, is now reaching Israel."

The report stated that twice as many arrests were made for drug offenses during the first half of this year as during the corresponding period last year. Pushers of hashish and heroin are increasingly active in cafés frequented by teenagers, as well as in the universities and even some secondary schools.

American students and tourists are partly responsible for bringing the drug problem to Israel. But police officers allege that an Arab extremist organization is supplying drugs free of charge to pushers in the universities and technical colleges in the hope of corrupting Israeli youth.

A waiter told me my car was at the door.

It was a blue-and-gold Cadillac. The driver wore a blue-and-gold cap. He gave me a blue-and-gold grin (blue jowls, gold teeth) and a note written in a vigorous scrawl: "This is to confirm the phone call. The driver knows where to take you."

There was no signature. I thought of Hamam. If someone was running short of lobster bait, this was one way of taking delivery. They didn't even have to pull a gun on me. All the driver had to do was open the door, and, like a nitwit, I would get in.

He opened the door. I got in.

7

We oozed up the mountainside east of Beirut like a bee up a honeysuckle. After a few miles we turned off the Damascus highway onto a well-paved secondary road that overlooked the bay like a balcony. To the west, vineyards and orchards billowed down to the coastal plain. East of the road were pink and blue villas on whose porches elegant refugees from the clamor and stickiness of Beirut yawned and pondered the problem of killing the long, bright afternoon.

We crossed a stream that danced down the hillside on silver steps. Then we climbed through the fringes of a sweet-smelling pinewood. In a clearing in front of two old stone houses, women wearing white Druze headcloths were spreading out pinecones to dry in the sun. Beyond the wood, orchards began again—lush, well-tended orchards, terraced and irrigated, and dominated by a peach-and-cream mansion that would have brought a gleam to the eye of Kubla Khan. It had Moorish arches, a Greek colonnade, a Spanish turret, and latticed Turkish balconies. A guard at the gates looked me over and let us into a fragrant drive shaded with parasol pines.

A massive Sudanese wearing a white galabia, crimson sash, and dark-red tarboosh* was waiting on the blue-veined marble steps that rose gently to the Moorish entrance. The vast hall inside was simply furnished with white armchairs arranged in circles around big brass-and-silver trays on inlaid legs. On each tray stood a silver cigarette box and a silver vase containing three or four roses. Damascene lanterns hung from the ceiling.

---

* A galabia is a long nightshirt-like garment; a tarboosh is a brimless hat made of red felt, and is sometimes called a fez.

A single huge scarlet-and-bronze Mahal carpet glowed in the center of the marble floor.

The Sudanese installed me in an armchair, refused to allow me to refuse a cigarette, lit it for me, gave me *Time* and *Newsweek,* and walked off. Almost at once a scrawny hawk-nosed Arab came in, carrying a coffeepot and a tiny cup, and served me a tot of the refreshing bitter coffee that is the symbol of Bedouin hospitality. I drank and held the cup out, and he refilled it. I drank again and wiggled the cup slightly as I held it out the second time. He took it and loped away.

Time tiptoed by.

A voice said: *"Ahlan wa sahlan!* Welcome!" It belonged to a thick squat man of about sixty in a well-cut olive-green suit, a white shirt, and a red brocade tie. "Mr. Alan? My name's Assury. Edmond Assury."

He looked a little, but only a little, like a peasant who had prospered. His head was tall and blunt, an old Hittite rock from any Lebanese hillside, with a rough grinning dent for its mouth. He had short mosslike hair, most of it still black, and a mustache the size of a postage stamp. The eyes were dark and shrewd, set deeply back beneath bushy eyebrows: eyes that were more used to taking than giving. The third finger of his right hand was missing, which made his handshake messy.

"Glad to know ya," he said. "Let's get outa this railroad station to someplace we can talk."

He led me through a broad hallway and dining room, over a Nizam's nestegg in Kashani carpets, to a semicircular balcony overhung with roses on the northwest side of the house. A tiny wall fountain whispered at each end of the balcony where the stone balustrade met the house: one jet was spewed by a grinning old man, the other by a scowling infant. Beneath us, rivulets flickered through the garden like serpents' tongues. To the north, green hills reached up to gray crags. Down on the coast, Beirut stewed in a steel-wool haze.

I said: "Whoever picked this site for a house was a genius."

Assury bowed his head. "I was twelve years old when I decided on it. I used to sit on this ridge and watch the family's goats and dream. One day, I realized dreaming's no good: it's education and planning that count. So I went to America, earned money, got myself an education, and came back. But it's a long story: I won't bore ya with it."

We sat in dove-gray armchairs whose seat cushions were covered with gazelle skins—which biased me against Assury a little because I happen to be pro-gazelle.

"D'ya use arak?" he asked.

"For everything," I said.

He pressed a buzzer. A minute later two servants carried in a big brass-and-silver tray of *mezze* and set it on legs between us. A third parked at Assury's elbow a smaller tray holding a carafe of arak, a jug of water, tinkling ice cubes, and glasses.

"Telepathy?" I asked.

He chuckled. "No. Rings. Twice for soft drinks, three for arak, four for coffee."

"And one long one for a man with a gun."

"How d'ya guess? Now ya know all my secrets."

The servants went away, closing glass doors behind them, and Assury served the arak. It tasted like a memory of young love.

He said: "I'm a businessman, Mr. Alan. I go straight to the point. I discuss what interests me, and the hell with small talk."

"I don't go for small talk either."

"Fine. I first heard of ya through the Sûreté, where a coupla kind folk keep me informed on current affairs. I know ya were with Arnold Amery when he was killed last night, that ya were present at another sudden death this morning, and that ya'll need a file and a rope ladder if yar relations with the Sûreté get any worse. Tell me what you think of the squid: I invented the recipe."

We each speared a slice. It was superb. I told him.

He resumed: "I knew Arnold. Nice guy. Good taste in arak and scenery, like yaself. I never knew much about his private affairs; but I did know he was worried about the business. The last time I saw him he'd just had his office burglarized."

"He told me about that."

"Good. I gathered he trusted ya. Now here's where we get together. First, we were both friends of Arnold's. Second, we're both nosy characters. I admit it: I like to know what goes on. As for yaself, if ya didn't like nosing around, ya wouldn't be a newspaperman."

"Inspector Bliss warned me to restrain my curiosity."

"Sure; but ya gonna nose around just the same—because ya built that way, because ya were Arnold's friend, and because ya'd like to see justice done. So my idea is: let's coordinate our nosing; let's exchange notes. Try the green olives—they're from my trees; the black ones aren't so good."

I took a green olive.

"Justice," he repeated. "The blindfolded goddess. In the Levant she wears earplugs, too. Ya know as well as I do how we run things in this little republic—well, maybe not quite as well or ya'd have a house on a hilltop here, too. Anyway, ya know that whoever finally takes the rap for last night won't be the guy that should. Ya stand a fair chance of taking it yaself."

I asked: "When Arnold told you he was worried, didn't he say why?"

"No. I was hoping he told you something."

"He didn't have time."

"And Hamam: what ya get outa him?"

I hesitated. "Only one thing . . . of doubtful value. I'll tell you about it in a minute. What's your theory?"

"My guess is that some rival group may have ideas of taking the company over—or, at least, grabbing one of its concessions. But, if so, what's attracting them? The company doesn't mine anything extraordinary—copper and chrome ore, mainly, isn't it? Anyhow, there's the problem: Who's trying to muscle in and why? I guess ya've had experience of nosing out things like that. I've been looking at that magazine ya work for—*Outlook*."

69

"Don't believe everything you read in the papers."

"I don't. I own three."

A car door slammed. Assury listened for a moment. Then he said: "Well, are ya game?"

"To go into competition with the Sûreté?"

He gestured impatiently. "To follow yar nose; to see what ya can dig up. I'll pay all yar expenses, of course, and compensate ya for loss of earnings during the inquiry."

I shook my head. "I don't like that word 'inquiry.' When I set out to trace Hamam this morning, I didn't kid myself I could beat the Sûreté at their own business. I just hoped to gather a few facts—facts that might help me if the Sûreté tried to pull a fast one, and facts I could use in the account of Arnold's murder I'll be telephoning to my office later this afternoon."

Assury shrugged. "Well, there's my idea."

"It's a tempting idea; and if I had to bribe anyone above the rank of corporal I'd be glad of your help. But I'd rather not be under any kind of obligation. What would I do if I discovered it was you that hit me on the head last night?"

He laughed. "Never turn your back on me again."

Through one of the glass doors I saw a gleam of golden hair. Assury saw it, too, and beckoned. The door opened.

"Ya just in time, Anna," he said. "Mr. Alan suspects it might have been me that dented his thoughts last night."

She was now wearing a white dress that made her tanned arms and legs seem to glow. I stood up and Assury introduced us. Her handshake was firm. Her smile set termites gnawing at my spine.

"Anna looks after my foreign real-estate investments," Assury was saying. "She can rattle off the property and tax laws of a dozen countries."

She sat down, refused an arak, and looked me over in quick careful glances, while seeming to give Assury most of her attention. Her face was both alert and discreet. It hinted of high adventure but warned of glaciers: it didn't preclude going places with you, but you'd have a tough selection board to pass first.

Assury pressed his buzzer twice and told her: "Mr. Alan doesn't want to be under any obligation to me—"

She said: "He's heard those bazaar rumors, too, has he?"

He grinned. "But he's almost agreed to join forces with me in inquiring into what happened last night."

"Almost," I said. "Before we sign the treaty, may I ask you two indiscreet questions?"

"Shoot!"

A servant came onto the balcony and offered Anna a choice of soft drinks. When he had gone I said: "We've been talking about concessions and company matters, but Arnold may have been shot for some other reason—or by accident. Have you any idea who may have killed him?"

Assury replied at once: "Would I be asking ya to help me dig around if I did?"

"You might. Would you be inclined to buy a piece of Levant Mining & Chemicals if the opportunity arose?"

"Not under present circumstances. I'd need to know more about their operations and cash flow. Arnold's murder may have been a coverup for something smelly within the company. Do we sign?"

"I guess so. First, though, I'll have to ask my boss in Cyprus to extend my leave. I don't think he'll object—unless someone in the office has been taken ill. The paper gives me a bit of unpaid leave every year for freelancing."

"Fine. When will ya have his answer?"

"I'll be telephoning him when I get back to Beirut."

"Will ya avoid mentioning my name on the phone? Tell him about me—about our understanding—in a private letter, if ya wish; but the phone isn't always as private as it oughta be."

Anna said: "I believe you write for *Outlook*, Mr. Alan."

"Yes."

"Do you write also for *Insight?*"

"Sometimes."

"It's run by the same people, isn't it?"

"Yes." I wondered how much she meant by "the same people."

Assury refilled our glasses. "Ya were gonna tell me something Hamam said. Something of doubtful value."

"I asked who his boss was. He took some persuading. In the end he named a friend of mine: Julien Montrand. I learned later that he used to work for Julien but got fired for theft. I guess he was just stalling—and trying to harm Julien."

Anna and Assury looked at each other.

"Ya call that of doubtful value?" Assury asked. "There's a possible member of the rival group I was talking about."

"There is another factor," Anna said. "Their 1940 defeat left the French with a painful inferiority complex. They have never got used to the fact that they owe their liberation to the British and Americans. Hence the Gaullist myth. So they are constantly tempted to do the British and Americans down, to—"

I shook my head. "That used to be true of a certain type of provincial bourgeois and petty official, but they're dying out. Julien's not that kind of Frenchman. And he's not a crook."

"That's just the point," Assury said. "He isn't—in the ordinary sense of the word. Everything about what happened last night reeks of amateurs. Professionals would have dumped Hamam in the sea. To take him home and call a doctor was crazy, though they seem to have wised up later and sent somebody around to poison him."

"Bliss's assistant," the girl said. "Wasn't he involved in—"

"Bliss's stooge could have done it," Assury said. "But so could Mr. Alan and half the population of Beirut. Something else: professionals would have had an expert to pick Arnold's locks, not a two-bit chiseler. All this jibes with Montrand running the show. He wants facts about Arnold's business, but he's not going to pick locks himself. So he hires Hamam. Hamam's previous thieving would give Montrand a hold over him."

72

I shook my head doubtfully.

Anna said: "I wonder if Monsieur Montrand has as much confidence in you as you have in him? When you were with him in the club, did he tell you he was going to Aleppo?"

"No."

"He is going tonight." She took two sheets of paper out of her big white bag and gave them to Assury. "Green Flag," she told him. "I called there to show Farid the plans of the Iskenderun motel and he asked me to bring these."

Assury glanced at the papers and handed one to me. It had about thirty names typed on it in Arabic, followed by eight in Roman characters.

He said: "This is a list of the people who've traveled to Syria in the last twenty-four hours in Green Flag taxis. Ya know the system, don't ya? Green Flag run regular services between Beirut and every town in Lebanon and Syria. Most people pay only for a seat and share the taxi with four or five others; those who can afford it have a car to themselves." He showed me another list. "These are reservations for tonight or tomorrow morning."

On this one there were only nine names. Six were Arab and three Western European:

Montrand, Julien—French/m/businessman—Aleppo 22h.

Blane, Henry—British/m/businessman—Aleppo 23h.

Wilson, Harold—British/m/entertainer—Damascus 11h.

"Green Flag Transportation is one of my companies," Assury went on. "They have to make these lists for the police, so they give me a copy. One of my secretaries spends an hour a day on these and the airlines' passenger lists: ya'd be surprised how much useful information—business and political—he squeezes outa them."

You'd be surprised, I thought, to learn that someone in our Cyprus office spends several hours a day studying passenger lists from all over the Near East. I said: "Julien may have decided to go to Aleppo after he left me. Anyway, he's under no obligation to tell me his plans. He's probably hoping to sell more machines in the northeast now that the Russians are backing the Euphrates irrigation scheme. Aren't they inaugurating a new canal this week?"

Assury nodded. "Yeah. Green Flag are having a great week running Commies up there to cheer. We oughta call it Red Flag Transportation. And the plane service to Aleppo's booked solid."

"I've just remembered," Anna said. "Pete McGlint is trying to get on a plane to Aleppo. He told me at lunch."

"I saw him this morning, too," I said. "And he didn't tell me his travel plans, either. Maybe I ought to grow long, golden hair."

She looked at me rather haughtily.

"How d'ya like that!" Assury exclaimed. He was scanning the list of taxi bookings. "Two of the guys in the Arabic list are Rooskis. Farid usually lists them with the Europeans."

"What are their names?" I asked.

He squinted at the paper. "Nov-nin-ski, trade official, and Stro-go-nov, geologist. About the only part of northern Syria likely to interest a geologist is the Kurd Dagh*—where Arnold's company has a concession."

"I'm beginning to like the idea of a trip to Aleppo," I said. "If only to see what all these people are up to. Though I'll probably find they're attending a Rotary convention."

Anna said: "You won't get on the plane."

"You could go by road, though," Assury suggested. "Book a Green Flag car. I think that's an idea. All expenses on me, of course."

"What about the Sûreté? They may not want to part with me."

"I'll fix that."

"Can you give me a card with a few words on it? Something to open doors and influence people?"

"I never give open introductions. But I'll have two letters of

---

* The mountainous Kurdish region north of Aleppo.

74

accreditation sent to yar hotel before ya leave: one from a right-wing paper I own in Beirut, the other from a left-wing paper I own in Damascus. They'll establish that ya've a link with me and give ya some protection—provided ya show the right one to the right people."

Anna laughed. "And the left one to the left people."

Assury gave me the telephone number of his Beirut secretariat and said: "Let me know where you stay in Aleppo. If anything interesting develops this end, we'll call ya—or, if it's confidential, I'll persuade one of my bright young men to go to Aleppo."

"Discrimination!" Anna exclaimed. "I know at least one bright young woman who could be persuaded to go to Aleppo. I love those bazaars—and the citadel by moonlight."

"Nix on the moonlight," Assury said. "Aleppo's a tough town. Ya'll get yar throat cut."

"With Mr. Alan to protect me?"

I stuck my chest out a quarter of an inch.

Assury grinned. "Okay. Have it yar own way. Looks like we got a swell team. Enthusiasm, heroism, self-sacrifice . . ."

I'd expected him to resent her suggestion. I suddenly realized that, as a girl, she just wasn't there so far as he was concerned.

"Especially self-sacrifice," Anna said. She smiled and stretched out her legs languorously.

75

8

Assury accompanied us to the car. The driver was leaning against it, talking to a youngish man with a round face, fair hair, and handsome hazel eyes. Assury called the driver to give him instructions and I strolled on four or five paces, then stood, waiting to say goodbye. Anna walked straight on to the car.

The fair man was wearing a white naval-style cap, a white jacket over a horizontally striped tee-shirt, and navy-blue trousers. He might have been an actor, a yacht-owning playboy, or a seafront barman. He ignored Anna, but I expected him to touch his cap as she drew near him and maybe open the car door. He thrust his hands into his pockets and turned his back. She opened the door herself.

Assury took my arm. "Meet Jemal," he said. "Lebanon's answer to Sir Francis Drake. He's in charge of my harem."

"Huh?" It was stronger than me. It leaped right out.

Assury laughed. "I have a yacht. It's called *My Harem*. Ya shoulda seen the American ambassador's wife when I invited her husband to spend a weekend in *My Harem*. He accepted, too."

The fair man beamed at us. He had the smooth skin and long eyelashes of a girl. He wore a discreet perfume, not the usual violent patchouli Arabs favor.

"This is Mr. Alan," Assury told him in Arabic. "Folks that are nice to him get their picture in the paper."

Jemal looked as if he would like having his picture in the paper. He smirked and gave me one of those long, clinging handshakes that set you wondering when you're going to get your hand back. Then he fondled Assury and Assury pinched his plump cheek and kidded him. In the Cadillac Anna rolled her big eyes impatiently. At last Assury disengaged and gave me his three-fingered hand to shake. "Good hunting," he said. Jemal sat next to the driver and I got into the back with Anna. We moved silently forward.

The soundproof window behind the front seat was closed. I said to Anna: "I'd never have thought it possible, but Jemal doesn't seem to love you. What's wrong with him?"

"His glands, I suppose," she said.

"Huh?"

"He is jealous of me."

I nearly said it again. I bit my bottom lip and cast around. "You mean—he wants your job?"

She said: "I do not like the sound of that."

I gaped at her. "I didn't even hear the sound. This conversation's going way over my head."

She thought for a moment and said: "Let me put it like this. I heard Edmond Bey catch you with his silly gag about *My Harem*. If he had a real harem, its occupants would not be women. You know the Levant well enough, I believe, to understand me."

She was blushing, but I plowed on: "I still don't see what Jemal's got against you."

"Really . . ." Her flush deepened. "Jemal was once Edmond Bey's special favorite. Now, there is still, as you saw, a playful kind of affection, but that is all. Perhaps it is because Edmond Bey is becoming old. But Jemal, in his primitive little mind, thinks that I have supplanted him in Edmond's . . . esteem."

"And converted Edmond to orthodoxy?"

She looked out of the window. The blue-and-pink villas flashed gaily by. She said: "I hope I do not sound censorious in telling you this. For me, it is convenient that Edmond Bey's tastes lie in that direction. It might be difficult for me to work with him so closely and to visit his house so freely if they were orthodox."

"Somebody told me you work for a lawyer: Anis Salem."

"I work with him. We are both part of Edmond's empire."

"Was it Salem who telephoned me?"

"Yes. We had been wondering how to contact you. When I saw you in the club I telephoned him. He checked that Edmond Bey was free and called you back."

We swung onto the Damascus highway and plunged toward Beirut. The far horn of the bay was doing a bubble dance in the heat haze. I looked at Anna's eyes. Their blue was midway between the rich royal blue of the sea and the paler blue of the afternoon sky.

I said: "I don't like this grudge Jemal's got against you."

She shrugged. "I hardly ever see him."

The air began to get heavy and damp, and soon we were in the steam-laundry atmosphere of Beirut. We pulled up in front of a glass-and-concrete office block. Anna jumped out.

"Goodbye," she said. "Enjoy Aleppo."

"Especially the citadel by moonlight."

"Remember what Edmond Bey said."

"I've never had my throat cut in Aleppo."

"There's a first time for everything."

From my room in the Saint-George, I rang the Stanhope Club and asked the receptionist where Blane was staying.

"At the Normandie," she said.

I booked a call for Cyprus and got out my poppet. What we called a poppet looked like a small Japanese tape recorder. Our version was equipped with a cassette of pop songs on any of which it would superimpose a spoken message at very high speed. First, you recorded your message. Then, by adjusting a dial, you chose a pop song to camouflage it. Next, you set another control that would decide whether your message was played ten, twenty, thirty, or forty seconds after a synchronization note at the beginning of the song. Finally, you pressed the "play" button, and the song and your message could be telephoned or broadcast—or recorded on another cassette for delivery by mail or courier. The message could then be erased, but not the pop songs, which were used over and over again.

78

The speeded-up spoken text rarely lasted more than thirty seconds and sounded like a mild case of tape flutter or radio interference. The combination of speed and pop song acted like a scrambler; it could be unscrambled only by a special receiver-recorder adjusted to filter out the pop song and slow down the message. It was not a system for top-secret communication, of course; and, except in an emergency, no sane person would use it in Russia or any other state where the authorities were both instinctively suspicious and educated in electronics. But it was useful in most Near Eastern and Mediterranean countries.

I recorded a message for O'Neill—a few facts and impressions to supplement what I'd be telling him on the open wire— and waited for my Cyprus call. When it came I greeted Heather affectionately, for the operator's benefit, and asked where the sun had been burning her lately.

"In my back garden," she said.

After a minute or so of chitchat—she was good at the dumb-office-bird act—I said: "Poppet, I've found that old Beatle song you wanted. I bought the record at a junk stall for twenty-four pesetas. It's a bit rough, but I've taped it."

"Twenty-four pesetas!" she exclaimed. "Since when are you in señorita country?"

"I meant piasters, Heather honey. Twenty-four piasters."

She knew now that I was going to play pop song number two and my message would start forty seconds after the pip. She would be adjusting her receiver as she said: "Can you play it for me now?"

"The song? It would sound awful over the blower."

"Oh, please!"

After I had played the tape and she had told me it was smashing—which meant reception was good—I talked to O'Neill. I gave him an account of the deaths of Arnold and Haman but said nothing of my involvement or Assury's interest. I had covered these in my poppet message.

"I'm sorry about Amery," he said; "but there're the makings of a story there. I've recorded it, and— Hang on a minute. I've got to take another call. Don't go away." Heather would have brought him the unscrambled recording of my poppet message. She twittered to me while he listened to it. Then O'Neill came back.

"Don't be too sanguine," he said. "London won't give it a lot of space. But it's worth following up. Your other piece is interesting, too. I should accept that fellow's offer. Expenses and all. If, that is, you really want to go north to see that ditch."

"Most of my pals are going. So is the chap I skylarked with. There may be a story. But I don't want to use up leave."

"I think we can fix that. Know anything about newts?"

"I've heard the females are rather crude little minxes."

"You've got yourself a job. I hereby appoint you our roving ditch-watcher."

A few minutes later Anna telephoned. "Will you be there for another quarter of an hour? We'd like to send you an envelope. It is important that you receive it personally."

"I hope it's equally important that you bring it personally."

"I am not a postman, Mr. Alan," she said.

Squelch.

The blue-and-gold Cadillac drove up to the hotel in due course. The driver with the blue-and-gold cap grinned brightly and gave me a manila envelope. It contained the two letters Assury had promised me and the equivalent in Lebanese and Syrian currency of about one thousand dollars.

I walked over to the Normandie. Blane was standing just inside the lobby. He was wearing a fawn tropical-weight suit and peering out at the sky like an old Africa hand waiting for his sundowner.

"Excuse me," I said. "You are Colonel Blane, aren't you?"

He shook his head. "You've muffed your line. You should have said: 'Colonel Blane, I presume?' And I'd have replied— what did Livingstone reply?"

" 'Right on'?"

"No. That would be the American consul." We shook

hands. "Aren't you Ray Alan of *Outlook?* Don't ask me why, but I associate you with Cyprus."

"We met at one of the High Commissioner's parties a few years ago. Queen's birthday, I think. I've seen you once or twice since, but usually you were in uniform. So I wasn't sure—"

"And I've pruned the fungus." He touched his mustache.

"That's why you look different. It used to be rather raffish." His eyebrows shot up. "I mean RAF-ish."

He laughed, then frowned. "I heard at the club that you ran into trouble last night. Sad about Amery. Nice chap. Hope they get the devil who did it. Are you here for long?"

"I should be going to Aleppo to see a new irrigation scheme. But I can't get a seat on a plane, and even the taxi services are booked up. I was at the Green Flag office an hour ago and saw your name on a list of reservations. I'm wondering if—"

"You'd like to share my taxi? Gladly! It's a boring trip alone; and two's an alliance if you run into trouble. I'm going overnight, though. Too hot in the daytime. Leaving here at eleven o'clock. Will that be all right?"

I looked at my watch. I had a lot to do. I wanted to see our Beirut correspondent. And I intended to have a chat with Ondine, the girl at La Sirène, even if I had to dive into the sea after her.

"Yes," I told Blane. "That'll be fine."

I met our Beirut man in an imitation English pub. It sold afternoon teas and a variety of beers, stouts, and pies, and was decorated with horse brasses, hunting prints, a microskirted English barmaid, and a dartless dartboard. "Two Arabs had an argument in here last month," the barmaid explained, "and began using the darts as missiles. So now we don't leave them lying about."

Our correspondent wasn't thrilled by my clomping around in his parish, but he wasn't grievously irked, either. He knew he might be given an assignment in Cyprus or elsewhere at any

81

time. Tossteam often adopted the Mafia's technique of bringing in an agent from another area for a specific operation and then rushing him out.

We drank tea and ate fruit cake. I took out of my wallet the envelope containing the white powder I had found in Arnold's bathroom.

Our correspondent blinked. "Sodium bicarb? I thought you had the digestive system of an ostrich. Remember that raw liver the Jaulani Bedouin fed us on?"

"I found this in Arnold's flat. Could you get it analyzed?" I tore a page out of my notebook and poured some of the powder onto it. "It was disguised as talcum powder."

"Who says it isn't talcum powder?"

"It doesn't feel quite like it."

He rubbed a little between thumb and forefinger, raised his fingertip halfway to his mouth, then lowered it, grinning. "I'm an only son," he said. He folded the paper carefully. "I'll get it done tomorrow morning. If we were in Alexandria or Marseille, I'd say this would have a bitter taste and a good sniff of it would whoosh you over the bar. But Lebanon's not heroin country."

9

Dusk had already come to the web of alleyways behind the waterfront, but the sky and sea were still luminous. The lamp over the entrance to La Sirène had not been switched on yet. The arched double door was shut. I pushed it.

One half creaked open. In the entrance hall a dying strip light flickered like a moth in a spider's web. I went in.

The door of the owner's office was closed. Opposite it, on the right of the hallway, the side nearest Ondine's steps, I saw a dark corridor with a curtain drawn across it. I went behind the curtain and switched on the little flash Julien had given me. The corridor was about five yards long. Three doors gave onto it. Two, side by side, looked like closet or storeroom doors; the third, down a couple of steps, blocked the end of the corridor. I wanted it to be a cellar door.

It opened silently on well-oiled hinges. Stone steps went down to a corner and a glow of light. I snapped off the flash and closed the door behind me. Slowly, cautiously, I felt my way down, toward cool dank air and mingled odors of aniseed, spices, wine, and the things of the sea. At the corner I saw a big cellar below me, lit by a dusty lamp, with a shadowy array of barrels and crates and racks of bottles around its walls. I went down the last few steps.

A man laughed.

A half-open door, only three or four paces beyond the bottom step, led to another cellar. The laughter came from there.

"La, la!" a woman's voice said. No, no. Then, to show how determined her "no" was: *"El-bab!"* The door.

I froze. Footsteps approached. I saw an elbow and a powerful shoulder. The door slammed. A key turned. There was a pause.

"You're going to tear it," the woman said in Arabic.

"No; I'm going to take it off," the man replied.

"*La, la!*" the woman said again.

Someone in there had been reading too much early Aldous Huxley. He would probably hate an interruption. But I had to talk to his playmate. I knocked on the door.

Nothing happened. I knocked again. Light footsteps . . . and the door opened. Ondine stood there, flushed and feline, in a long black-and-silver brocade robe. She stared at me, puzzled, then recognised me and asked in English: "What you want?"

"To talk to you," I said. "Privately. It's very important."

She clicked her tongue against her teeth. "You no can come here. If the boss catch you . . ."

"The boss is my friend. I'm helping him. Because if I don't talk to you, the police will. The Sûreté."

"Why the bolice want to talk with me?"

"That's what I've come to tell you."

She sighed in bewilderment, shrugged, looked quickly over her shoulder, and stood aside to let me in. She shut the door behind me and turned the key.

This one was a cellar out of *Homes & Gardens.* It was lit by a wrought-iron floor lamp with a big orange shade; its walls were pink; and it contained a divan, armchairs, a low table, a television set, a tape recorder, and a long dressing table with three mirrors and enough bottles to start a drugstore. There were rugs on the floor; and a waterpot like the one that had poisoned Hamam stood on a plate in the far corner. Two sliding closet doors, partly open, revealed a dark-blue abaya* and a red dress. There was no sign of Aldous, but a closed door on the right explained that.

Ondine stood uneasily in the middle of the floor. Her wide

* Cloak.

green eyes were worried. She said: "Tell now. What the bolice want?"

I stood with my back to her dressing table to have a view of the doors. I said: "The friend I was with last night—you remember him?" She nodded. "He is dead. The Sûreté are looking for his murderer."

"I know nothing."

"You said something that disturbed him. Something about a city in the sea. What did you mean?"

Her eyes were less apprehensive now. She said: "Nothing. People think I live under the sea. I try to make one joke. That is all."

I shook my head and smiled and waited. She watched me tensely. I leaned back against her dressing table and toyed with a heavy cut-glass bottle, the shape of a hand grenade, labeled *Coup de foudre*. There was a thick, sepulchral silence you could have cut with a knife. She didn't like it and began to fidget. Aldous didn't seem to like it, either. His door opened suddenly and he stepped forward, knife in hand, all set to cut the silence and anything else that needed seeing to.

He was the bouncer. His placid buffalo eyes focused on my tonsils. Ondine laughed nervously and rattled off a quick Arabic sentence to tell him what I wanted. He sneered and began flicking his knife against his left thumbnail.

I understood his reply but didn't react. Ondine translated: "He say you must go quick and never come back. And if ever you tell anybody you saw me down here . . ."

"I can guess the rest," I said. "He'll take knife-throwing lessons."

She told him what I had said.

I didn't see him move. There was simply a steel arc and the knife was quivering in the edge of the dressing table an inch from my right hand. I didn't mind about the dressing table. It was oldish and scratched and there were probably plenty more where it came from. But my right hand was still fairly new and still fairly useful for picking up glasses of arak and things, and

85

there were no more in stock. I didn't like people using it for target practice. I hurled the grenade-shaped bottle labeled *Coup de foudre* at Aldous's head. It smashed into his cheek and fell, without breaking, to the floor.

Wailing, Ondine darted forward and scooped it up.

Aldous lowed, shook his head, and staggered forward, blood trickling from a cut under his eye. He wiped it with the back of his hand, pretending to be more dazed than he was, and rushed at me. I took a liter bottle of eau de cologne from the dressing table and tickled his nose with it. He shot a kick at me that would have cracked a safe. I leaped aside and his shoe grazed my thigh. The kick unbalanced him, but he recovered quickly and pulled his knife out of the edge of the dressing table. As he swung around after me, I closed in again and stroked him behind the ear with my bottle. His knees quivered. I got two hands on the bottle neck and gave him a playful pat on the base of the skull that shattered the glass and drenched him in eau de cologne. He dived forward onto the rug, his teeth bared as if he intended to take a bite out of it.

I selected an unopened half-liter bottle of eau de quinine and held it at the ready. My hand was trembling.

I told Ondine: "Help me get him into the other cellar."

I put his knife in my pocket and took his right arm. She took his left, and we dragged him through the open door into the cellar where he had been hiding and dumped him on its bare cement floor. In the middle of the floor, steps and a handrail went steeply down into softly stirring water and on, beneath its surface, along a cement-lined trench to the salt-encrusted seaward wall.

"Is there a door down there?" I asked Ondine.

She nodded and tapped a long iron bar with her foot. One end of the bar curved down into the water, the other was hooked into a slot in the floor beside the steps. I picked it up and pulled. The water in the trench shuddered, and I could feel a heavy door opening. I pushed, the water swirled and rippled, and I felt the door close again. I took the knife out of my pocket and threw it into the deep end of the water. Aldous didn't mind. He was snoring as contentedly as if they'd mixed the cement with swansdown.

A clothesline was slung across one end of the cellar. There was an abaya like Ondine's hanging on it, a couple of head-cloths, a man's swimming trunks, and a big towel; and, on the floor nearby, a bathmat, an electric heater, and a pair of sandals like the ones Ondine wore for her act, but bigger and sturdier. I had a closer look. Strips of lead were riveted across the soles of the sandals. The abaya was made of polyester and had a weighted hem and straps inside it to prevent it from flapping open.

"So that's how you work it," I said. "You disappear behind the orchestra—I suppose there's a flight of stairs backstage—and a man dressed like you strolls out onto the quay, goes down the steps, vanishes under the water, and pops up here. Not this man, though."

"No. My brother."

"But there's nothing illegal in any of that. Why were you so worried about the police?" I looked around the cellar. "Were these steps and the door made just for your act?"

"No. They here before. But old and tumbling-down. Once one big smuggler live here."

We went back to her cellar. I locked and bolted the door. Aldous smelled like a rose garden, but he wouldn't be feeling too friendly when he recovered.

I said: "This place could still be used for smuggling, couldn't it? Canisters full of hashish could be attached to a cable and let out through the underwater door. A launch would tow them to a ship. Stuff coming into Lebanon—Swiss watches, for example—could be delivered here in canisters in much the same way. And if the customs ever called, your act would explain why the steps and underwater door are kept in such good repair."

She frowned. "You working with the customs?"

"No. I'm all for free trade. I won't tell the customs anything if you tell me what I want to know. The City in the Sea—remember? What does it mean?"

"I tell you: it mean nothing."

I tucked the eau de quinine under my arm and looked her dressing table over. In the middle was a bottle of that Chanel number they all have to have. The supervamp size, pride of the collection. I held it upside down and pretended to be easing out the stopper. I said: "There are probably cheaper forms of chemical warfare, but if you insist . . ."

She yelled anxiously and leaped toward me with all her claws out. I brandished the eau de quinine. She stopped dead, put the beginnings of a smile on her lips, and tossed her head back haughtily. Then, slowly and provocatively, the big green eyes mocking me, she walked right up to me and took the Chanel out of my hand. I let her take it but grabbed her forearm, and we stood looking at each other.

Soon her smile broadened and the mockery went out of her eyes. She said softly: "'*Ya habibi,** you forgetting something. You forgetting this the Arab world and I am a woman. I am used to being bullied. From a Western man I want gentleness, like in the cinema; I want charm and seduction, not threats with bottles."

"I'd love to seduce you, angel, but there just isn't time."

The mockery came back. "Does it take you so long? Ah, yes—I have seen this in American films. Much singing and dancing and arguing and kissing and offering flowers and going out to dinner . . . Here, a man just gives money to the girl's father."

I let go of her arm. "I haven't any money to give your father," I said, "but I'll gladly take you out to dinner this evening."

She laughed dryly. "And we both die this evening. No. But you not bullying me now, so I tell you. Two English came to La

* Oh, friend.

Sirène three days ago. Well, one was English; the other speaking English but I not understand him good. Maybe he French. It was he that said it. He drinking much arak. I went to their table like I went to yours. He said: 'She must be from the City in the Sea—you not think, Benny?' Something like that. And he said again: 'The City in the Sea!' Then he laugh much. So I think it one English joke and I say it to your friend, but he not like it. That is all."

"The other man's name was Benny?"

"Benny or Danny—one of these names."

"Could it have been Denny?"

"*Yimkin.*" She shrugged. "Maybe."

"What did Denny look like?"

"Like this." She made a priggish, disdainful face. "He no smile easy."

"And the man who spoke?"

"He not beautiful, that one." She held up a fist. "The face like this."

"Was he tall?"

"*Taweel?* I think no, but I not see him standing."

"Did the other man, Denny, call him by his name?"

"*La.*"

I thought I heard Aldous stirring. I wanted to be out of there before he kicked the door off its hinges. I said: "Thanks for telling me this. I'd like to apologize to your friend for breaking that bottle on his head, but I don't want to seem tactless."

She said glumly: "He not my friend. He my husband."

I patted her arm and went out into the cellar with the barrels and crates, up the stairs, and along the corridor to the entrance hall, still carrying the bottle of eau de quinine. A waiter was standing in the doorway looking out at the dark square. He turned when he heard me. I gave him the eau de quinine.

"I brought this for the doorkeeper," I said. "The man in the sailor suit. I can't find him anywhere. Will you give it to him?"

The waiter asked: "He one friend of you?"

"He helped me last night. The boss knows all about it."

He looked puzzled, but he let me pass. The outside lamp was on now and two bats were pretending to be Lebanese taxi drivers and whizzing after the insects it attracted. I did a passable imitation of a Lebanese taxi myself getting away from there.

10

I showered, changed, paid my bill, packed my suitcase, left it at the Normandie, and ate dinner in a quiet little Armenian restaurant: *tutmaj* (a soup made with yogurt, eggs, onions, and mint) and *lahme b'ajeen* (thin discs of light pastry covered with finely chopped lamb, pine nuts, pomegranate seeds, tomato, onion, and other vegetables).

A little before eleven I met Blane in the Normandie bar. He questioned me about Arnold until the car arrived. It was a big green Ford with a V-shaped dent in its left rear door and crossed green flags painted on its rear window. The driver seemed annoyed when Blane told him I was coming along; but he gave us a clean pillow each and drove off at once.

The lights of Beirut slid away. We chatted sleepily about the irrigation scheme I had told him I was going to see. I leaned back in my corner and watched the moongleam quivering and fraying along the empty shore. We were taking the coastal road to just north of Tripoli and then striking inland to Homs and Hama.

Dimly, I remembered hearing someone say that Blane might have come to the Levant to drive a truck for one of the oil companies. It sounded like the sort of thing I would say, but I couldn't be sure.

I yawned and asked: "Are you in oil?"

"No," he replied. "In tomato sauce."

"Say that again."

"Tomato sauce. And tomato purée, tomato ketchup, tomato soup, tomato juice, canned tomatoes, tomato sandwich spreads . . . Everything that can be done to or with a tomato—we do it."

"You should be popular with the politicians. Who's we?"

"Tom Ato Enterprises."

"You won't do much business in Aleppo. Syrian mobs throw rocks."

"We're launching tomato-juice drinks in the Moslem world."

"Have you been out of the army long?"

"Three years. I worked for TOP—Trans-Orient Pipelines—for two years. Organizing transport, my old army job. Then I thought I'd take it easy in Cyprus. But being idle nearly drove me round the bend, so I joined Tom Ato. It sounds a silly business, but I'm concerned with transport and distribution."

The next thing I knew was that a guard was yawning at us outside a frontier post and asking for our passports. We were leaving Lebanon. A few minutes later another guard yawned at us outside another frontier post, and a customs man looked us over. We were entering Syria.

Suddenly the sky was pink and all the sinners in hell were moaning. There was a rusty hinge where my neck had been. I blinked out of the window. The moaning came from great wooden waterwheels through which the rising sun was skimming golden pebbles across a river. We had reached Hama, a shabby sullen town on the Orontes that looks as if it has been dumped there out of a sack. The car halted beside a dingy building plastered with posters showing American teenagers knifing and strangling each other.

Blane rubbed his eyes and said: "Hama already? Good show. I told the driver to break the journey here. Thought we could wash and have breakfast in the hotel."

"If this is the hotel you're thinking of," I said, "it's closed. It's now a cinema. As you can see, it's giving the local Moslems an intensive course in Christian civilization."

He frowned. "Hell! I was counting on that." In Arabic, he asked the driver to take us to a café.

"They won't serve you," the driver said. "It's Ramadan.

The café owners are all Moslems here." Ramadan is the month during which pious Moslems fast from dawn to dusk and feast, if they can afford to, at night. "I'm a Christian," he added. "I have a flask of coffee. I will serve you a cup, if you wish, when we get clear of the town."

"Thank you," Blane said. He turned to me. "You see: Christian civilization has something to be said for it."

We drove on, across a cobbled square where men in black-and-yellow robes were setting out market stalls, and over a narrow bridge, overtaking three haughty camels. As we picked up speed, a mangy pye-dog hurtled toward the car, snarling. We felt a soft thump and heard a hideous yelp. The driver cursed. I looked back. The dog lay on its side, twitching. A boy ran up and threw a rock at it.

For miles there is nothing but the straight simmering road and the parched steppe. Occasionally a tawny village flashes by—a village so old that its core is a great adobe mound. The steppe is almost treeless, so there is little wood for building or burning: many houses are simply mud igloos, and the villagers' fuel is a mixture of chaff and dung, which the women knead into flat cakes and dry in the sun. Downwind from the village, its smell accosts you—the patriarch of smells, a hundred centuries old: a cloying redolence of food and excrement, joy and anguish, copulation and death. Man's most enduring creation.

A dust devil whirls over the steppe. The road ripples with heat haze and plunges, a short way ahead, into a phantom lake. Suddenly, like a mirage, a mighty citadel appears, riding above the haze, receding, shimmering. The road runs over a succession of low ridges, and as it falls and rises, the citadel vanishes and reappears, each time in firmer focus. The mirage hardens and deepens to include a honey-colored panorama of minarets and domes and tall houses. The road swings over a low shoulder of rock and rides gently down into Aleppo.

Aleppo's best hotels were bulging with officials and dignitaries on their way to the Euphrates ceremony. The fourth one we tried was a rambling old place on the edge of the suq.* Its plumbing had gone out of order at about the same time as the Ottoman empire and nobody had done very much about it. But it had vacant rooms and I noticed the name "Julien Montrand" on a registration card on the receptionist's desk. I recommended it highly to Blane.

I washed, shaved, and sent a wish-you-were-here cable to Heather to let Cyprus know my address. Then I wandered through a dim bazaar and then out into the glare of an unshaded street. Nobody was following me.

The air was hot and desiccating, even for Aleppo. A beggar's parched voice whined for baksheesh. A contemptuous-looking camel dumped a load of sheepskins beside me and stirred up a column of dust that followed me down the street like a tame jinn. A silversmith began making tantalizing tinkling noises that sounded like ice cubes plopping into glasses. I took a shortcut back to the hotel.

Julien was in the lobby, putting on a hat and sunglasses in front of a speckled gilt-framed mirror. He looked startled when he saw me; then he gripped my hand. *"Vive la presse!* I might 'ave known. NORTHERN SYRIA—VORTEX OF THE POWER STRUGGLE. There is your 'eadline, ready-made. I'd make a good editor—no?"

"No. Editors don't write headlines. They just sneer at the people who do."

"The Russians arrived first—but I was forgetting: you told me about Strogonov. Then came the British, complete with a dazzling Russian-speaking blonde."

"Come and have an arak," I said. "I talk nonsense best with a glass in my hand."

"No; I must go. With regret, for I am fascinated by your failure to ask me about the blonde. That suggests you know about

* A vast central warren of covered bazaars.

'er already, *n'est-ce pas?* I wish I 'ad time to watch your meeting in the bar—your avoidance of each other until someone, McGlint per'aps, introduces you . . ."

In the bar things worked out as he had said. It was a long, bleak room, like an old railway snack bar, furnished in dark wood and dominated by a fearsome ceiling fan. Anna and McGlint were standing at a half-shuttered window looking out toward the citadel. Anna wore a short-sleeved oatmeal-colored dress made of a rippling synthetic material that became iridescent when she moved into a shaft of sunlight. A combined headcloth and snood of the same fabric enclosed her hair. Two middle-aged Syrians, the bar's only other occupants, sat at a table flicking their eyes over a catalogue and Anna's contours.

She looked through me, like Marie Antoinette meeting an undergardener, when McGlint called me over. But when he introduced us she smiled and gave me a firm handshake, and I began to have termite trouble again. McGlint was unexpectedly friendly, watched the barman to be sure he served me Zahle arak, made a good story of his negotiations for a seat aboard a freight plane, and then, obligingly, went off to answer the telephone.

Anna said: "I came on the same plane. We arrived only half an hour ago. Fortunately, I did not have any of Pete's problems."

"Pete wouldn't have had any," I said, "if he'd been cast in the same mold as you."

"Edmond Bey has an interest in Levant Airways. They could not refuse when he asked them to squeeze me aboard."

"I wouldn't have refused, either."

She ignored that. "Tell me now: what did you do with the gun that shot Arnold Amery?"

I watched the ceiling fan go round, ready to chop my head off if I annoyed it. "I can't remember having seen it. Why do you put the question like that? You sound like a Sûreté man."

"The Sûreté think they have the gun. It was found in— Pete

95

is coming. This evening, can you— No; I will come here. Between six and seven."

"Aren't you staying here?"

"No. Pete is; and he invited me for lunch. Tell me who built the citadel."

"Mainly a chap called Malik, son of the great Salah ed-Din. It's mostly twelfth century—"

"That wa' the manager oot at number two mine," Pete broke in. "I'll be goin' oot there. If either o' ye'd like a nice dusty jeep ride, ye'll be welcome to come along."

We had lunch together. At first, McGlint seemed pleased I had come to Aleppo and, apparently, dropped my interest in Arnold's affairs. When he learned I had traveled with Blane, he looked annoyed.

Over coffee I asked: "How did you like La Sirène—and Ondine?"

His small eyes opened wide. "Pretty fair. But how did ye know I wa' there?"

"Didn't you tell me? You were there three or four nights ago, weren't you?"

"Aye; but I didna tell ye."

I shook my head. "I'm sorry. So much has happened lately and I've had so little sleep . . . It's Julien I'm thinking of. But maybe you were there together."

"No; I wa' with Denny. I didna see Julien." He frowned into his coffee.

Anna sat still and tense, her keen eyes flashing from one to the other of us.

After lunch I undressed, lay on my bed, and stared at the cracks in the ceiling, searching for a pattern in them. After what seemed like two minutes I was forcing my eyes open, feeling thirsty, and realizing I had fallen asleep. I put on my dressing gown and slippers and explored a meandering corridor in quest of a bathroom.

I found one and had a shower. On the return journey I noticed two solidly built men walking ahead of me. One of them stopped at my door. I sidestepped into an alcove and rumpled up my towel and refolded it slowly, watching them.

The other man clicked his tongue. They moved on to the next room—Blane's. They looked at each other and one of them rapped on the door. When Blane opened it, they walked him back into the room. I heard the word "Sûreté." The door slammed.

I sprinted to my room, locked myself in, and put an ear to the wall. I heard a muffled protest from Blane and a scuffle of drawers being opened and shut. At last Blane's door creaked and clicked, and footsteps and voices moved off down the corridor.

I opened my shutters and leaned out the window. High above the flat rooftops, the citadel glowed like the crucible of a solar oven. But the afternoon was dying, and long shadows lay across the square in front of the hotel.

Blane and the Sûreté men emerged onto the sidewalk and got into a gray car. It drove off across the square into a narrow street that led southward through the suq. The only thing wrong with that was that the Sûreté HQ was in the modern quarter to the west.

11

I dressed quickly, went down to one of the cafés in the square, and shut myself in its telephone booth. I called the Sûreté and, after a volley of crackles and buzzes, was allowed to talk to an officer named Captain Azzam.

"Good evening, Captain," I said. "This is Smith-Jones of the British consulate. I understand that a British subject, a Mr. Henry Blane, has been called to the Sûreté for interrogation. Two men, claiming to be officers of yours, arrested him in his hotel and drove him away in a gray car. Would it be possible for you to give us any information on this?"

A brief electric storm. Then he assured me that the Sûreté had no interest in anyone called Blane.

"The men were not wearing uniforms," I said. He remained silent, so I added: "If there is some confidential angle, perhaps you would prefer to speak to the consul personally . . ."

"No, no. It is not necessary."

"Is it possible that some other police service may wish to interrogate Mr. Blane and have forgotten to inform you?"

"No, I think not."

"Would it be possible for you to ring the consulate if you trace him or get any information?"

For the first time he said, "Yes." I gave him Blane's description and the name of the hotel, and we said goodbye.

From another café I called our Aleppo stringer. He was also the correspondent for three Arabic papers. I told him about Blane's arrest, much as one of his regular contacts would, and added: "The strange thing is that he was driven southward from the hotel, into the suq, not toward Sûreté HQ. And I understand that the British consulate has been told the Sûreté's not interested in Blane. That's not for publication, though. There used to be a lockup in the suq, didn't there? Do you know if it's still used—and by whom? That's only idle curiosity on my part, of course, but it might garnish the story." "Idle curiosity" in this context meant: "Please find out."

"I don't think it's used," he said. "Anyway, thank you for the information. It will make a story. I hope I'll see you while you're in Aleppo. I still have some of that yellow arak from Idlib. Where will you be in about half an hour?"

"At the hotel."

"Good. If I can free myself, I'll ring you and we'll arrange to meet. Keep the line clear!" That meant he would be sending me a message—not by telephone.

I went back to the hotel, up to my floor, and stood outside Blane's room. They were not self-locking doors and I had not heard the Sûreté men turn a key. There was nobody in the corridor. I tried Blane's door. It creaked open.

The shutters were almost closed and there was a strange golden half-light in the room. I stepped inside. A red handbag lay on the bed. A hint of perfume reached me. The door was pushed to, and a young woman with a loose red scarf over the back of her head stepped from behind it.

"*Chéri!*" she said.

But at once she gasped and raised her hand to hide her face. She was slim and compact, and an unbelted linen dress the color of Aleppo stone at sunset understressed her figure intriguingly. Her lips and nails were the same bright red as her flimsy headscarf. Lustrous black hair, pulled tightly back from the temples, and a solemn, symmetrical face with big dark eyes and a fine longish nose gave her a Neapolitan look.

Her right hand was clasped behind her back. A glow in a mirror on the wall behind her warned me that she was holding something metallic.

"Who are you?" I asked in French; and while she was deciding what to reply, I sprang forward and hugged her tightly, gripping her forearms with both hands. Slowly, I reached for whatever she was holding. With a flick of her fingers she tossed it onto the tiled floor, no doubt hoping I would chase it. When I failed to cooperate she gave me a jab in the thigh with what felt like an armored knee, twisted out of my arms, punched me in the stomach, and tried to scamper away.

I dived after her. We both went down with a smack that must have been heard at street level. I rolled her over onto her back, and crawled over her to grasp what I now saw was an unopened purse-size flick-knife. It was inscribed *A girl's best friend.*

I sat on her thighs and flicked the knife open. Defiance blazed in her eyes, though with an occasional flicker of fear.

"Don't make any sudden move," I said. "I'm not used to threatening people with knives. I wouldn't want there to be an accident. Tell me why you wanted to kill Blane."

"Kill him?" Her eyes dilated. "I did not wish to kill him. Holy Mother of God—I swear it!"

"You weren't going to trim his mustache."

"I wished . . . to scare him a little—to teach him a lesson."

"Why?"

She hesitated. I narrowed my eyes and twiddled the knife like when I played the third robber in *Ali Baba.* That upset her.

"He was here working for the pipeline company. We became friends. He dishonored his word to me and cheated my uncle. I frequented him more than is customary here. When he went away, some people mocked me."

"How did you know he was coming here again?"

"My uncle Walid—" She broke off, fear in her eyes.

I pointed the knife in the direction Blane had been taken. "Does your uncle live in the suq quarter?"

She nodded.

"Would he harm Blane?"

"Of course not. My uncle is a good man."

"What business is he in?"

She took a deep breath and her breasts thrust up against her

100

dress like neat, neighborly molehills. "Let me go. The floor is hard."

"When you've told me what your uncle does."

She tried to roll over and throw me off. I shut the knife and flicked it open an inch from her fine nose. She said: "He has a coffee shop."

"What's your name?"

She didn't want to tell me, but at last she said: "Salwa."

It didn't fit her. "Which of your parents was Syrian?"

"My mother. My father was a doctor at the Italian hospital. He went back to Italy without her."

"The girls in your family don't have much luck with their European friends."

The warmth and resilience of her thighs were doing things to my hormones or whatever it is. I dismounted and knelt beside her to help her to a sitting position. I slid the knife under the bed.

"If you see Colonel Blane," she said, wriggling cutely to ease her cramp, "give him the knife as a souvenir. But do not worry: I will not come back."

"Please do; but come to room 25. There's a rug."

She smiled bitterly. "So Western; so plausible. So fair of speech and black of heart. Drawn like a moth to the light of love and the flame of hate."

"Even poets exaggerate.* Which way are you drawn?"

"Once, I thought that my vocation was love. Now I know myself to be talented for hate."

"In the cause of human happiness, you should give your original belief another chance."

A hundred miles away someone was knocking on a door.

Still kneeling, I put my hands on her shoulders and leaned toward her. She jerked back, startled, then relaxed a little. We were scrutinizing each other, face to face, when the door opened.

* She was quoting the poet N. Al-Ayar.

Anna's voice asked contemptuously: "Are the beds here so uncomfortable?"

Salwa leaped to her feet, snatched the red bag from the bed, and ran out of the room. Anna scarcely glanced at her. She was staring at me—sternly, at first; but as I got up and walked stiffly toward her, her lips pouted mockingly.

"She pulled a knife on me," I said. "I was grilling her."

"That's a new name for it."

"If only you were a suspect!" I put my hands behind her shoulders and kissed her cool lips. I was as randy as six sailors. She stepped back into the open doorway.

"It seems you think I am," she said icily.

"Not really. Tussling with that girl aroused the ape in me."

"If ever I need your ape, I will arouse it myself. Can we talk business now? I have not much time."

Her face seemed different. Darker, perhaps. But the light was dim. She was wearing a pink dress and another of those headcloth-and-snood things, the same color.

I asked: "Why are you hiding your hair?"

"People aren't used to blondes here. They think I'm a cabaret girl or worse, and make crude remarks, if I go out with uncovered hair. Now can we talk of serious matters?"

We shut Blane's door and went into my room. I offered her the only chair and said: "I heard you knock . . . but where were you knocking? Here or on Blane's door?"

"Both. I tried here first. But I wasn't sure of the number, so when I heard a noise in the next room I went there. That's Colonel Blane's room, is it? But why were you there—and that girl?"

"I was going to search it when the girl ambushed me." I told her about Blane's arrest and the Salwa interlude.

She said: "Pete dislikes Blane. He suspects that Blane has some unsavory local involvements. He may be right. But we must not let Blane's activities sidetrack us."

"We can't be sure they're a sidetrack. They may have some bearing on Arnold's death."

She got up and walked to the open window to help her think. The citadel and the tip of a tall minaret were floodlit by the setting sun. The edges of the square were deepening drifts of shadow.

Anna shook her head. "So far as I know, Blane arrived in Beirut only a few weeks ago. He seems completely tied up in his own affairs. He probably made use of this girl while he was here laying pipelines and things. She certainly seems easy to make use of."

"Please," I said. "I blush easily."

"She told you that he cheated her family. He may have become involved with them in black-market activities or the sale of pipeline-company property or smuggling or something."

"An officer-and-gentleman? What have you got against Blane?"

She looked surprised. "Nothing. But one must be realistic. There is something about the Levant that dirties Western hands."

"You may be right. But—"

Someone knocked on the door. I opened it and saw a bright-eyed, curly-haired boy of about eleven—our stringer's son. He gave me an envelope. The unsigned typewritten note inside it read:

El-Beyt el-Basha is not now used officially. It is occupied by a semipolitical group once supported by the army. I do not recommend a visit. It is of no architectural or other tourist interest, though I understand that a friend of yours may have visited it recently.

I thanked the boy, asked after his parents and brothers, gave him the price of two liters of soda pop, and hoped he wouldn't burst. We shook hands and he ran off down the corridor.

103

"News from Salwa?" Anna asked, a little too sweetly. I showed her the note. "What's the Beyt el-Basha?"

"The House of the Pasha," I said.

"I know that much Arabic."

"In olden times it belonged to an eccentric pasha whose hobby was to abduct beautiful women and try love potions, drugs, and spells on them in order to discover the secret of passion."

"What a pity he never met Salwa!"

"Miaou. During the French mandate, it was used by the Deuxième Bureau as an interrogation center and lockup. Then the Syrian Sûreté took it over. When Blane was arrested and driven off in that direction, I asked a friend if it was still in use. This is his reply."

"You are very concerned about Blane."

"Fellow gringo and all that. If I were in a Syrian dungeon, maybe Blane would try to get me out."

I made a taper of the note and burned it over the washbasin, turning a tap on to flush away the ash.

Anna shrugged. "We are wasting time. You don't know that Blane has really been arrested. This may simply have been an attempt by Salwa's family to intimidate him. Anyway, it's not—"

"That's an idea! They may have taken him to her uncle's coffee shop. If only I knew where it—"

"If only!" she exclaimed. "You could go there and get beaten up and your new friend Salwa might or might not console you." She sighed. "There is a lawyer here who handles a little business for Edmond Bey. If it will ease your mind, I will ask him to make inquiries about Blane. He is a friend of the new chief of the Aleppo Sûreté, Major Yazid. Yazid will tell him in two minutes what it would take us two weeks to discover. Now let us return to our problems. As I told you at lunchtime, the Beirut Sûreté think they have the gun that shot your friend Amery. It was found in the bar of your hotel. Are you certain you never handled it?"

104

"Completely. I never even saw it."

"Good. That is one possible complication less. Edmond Bey wanted to be sure."

The citadel was a dark lilac glow now, like the embers of a dying campfire. Lights were flashing on in cafés across the square. Constellations shone in Anna's eyes. There was something luminous about her in the grayness of the room.

"I am going," she said. "I must see the lawyer I told you about; and there is a restless glitter in your eyes. Keep out of the way of the Syrian Sûreté. They are rather anti-Western just now."

"Keep out of their way yourself. They'd love to grill you."

She looked surprised. "You're a Westerner, too."

"I have a Lebanese passport. Edmond Bey got it for me."

"Isn't it a bit precarious?"

"Not so long as his influence lasts. I treasure it. A Lebanese passport is a wonderful thing to have—when the only alternative is no passport."

"Is that the only alternative?"

"My father had a Polish diplomatic passport."

"Was he a Communist?"

"No. He was a Socialist. But he thought it might be possible to democratize the Communist regime from within. So he worked with the Communists while reading Western papers and teaching me English and French. In the end he was warned by a friend that he was due to be purged. When the government recalled him, he stayed on in Beirut. And when he and my mother died, I suddenly found myself a minority of one in an unimaginably huge world."

Somewhere on the ramparts of the citadel, now a muddy smear against a copper-red sky, the Ramadan cannon roared—the cannon that tells Moslems the sun has safely set and they may end their daytime fast. Minarets stood out one by one in garlands of fairy lights, and the muezzin began crooning over their loudspeakers.

Anna said: "Goodbye. I will come tomorrow if I have news."

105

She held out a hand. I raised it gently and kissed it. If diplomatic courtesies were what she had been used to—well, what the hell. She was so astonished she almost walked into the door.

Without her, the room was dingy and dark. I switched lights on, slipped off my shirt, and splashed water over myself. Across the square kids were letting off firecrackers. Across the square was the narrow street down which Blane had been driven.

Sidetrack, Anna had said. I remembered that card of Blane's, taped to the fragment of blue-and-white carton, on Arnold's desk. A crude red herring . . . or a clue planted by a disgruntled accomplice? I needed to know more about Blane. And I was still a journalist of sorts. It was as hard for me to turn my back on the Blane story as for a cat to snub a sardine.

So I asked the wet ape in my mirror: Who in Aleppo knows anything about Blane?

Blane, it replied.

I nodded admiringly. With you on the payroll, who needs a computer?

Pete dislikes Blane, Anna's echo said. He had certainly been fazed by my traveling with Blane. Why?

I grabbed the telephone.

There was no reply from McGlint's room. I asked the switchboard girl, who was also in charge of keys and mail, if she had seen McGlint go out.

"No," she said. "I mean yes."

"Try again."

"He going out just now. You want talk from him?"

"I want much talk from him."

McGlint sounded grumpy. When I asked if I could see him, he said: "Not noo. I've an appointment."

"I want to talk to you about Blane. He's been arrested."

"What for?"

"I don't know."

"Who arrested him?"

"Two plainclothesmen."

"So what? Am I supposed to weep or cheer?"

"Blane may need help."

"That's a matter for the consul. Anyone else who pokes his nose in may well land in the clink, too."

"Have a heart! For me, if not for Blane. There's a hundred quid's worth of story in Blane's adventure. BRITISH OFFICER SEIZED BY SYRIAN SECRET POLICE. You know how Fleet Street loves that sort of thing."

"Aye. Every year British, American, and other Western riff-raff are caught here or in Turkey smugglin' dope to pay for their summer holidays. So consular officials lose their sleep and all of us who work here suffer embarrassment while Western papers weep crocodile tears over decent Christian kids victimized by cruel Orientals. But if an Arab or a Turk is caught pushin' dope in England, he's a vicious wog corruptin' our youth."

As excitedly as I could, I said: "It hadn't occurred to me that Blane might be in a dope racket."

"For Christ's sake! Nobody said he is. He may simply owe the Syrians some tax. My point is: there's no reason to make a hero out of him."

"He's going to be a hero or something when I cable London—there'll be interviews with his white-haired mother, questions in the House, the lot—unless you tell me why you think he's a bastard."

I heard him gasp. "I never said—"

"You don't like him."

"I don't like a lot o' people. I'm not wildly fond o' you. But I admit Blane's type gets ma hackles up. Devote forty years to a useful honest job and what are ye at the end of it? Just another bloody fool fit for the scrap heap. But make a career o' beatin' up Africans or Asians and ye get a medal, a pension, and the title officer-and-gentleman. I'm allergic to that kind o' gentleman."

107

"In addition, you think Blane's up to something."

"Perhaps. Perhaps ye're up to somethin', too."

"Come off it, Pete. We were both friends of Arnold's. You don't trust journalists—fair enough, I don't blame you—but I promise I won't quote you. Just tell me if what's worrying you about Blane has any connection with Arnold's murder. If it has, I certainly won't make a hero of him."

"Nothin's worryin' me about Blane. I couldna care less about him. But for Arnold's sake I'll tell ye this. I've a notion I saw Blane in Beirut one day last week wi' somebody who . . . who wa' no friend of Arnold's—I'll put it that way. The notion left me with another reason for bein' unenthusiastic about him. The Syrian police are welcome to him."

"An odd thing is that they didn't take him toward Sûreté HQ. They drove him across the square into the suq."

"Oh? Perhaps . . . but who cares? And I must go. This is costin' me money. I've a taxi waitin'."

I dressed again and went down to a smoky little restaurant near the hotel. I sat at the back, facing the door. I drank arak with plenty of water in it and ate a dish of hummus, three skewers of kebab, and a big disc of crisp Aleppo bread. Then I walked around the square to see if I was being followed and turned into the narrow street that led toward the House of the Pasha.

12

The garden smelled of fig trees, but all I could see over its twelve-foot wall and metal gates were the tops of two tatty palms. Three supersonic bats weaved around them like politicians at a cocktail party. The house was silent and secretive, with latticed Turkish balconies at the front of its two upper stories and narrow shuttered windows at the sides. To the right of the garden was an ancient crumbling khan*; to the left, a small mosque. Rival café loudspeakers a hundred or so yards away made a noise like a dog show, but here everything was calm: the merchants whose tiny stores slumbered across the alley from the House of the Pasha had rolled down their shutters and gone home to their Ramadan feast an hour before.

I climbed into the khan over a pair of sagging wooden doors that barred the lower half of a tall archway. The holes and cracks in the wood made them so easy to climb that I was sure there must be a guard dog inside. I picked up a few stones—Syrian dogs are noisy and look fierce but retreat under bombardment—and walked in the shadows around the khan's central courtyard, now a parking lot for an old truck, a cement mixer, and two battered cars.

Soon I found a flight of worn stone steps leading up to an abandoned gallery. I walked along it to the side nearest the House of the Pasha. It was littered with the junk and rubble of half a century. The moon slashed like a scimitar through gaps in the wall and showed me more steps that took me shakily onto the flat roof of the gallery. From there I could see into the walled garden.

* A caravansary: a combined inn and depot for merchants.

It was a leafy fragrant garden planted with fruit trees and shrubs. Beside the house, less than twenty yards from me, two men in light khaki shirts and trousers were drinking arak and eating olives at a small table. Above them a kerosene pressure lamp swayed on a long clothesline slung between a contorted fig tree and a hook in the garden wall. The house itself was in darkness. A side door a few yards beyond the two men was half open and looked as inviting as a rat trap. A gray car was parked in the driveway.

The younger and plumper of the two men was turned away from me. The one I could see most of was a big rawboned man with knobbly shoulders and a deeply lined yellow face and grizzled hair. He had a harsh voice and seemed angry. I soon saw why.

A bell clanged violently, and went on clanging and then tinkling and finally just quivering on a spring over the side door. The lean man got up and strode off down the drive. He had a holster on his belt that looked as if it held an elephant gun. He opened one of the big gates and let in a waiter with a tray on his head apologized for being late, while the guard cursed at him. The waiter set out dishes of food on the table, and then the guard accompanied him back to the gates, locked up, and returned to the table.

I liked his being hungry; and I liked the hook in the wall that supported the clothesline that held the lamp. It was embedded in the back wall of the garden, which was also the back wall of a row of flat-roofed garages or workshops opening into another alley behind the House of the Pasha and inaccessible from it. I went down into the rubbish-strewn gallery of the khan and shone the fountain-pen flash Julien had given me a few inches from the ground in search of something the shape of a walking stick. I found the remains of a shovel. Much of the metal had worn and rusted away, but what was left was still firmly attached to the haft. I went up the steps again, to the back of the gallery this time, and through a breach in the wall onto the concrete roof of the row of garages, feeling as conspicuous in the moonlight as a bishop at a rationalist congress. I crawled along the roof until I was level with the clothesline and then, cautiously, up to the edge.

It looked easy—too easy. The foliage was in my favor and the pressure lamp needed pumping and was getting dim. The men at the table were eating industriously. The thin one had his back to me now. He sounded happier, but he still had a voice to turn the milk.

The clothesline was knotted firmly enough, but merely looped over the hook. I lowered my ghost of a shovel over the edge, poked the shoulder of the frayed blade under the rope, rested my elbows firmly on the edge of the roof, and pulled sharply up.

The shadow of a branch leaped up the side of the house. Both men cried out, and there was a crash of metal on crockery, a clank as the lamp rolled over on the table, and a tinkle of breaking glass. Then, as the men jumped from their chairs, the lamp went out. While they were shouting curses and warnings at one another, I lowered myself over the edge as far as my arms would take me and dropped.

It was only a few feet more. I crouched there, my arms trembling, still gripping the haft of the shovel, waiting for someone to shine a light on me. But they were afraid the kerosene of the lamp might be spilling over the stuffed vine leaves and afraid to touch the lamp because it was hot. At last one of them struck a match and the other hooked the lamp upright with a fork or something. The match went out and I moved away along the garden wall until I had a corner of the house between them and me. Then I walked down a row of apricot trees and tucked myself between two bougainvilleas growing up the back of the house.

There was a silence, during which lights flashed on in the house. When I next heard their voices, they had brought out two yellow storm lamps and a flashlight. They hung the lamps on branches, and the big man, carrying the flashlight, went to inspect the hook in the wall.

111

"The rope didn't break," he called in Arabic. "It slipped off the hook. That idiot Fuad . . ."

He came straight toward me, keeping his beam on the ground as if following my footprints. He walked within three yards of me, went on a few more paces, and shone his light into a barred basement window. He crouched to look through it and grunted.

I could have laid him out there with the haft of my shovel, picked up his flashlight, walked casually to the table, dazzling the other man with the beam, and taken him, too. I could have locked them in a cellar, released Blane if he was there, and let us both out the front gates. But I didn't know how much law they had on their side. If theirs was one of the Syrian secret services, they would catch up with us somewhere. The moment I started batting folk over the head I should lose whatever fragile protection my status as a newsman in pursuit of a story might confer. So I let the thin man grunt again, stand up, and walk slowly by me to the corner of the house and around it to resume his meal.

I put down the shovel and crawled out of my shelter to have a look at that basement window. The moonlight showed me four or five of them, all barred, about a foot square and ten feet apart. I lay on the ground, my body wedged between the wall of the house and a row of shrubs, and looked in. I saw a pale blur on the inside. So I got out the little flash, poked it through the bars, and switched it on. Beneath the window I saw a bare mattress. And then Blane came into my beam. He shielded his eyes and tried to look at me. I snapped the light off.

"Blane," I whispered. "Can you hear me?"

"Yes. Who are you?" It was like a voice from the tomb.

"Alan—Ray Alan. We shared the car from Beirut."

"Thank God! Can you get me out of here?"

"Keep your voice down. I'll need help. Tell me quickly who these people are and why they're keeping you here."

"They said they were security police."

"But what have they got against you?"

112

"I don't know. They haven't charged me with anything. Someone is coming to interrogate me later."

"But what about?"

"I don't really know."

"For God's sake!" I almost shouted at him. "I risk my neck getting in here and all you do is stall. You know damn well what they're after. What did you really come to Aleppo for?"

He hesitated, then whispered: "I won a fair amount of money here when I worked for the pipeline company, playing poker. You know how crazy the locals are about cards. I also did favors for a few Syrian businessmen, transporting things for them—things they weren't supposed to import without special permits. You know the bureaucracy here. Well, I couldn't get the proceeds out of Syria without attracting attention so a local lawyer made a few investments for me. Property, mostly. Now I want to sell out. That's all."

"That's not all," I whispered. "I happen to know about your pal Walid. Tell me some more."

"Don't believe a word he says."

"Could it be Walid who had you put here?"

"I don't know."

"What has Walid got on you?"

"Nothing. He bribed one of my drivers to carry hashish three or four times. I fired the driver. There's nothing more to it. How are you going to get me out of here?"

"I'd thought of asking the consul to intervene."

He didn't like that. "It's very embarrassing for me."

"You'll be even more embarrassed if they slit your throat."

"Well . . . go to the consulate only as a last resort. Haven't you any army or police contacts?"

"The influential ones were purged in the last coup. I'll go and see your lawyer. He'll know somebody. What's his name?"

He didn't like that, either. "I don't think . . ."

I lost patience with him. "All right. Don't tell me. If you're that thickheaded, the only way you'll get out of here is in a box. To hell—"

"Wait!" he whispered. "You're right. He's well-connected. His name is Mardam. Halim Mardam. Don't think I'm not grateful. You'll not regret having helped me. I'll give you a card with Mardam's address. Lend me your torch."

I passed it through the bars. "Here. It may be yours. I found it in the taxi. Have you lost one?"

"Yes. I wondered what had happened to it."

"Keep the beam down. Can I give Mardam a message?"

"Yes." He seemed eager all of a sudden. "Ask him to pull what strings he can, and to warn our friend in . . . on the coast, if there's any delay."

A twig snapped somewhere near me.

I turned my head. It was too late to try to wriggle back under cover. A huge dark silhouette, a faceless giant, blocked out the moon. As I pulled my arm clear of the bars, he bent down toward me. Blane, seeing that something was wrong, shone the narrow beam out of his window, and the giant suddenly had a face—a sneering, deeply lined face with tight sadistic eyes and a taut lipless slit of a mouth. The face bore down on me and got bigger and hands hovered over me.

I scrambled to my knees, but I was too slow and too late. The giant grabbed my throat with both his hands. I pressed one of my feet against the wall and thrust myself forward, trying to butt him. He took half a step back, still gripping my throat, snarling at me.

He was the big gaunt man with the harsh voice. I remembered the holster on his belt and grabbed the butt of his gun and tried to pull it out. He took his right hand off my throat and chopped at my wrist. I flattened his nose with the heel of my right hand, but I was too low to put my weight behind the blow and my fingers missed his eyes. While he blinked I seized his left thumb, twisted it back, away from my windpipe, and breathed again—but only for a few seconds. His right hand shot up and landed a glancing rabbit punch on the side of my neck. Then he pulled my head forward and tucked it under his left arm, passing his left forearm under my throat. He leaned

114

forward and, with his right hand, levered the forearm up against my throat. It felt like an iron bar.

I tried to use the wall as a launching pad again, but all my feet could find was shrubbery. The blood pressed against my eyes. I fumbled feebly for his gun to pass the time until my head exploded.

13

I was in a cellar—standing, somehow, though my ankles were loosely roped together. My wrists were tied behind my back. A man with a cloth over the lower half of his face was heating something over a charcoal brazier. He fanned it until the charcoal glowed and spat out sparks. Two other men seized my arms and dragged me toward him.

I was afraid for my eyes. I struggled and tried to kick the brazier over, but I couldn't move my foot far enough. Someone tripped me and I fell onto my knees, nearer the fire than ever. The charcoal crackled and sinister mauve flames shimmered over it. Its fumes were harsh, searing, overpowering.

Then I was sitting on Salwa's thighs again, but this time she was drenched in arak. Suddenly Ondine splashed ashore from out of a sea of arak, and her boyfriend broke a bottle of arak over my head. There was no getting away from the stuff.

Before long, all the girls I'd ever known in the Levant, and many more besides, had gathered round to see if I turned white when they added water. I was on the floor, of course. Where else would I be? I'd taken a ninety-nine-year lease on it. I was Drip Van Winkle, awakening in a disenchanted forest: a forest of legs—a few good, some still trying, most on the far side of despair.

"I don't mind the smell of arak," cried a hardy *sans-culotte* in raucous French, "and we can't leave him cluttering up the floor."

She sat me up and a man helped her haul me to my feet. I found I could walk, but the girl who had adopted me kept hold of me and led me to a less crowded inner room. She was plump, soft as a sponge, with sly little eyes and thick orange lips. The man followed and the three of us sat at a table.

There was a lot of smoke. There were bright colors on the tabletops, walls, and ceiling. There was music—sullen and sinuous, matching the smoke rather than the colors. It was hot. The crummier the women were, the less they wore. Their flabby off-white flesh looked as if it needed hosing down.

"Where are we?" I asked the girl in French. My voice was croaky. My throat felt as if someone had tied a knot in it.

"Chez Mimi," she said.

"In which town?"

She opened a mouth like a mailbox and laughed.

"My friend is not well," the man said in Arabic. "Give him his wallet back and bring us four cups of coffee."

Her mouth sagged shut and she scowled at him. She asked: "If you're his friend, why did you leave him on the floor like that?"

"Some others brought him here," he said, "and pushed him through the door. I followed them. I saw you take his wallet when we picked him up. Give it back. It will be empty."

He was a stocky nut-brown Syrian with a beaked nose and a small tight mouth. His hair was disheveled and he hadn't shaved for a couple of days. He looked as if he could be mean. The girl was taking no chances. She fished the wallet out of somewhere, slapped it on the table, and swaggered off.

The Syrian asked me: "Can you remember what was in it?"

I couldn't remember seeing it before. I opened it and found a credit card authorizing someone called Alan to telex and cable press messages. There were other cards, oddments, and a lot of money.

"Put it in your pocket," the Syrian said.

My pocket was wet and reeked of arak—like the rest of my jacket, which looked like a floor cloth.

"It was some temperance society," I said. "They put their goon squad onto me to scare me off arak. The hell with them. We'll—"

117

"That will be twenty liras," the girl's voice said. She reappeared carrying four doll's-house cups of coffee, a tall slender glass containing something dark and exotic, and a yellow plastic chip that recorded her percentage of the kill. "I had to order a drink for myself. The boss gets nasty otherwise. It's only a third of a bottle of Coca-Cola, but he charges you six liras for it. Don't take too long deciding who's going to come with me first or you'll have to buy me another."

Her small black eyes flicked from one to the other of us as if we were going to fight a duel over her. The Syrian ignored her and pushed three of the coffees to my side of the table. He watched me closely as I drank them. Then he swallowed his, helped me up, tossed some money onto the table, and steered me out. The girl stood in the entrance screeching after us as we walked off down a dark passageway just wide enough to admit a thin mule.

I had no idea where we were going. But the Syrian was my only friend in the world and I trotted along after him like a spaniel.

14

When the fog cleared again, I had a headache the size of Ulster and I was in bed looking at a ceiling of unpainted planks supported by rough round beams. It was a narrow bed in a long, narrow room with clean white walls. I sat up. A small uncurtained window at the far end of the room showed a rectangle of blue sky. To the left of the window was a marble-topped Victorian washstand with an enamel bowl on it and a broad mirror. The door was in the right-hand wall just beyond the foot of the bed. Both window and door were set in walls about a yard thick.

The House of the Pasha, I told myself. They've got you. You're a prisoner in the House of the Pasha.

There was a chair by the bed with my wallet on it but no clothes. No clothes anywhere. I was wearing a sort of long nightgown with thin blue-and-white stripes. I got up and walked to the mirror. The tiled floor felt like ice. The mirror showed me an unshaven Syrian peasant in a galabia that fitted him like a tent. He looked as if his donkey had died, the government had requisitioned his wheat crop, and his wife had given birth to a daughter. His eyes were something he'd picked up cheap in the fish market.

I heard footsteps and a knock. Slowly, the door opened. I expected a gorilla with a truncheon, but it was an entrancing dark-eyed girl carrying a tray. She was wearing a yellow dress with a tight waist and flaring skirt, a chunky black necklace as black and lustrous as her hair, and yellow sandals. On the tray were a glass, a steaming copper bowl, and a towel.

She smiled and said in French: "How do you like the galabia? It belonged to my grandfather. Walid's pajamas were too wide and too short for you."

I asked: "Did you dress me in it?" I sounded like an aging speak-your-weight machine.

She lowered her eyes. *"Non, monsieur!* Walid and Habib did that. Drink this."

I drank it. It tasted of old cigar butts. She put the bowl on the washstand and brought the chair up to it.

Her name came to me all of a sudden and I said it out loud—"Salwa!"—and she waited for me to say more.

When I didn't, she said: "Sit down and put your head over the bowl and breathe in the vapor. Put the towel over your head—make a little tent of it—to keep the vapor concentrated. Then go back to bed and sleep while your clothes are cleaned."

I sat down. "Who is Habib?" My throat hurt.

"He sometimes works for my uncle. He brought you here—do you remember from where?"

"There was a lot of smoke," I said. "And bright colors and a woman with eyes like a pig. Where are we now?"

"Chez nous. You are with friends." She draped the towel over my head and held her cool hand on my neck for a moment. "Breathe deeply. It will clear your head."

I heard the door close behind her.

This one smelled of capucines. It made my head feel as doddery as the House of Lords. After three or four minutes, I groped my way back to the bed.

The next thing I knew was that the rectangle of sky was turning orange. Someone had tucked me in again and left a red-and-gold brocade dressing gown on the back of the chair. I put it on and opened the door and fell over a boy who was sitting on the floor reading an Arabic horror comic.

"El-mustarah," I said.

He led me across a small reception room stuffed with red plush furniture and brass trays, and down a tiled staircase to the floor below. There was a smell of cooking and a bustle of

120

family life behind doors the boy ran ahead to close. The bathroom was spartan and its intestines hissed and clanked, but everything worked. The boy waited for me and escorted me back upstairs.

Ten minutes later Salwa came in with another glass for me to drink. "You look better," she said. "Can you remember things now?"

I tried to think of something in my life worth remembering. "What's the date?" I asked.

She told me the Moslem date and laughed. "We are Christians, but the calendar in the kitchen is Moslem."

"How many days is it since we first met?"

"Days?" She smiled. "Do you remember how we met?"

"You were behind a door . . . and we had a bit of a fight."

She looked at her watch. "That was twenty-four hours ago."

There was a knock at the door and a voice asked in Arabic if it could come in.

"My uncle Walid," Salwa said.

I had expected Uncle Walid to be an old boy in a tarboosh, dusty and maybe a bit dented by time and events. He proved to be a man of about fifty, dustproof and shock-resistant: a self-confident man who lived well and watched the world vigilantly through quick brown eyes. He was shorter than I but had more girth. He had a big nose and chin and the beginnings of a second chin. Vigorous black hair was brushed straight back from a high forehead. He was wearing a gray business suit, a shirt a few shades lighter, and a blue tie.

He gave me a hand to shake and went through the graceful Syrian hospitality ritual, inquiring after my health and assuring me that his house was henceforth mine. He had tried, he said, switching to correct but rusty French, to get me a copy of the *Daily Mirror,* which the Chamber of Commerce had informed him was the greatest English-language paper, but all he had been able to find was the *Times.* He laid it apologetically on the bed.

121

"If you feel well enough," he added, "I hope you will dine with us this evening."

Salwa dissented. "No, Uncle. He should have only a very light meal. If he is lonely I will keep him company. We can eat on a tray in the next room."

His mouth was smiling for my benefit, but his eyes were fixed on her, telling her no, he didn't want us to get too friendly, she had already made a fool of herself once with—

"Blane!" I exclaimed.

They both looked at me sharply.

"Blane," I said again. "He's in the House of the Pasha. I saw him. I'd forgotten. I ought to inform someone."

"You can inform me," Walid said. "I will do what is necessary."

Salwa looked scared. She was imploring me with her eyes—to do what? To avoid mentioning her visit to Blane's room?

I told Walid: "I think Blane is afraid of you."

He chuckled contemptuously. His smile had gone. "Blane is a stupid man, a dishonest man, and a dishonorable man. His stupidity one can pardon: it may be hereditary. His dishonesty . . ." He shrugged. "Honesty and dishonesty are in Syria a question of perspective. Our privileged class used to be the big landowners; now it is composed of army officers, many of them the old landowners' sons. To outwit such people in their own rackets is not dishonest, it is a sport. Honesty and loyalty to one's family and friends are what matter. That is why I say Blane was dishonorable. When he was here working with the pipeline company, we received him as a friend. But he cheated me out of a sum of money and, worse, behaved badly to my niece. When I heard that he was coming here again, I asked my niece if she wished me to settle that account. She replied that she did not." He turned to Salwa. "Have you changed your mind?"

"No," she whispered.

He looked at me again. "Blane came to Aleppo to close some kind of property deal. He was afraid he might run into me and get an unpleasant reception. So his lawyer asked me to overlook the past and even requested my services to protect Blane while he was in Aleppo."

"Has he so many enemies here?" I asked.

"No; but he is vulnerable. One or two people might be tempted to put pressure on him. I did not think the risk a great one. In fact, I considered his lawyer's approach a peace gesture. He offered me a satisfactory sum and I agreed. Now I am under a ridiculous obligation to do something for him. If you can tell me what you remember of the Beyt el-Basha, it may help me to decide what to do."

My headache was back and there were still gaps in my mind, but I was able now to distinguish reality from dream. I told them what I could remember of how I got into the garden and my talk with Blane. My voice began croaking again.

"What happened after they captured you?" Walid asked.

"I can't work it out. A man with a cloth over his face was heating something over a brazier. Two others dragged me toward the brazier . . . and then that man of yours was giving me coffee. There are gaps I just can't bridge."

"I can bridge one for you," Walid said. "They decided you were not dangerous to them. You knew nothing about whatever it is that interests them. You followed Blane out of curiosity. There was no point in keeping you there and giving the guards unnecessary work; there was no point in killing you— bodies are found, and you might have told someone where you were going. Perhaps they are not very sure of themselves. So they gave you henbane and kef."

"They gave me what?"

"Two herbs which, if taken together, efface one's memory of the previous few hours and even trouble one's remembrance of other things. The easiest way of administering them is to make the victim smoke them or inhale the vapor of the roasting seeds. That is probably what you saw the man heating over the brazier: he would wear a damp cloth over his mouth and nose to protect himself. Then they poured arak over you, and two of them took you out, supporting you as if you were drunk, and threw you into the entrance of"—he looked shyly at Salwa—"that place."

"But how did your man find me?"

"Habib? He's not really one of my men, but . . . that is unimportant. He and another man are keeping the Beyt el-Basha under observation from a coppersmith's shop opposite. They have been there since we first learned that Blane had been abducted and might be there. When two of the guards took you out, Habib followed them and brought you here. He didn't know you; but he thought you might have useful information for us. We saw from your eyes that you had been drugged: the pupils were like grains of maize. Salwa has studied medicine—and knowledge of herbal drugs is traditional in Syria—so she gave you antidotes to drink and inhale."

My throat was throbbing and my head felt as if someone had been boiling it to make soup, but there was a question I had to ask. "Who are those people at the Beyt el-Basha?"

"The Beyt el-Basha was taken over a few years ago by the army. Then, Communist officers on the general staff handed it to their friends in the PRM—the People's Revolutionary Militia. This was formed, you may remember, during the Turkish scare, when we were told by our government that the Turks were preparing to attack us. Its commander was the brother of the army chief of staff. After the Turkish scare, the PRM disintegrated, and in Aleppo it became just another gang—though one enjoying high-level protection and doing occasional odd jobs for its protectors."

Salwa put a hand on my forehead and said: "We are tiring him. He must sleep."

Walid smiled at her—a cold, artificial smile. "Please, nurse, may I ask the patient one more question?" He took my wallet from the chair beside the bed, opened it, and held up the plastic envelope containing the white powder I had found in Arnold's bathroom. "You will understand that we had to look in your wallet in order to identify you. I saw this. Is it . . . some kind of medicine you take?"

"No. I don't know what it is. I found it in the house of a friend in Beirut."

"May I take it and have it analyzed?"

"Yes." As I stared at it, the plastic envelope slipped out of focus and became two. "I'd like to know what it is."

He laughed. "Good. When I saw it I wondered . . . I looked for needlemarks on your arms. It's odd, isn't it? A few years ago one associated drug-taking with the Egyptians, the Chinese, the miserable of the earth; now the victims are prosperous Westerners."

"Don't worry. I'm not prosperous enough to buy dope."

"Is this connected in any way with Blane?"

He shook the little envelope. Its motion made me feel dizzy. I shut my eyes. "I don't know."

I heard Salwa say: "He must sleep."

15

When I awoke the next morning, the sun was shining through the little window and the name Mardam was dancing in my head. Halim Mardam, the lawyer Blane had told me to go and see. My mind was working again. I sat up and tested it. First, something easy. What's the purpose of existence? The development of consciousness. Who said that? Kant. Who won the Second World War? Japan.

All right. Now go and develop your consciousness. But try not to get it trodden on again.

I got up and leaned out of the window and watched a truck maneuver in the courtyard four stories below. It was a big yard surrounded by garages and warehouses. Uncle Walid appeared, got into a station wagon, and drove off under a porte cochere.

I went down to the bathroom for a shower and a shave. Walid still used soap and scythe, but he had borrowed a new electric shaver for me from a dealer in the suq. In my absence someone set out my clothes on the bed. They were clean and neat and I found sprigs of lavender in the pockets.

While I was dressing, a rich coffee odor crept up on me. In the next room Salwa was setting out a breakfast tray: discs of Aleppo bread, grape jam, melon, yogurt, goat's milk cheese, and coffee made the Italian way. She was wearing a simple cotton dress of the color people who have never seen the Nile call Nile blue. She still had one of the most graceful bodies I had ever sat on.

"You're looking remarkably well," I said.

She pretended to be puzzled. "You are the patient—or were."

126

We sat side by side on a red plush sofa and drank coffee and nibbled sporadically. After the meal I stroked her arm gently and thanked her for taking care of me. She took my hand in hers for a few seconds, glanced nervously at the door, and moved away from me three-tenths of an inch.

"Why are you afraid?" I asked, as if I didn't know.

"I'm afraid . . . of convention, I suppose. We are still fairly patriarchal here. Walid is the man of the house, I am a member of his household, and his honor is involved in whatever I do."

"In other words, before you sit in my lap, you must ask his permission."

"If he found me sitting in your lap without his permission, you would wish you had remained in the Beyt el-Basha."

"That complicates things. I saw him go out in a station wagon about half an hour ago. Unless you know where he's gone and we can telephone him . . ."

She smiled and took my hand again. "You are cruel to make fun of me. You forget that my friendship with Colonel Blane branded me as an errant soul."

"Let's talk about Blane," I said. "He worries me. I can't make up my mind about him—except that I'm a little jealous of him for discovering you first." She squeezed my hand and I felt like a louse. "Why did he really come back to Aleppo? To see you again?"

"No. To sell some property—buildings and land."

"Is Blane really an attractive sort of man to women?"

She said slowly: "I thought him the most charming man I knew. He was . . . oh, I was more impressionable then, of course, and it was a controlled, calculated charm—I can see that now. Yet . . ."

"Would you describe him as, on the whole, a good man? That's a silly question, I know. We're all a mixture of good and bad."

"I know what you mean. There is more good than bad in him. For example, he has a daughter. She is mentally subnor-

127

mal. He need not have told me about her; but he did. He's de-
voted to her."

"Is no reconciliation possible, then? Suppose Blane had
come into that hotel room, and not me . . ."

"Please!" She stood up. "Don't talk about that—ever. It
would be terrible if Walid found out."

She walked quickly out of the room, so that I wouldn't see
her cry.

The upper part of the house was silent, but the tiled staircase
took me down to a hallway in the rear of a vast clamorous café.
It was a few minutes to ten and not so much as a glass of water
could be served until sunset, but half the chairs in the place
were occupied by men playing tricktrack or dominoes or just
nodding to the rhythm of a braying radio. A yawning waiter
gave me the Aleppo directory. I telephoned Mardam's office.

A young man's voice told me Maître Mardam had not yet
arrived. "He comes in late during Ramadan. If you ring again
at eleven . . ."

I looked in the directory again and dialed Mardam's home
number. Someone lifted the telephone at the other end. In my
best Arabic, I asked: "May I speak to Maître Mardam,
please?"

I heard breathing. Then there was a click and a buzz.

I read Mardam's home address again and went out through
the courtyard. In an open garage doorway one of Walid's men
was taking a tire off a bright red wheel. Another wheel, the
same color, was leaning against the wall beside him. The tires
were Dunlop tubeless, made in England.

"That's a nice color," I said.

Walid's man agreed, smiling.

"I didn't know Walid had a car this color."

The smile faded.

"Aren't they from one of Walid's cars?" I asked.

He shrugged. "It's a job he asked me to do for someone."

I walked out under the porte cochere in search of a taxi. I

found one near the citadel. The driver was pasturing a small goat at the foot of the great mound on which the citadel stands. There were only thistles and parched brown grass on the menu, but the goat seemed to like them and I had to help the driver bundle it into the trunk of his taxi.

"I buy him for the big feast after Ramadan," he explained. "He is cheaper now. Are goats cheap in London?"

"Very expensive, and very hard to find in the shops."

"Ah. So that is why the English eat the insides of pigs. It is sad that capitalism drives people to such extremes."

Mardam's house was the last of twelve along a new avenue in what had until recently been a pistachio plantation. I told the driver to take me to Number 2. I paid him and stood at the gate of Number 2 while he drove off. When he was out of sight I walked on.

Mardam's gate was unlocked, which was unusual for suburban Aleppo. A little paint was missing from around the slot in the metal post into which the lock engaged. The gate opened with a creak that silenced the whirr of cicadas and crickets. I only notice them when they stop. Then, as my feet began crunching along the gravel drive, they started up again, sector by sector, until the air was vibrant with them. The drive had a border of roses and was lined on one side with pistachio trees and on the other with a trellis up which vines were being trained to climb. In a few years' time it would be a pleasant shady walk. Meanwhile, the sun was playing on the back of my neck like an acetylene torch.

Fifty yards from the gate, the drive looped around four young Aleppo pines and splayed out in front of the house—a big stone bungalow with a red tiled roof that sloped down to shade a broad veranda. On the left, a ramp led gently into a basement garage. Beyond the ramp, partly camouflaged by evergreen roses, a barred enclosure contained a king-size kennel. A wolf-like object sprawled inside the bars. I walked over and threw a handful of gravel at it. Only flies moved.

I went back to the house and climbed five pink steps onto

the front porch. A bronze Assyrian bull, about ten inches high, was set in a niche to the right of the door. I patted its head, it nodded, and a mellow tone sounded within the cream stone walls; but nothing else happened.

The door was massive, handsome, and as hospitable as John o'Groat's on a Sunday afternoon. Green roller-shutters and tough mosquito screens covered all the front windows. I followed the veranda to the right to inspect the rest of the fortifications.

Around the first corner, I saw a big glass door. The shutter in front of it was raised; but the glass was tinted and showed me little more than a reflection of the garden and, when I drew level with it, my own silhouette. As I paused there, wondering whether to knock, I noticed that the glass door was ajar. And while I stared at it, it moved slowly, closing to the width of a pistol muzzle.

A harsh metallic crash made the whole veranda vibrate. I jumped and skidded around the next corner.

A few yards in front of me, a middle-age woman with a blue tattoo mark on her forehead had just replaced the lid of a metal garbage can. It was in a recess near the kitchen door. She closed a screen door over the recess and returned to the kitchen.

I waited for my breathing to approach normal and followed her. She was mopping the kitchen floor now. I wished her a good day. She went on mopping. I knocked on the open door. She mopped some more. I was beginning to feel tired of the Mardam way of life when she turned brusquely and shook the mop in the doorway, right in my face.

She didn't mind. She pulled her apron up over her mouth and said: *"Naam?"*

I asked her if Maître Mardam was at home. She shook her head and pointed to her ear. I shouted my question.

"He is sleeping," she said. "During Ramadan he sleeps late every morning."

"Is anyone else at home?" I shouted.

She raised her head sharply and clicked her tongue. The rest of the family, she explained, had gone to spend the summer in Lebanon. He would be following them in four or five days. She resumed her mopping.

I thanked her and tramped off down a gravel path that led around the house back to the loop in the drive. From there I returned to the veranda and the unfastened glass door. Maître Mardam wouldn't like that flapping while he slept.

It couldn't be fastened from the outside. I wrapped a handkerchief around my right hand and pushed. The glass door swung inward. Whoever last went out that way had had no option but to leave it open. I might be doing the family a good turn by going in and locking up properly. I might also, of course, meet a duplicate of that wolfhound, but life is like that: the philanthropist must expect to lose the seat of his pants from time to time.

I stepped forward.

I was in a big living room with shelves of pottery and plants around the walls, a vast Tabrizi carpet in the middle, and a lot of heavy armchairs. Arched double doors of opaque glass led from one end into a shadowy dining room and from the other into a long, cool hall. I chose the hall.

Gently, while my friend in the kitchen made reassuring noises with a washing machine, I knocked on doors and then opened them. I found a bathroom, a box room with a trap in the ceiling that gave access to the roof, a girl's bedroom that contained only a nostalgic aroma of girl, and a man's bedroom that looked as if it ought to contain Mardam but didn't.

The next door took me into Mardam's study. It was a big comfortable room, with deep armchairs, books around the walls, brocade drapes at the windows, and a blue silk prayer mat on the floor. My eyes were used to the shuttered dimness of the house by now and I saw that nobody was sitting at the massive desk. There wasn't even a chair behind the desk. If there had been, I wouldn't have looked closer, and I wouldn't

131

have seen the man lying behind the desk, on his side, still in a sitting position in his tipped-over chair.

I touched his cheek and neck. He wasn't cold yet; but he was dead.

I looked out into the hall. Nobody. Still gripping a handkerchief around my hand, I shut the study door. There was a key beneath the door handle. I turned it. Back at the desk, I switched on a small lamp. It showed me a man in his late fifties: a worried-looking man whose worries were all over now, though he had paid for his release. His jaws were twisted in a memory of agony. The lips were blue. His eyes were trying to look up into the inside of his forehead. He was wearing pajamas and a dressing gown. I could see no blood on him. I looked at the soles of my shoes to be sure I hadn't trodden in any blood.

Out, you idiot, my mind was shouting. Out. Fast.

I reached over the desk to switch the lamp off and something stopped me. A scrap of blue-and-white card, lying in the middle of the desk. It bore the words *Superfine Talcum Powder,* in English and Greek, and, in smaller letters, *Made in Cyprus.* I had seen something like that before. On Arnold's desk, after he was shot. There was no visiting card behind this one.

The insects in the garden had stopped whirring. As I listened, they started up again, sector by sector. I switched off the desk lamp.

Footsteps were crunching along the drive. Soon I heard voices. They were speaking French. One of the study's two windows was open and I looked through the narrow slots of its shutter. Slowly, distorted at first by the mosquito screen outside the shutter, the newcomers took shape. Gradually, like figures on a print in a darkroom tray, they became distinct. There were two of them.

One was a burly, plump-faced man with thin hair, a pencil-line mustache, and thick lips. Mirror glasses hid his eyes. He was wearing a rust-brown suit and carrying a leather-covered officer's swagger stick. He spoke with a Syrian accent.

The other was Julien Montrand.

16

I shut the study door and tiptoed down the hall to the box room. Dominating the trunks and boxes, the vacuum cleaner, and the thick winter carpets—rolled up and wrapped in plastic bags—was a tall aluminum stepladder. While Julien and the Syrian were ringing the doorbell, I climbed up to the ceiling trap. It opened easily and I hauled first myself and then the ladder, hooking my feet under the top step, into the roof space. There was nothing up there but two big water tanks, spare tiles, and ocherous dust. I piled a few tiles on the trapdoor and stepped from beam to beam to where the ceiling of Mardam's study would be. The roof tiles just above my head felt like a furnace. I took my jacket off.

Like me, they had gone at last to the back door. The Syrian was shouting at the woman in the kitchen. Soon I heard them talking in the hall and knocking on doors. A brief silence. One of them said: "He must have gone out without the woman seeing him." And then the Syrian went into the study and found Mardam.

I heard him call Julien. A moment later he exclaimed: "No! Let me do it. Don't touch anything." A shutter was raised.

Julien murmured something.

"One must not jump to conclusions," the Syrian said. "Maître Mardam was *cardiaque*. His doctor has been urging him to retire."

Julien said: "A heart attack can be provoked by shock—bad news, unwelcome visitors . . ."

"I agree; and if he had any such visitors, we shall find traces of them. Let us look around quickly and then I will telephone my office. Be careful not to leave fingerprints."

For the next few minutes I heard them opening doors and moving about the house. The Syrian officer shouted questions at the woman without telling her Mardam was dead. He found the open glass door and asked her if she had touched it. She said no. He tried the telephone and found it was out of order.

"It may just be a coincidence," he said. "We'll see."

He was silent for a minute or two. Then he shouted to the woman in Arabic: "Go to the end of the drive. You will see my car. The driver's name is Ahmed. Give him this note and come back."

When she had gone he resumed in French: "I must say I am grateful to you for reporting the disappearance of that journalist and for the background information you gave me: the murder of his friend in Beirut, the presence in Aleppo of Mag— *Shu ismo?** The mining-company official?"

"Mac-Gleent," Julien said.

"Magklee— Why do the English have such horrible names? I confess that when you first mentioned the journalist I was not greatly interested. I know Western journalists. They get drunk, hire a camel, and wander off to write an article on 'How I Defied the Desert.' The English, especially, are prone to imagine they are Lawrence of Arabia when they've had a few araks. But then Maître Mardam reported that his client Blane had been arrested by men claiming to be Sûreté officers. We knew that already: someone had telephoned from the British consulate. What was new was that Mardam thought Blane might be at the Beyt el-Basha."

"Why did he think that?"

"He wouldn't say. And this morning a man I've had checking on Magklee's activities, since you told me about his boss's murder, tailed him to the Beyt el-Basha. So there we have two Englishmen, both linked—one directly, one by Mardam's supposition—with the Beyt el-Basha, which, as you may know, is a base of the People's Revolutionary Militia. What are they up

* What is his name?

134

to? And a third Englishman—the journalist—has disappeared. How does he fit in?"

"Alan? He may simply have followed Blane and been captured."

"Journalists!" the Syrian exclaimed. "Like maggots on a carcass. What is this one—a connoisseur of dirty underwear? Or one of the so-called serious ones, subsidized by a bank or the CIA?"

"He is not very intelligent." Melting up there in the roof, like a superannuated waxwork, I couldn't disagree. "But he is harmless. We've been friends for a few years and I'd like to know what's happened to him. I think you'll find him where you find Blane. You'll be taking a look at the Beyt el-Basha today, no doubt?"

"This evening. After dark. That is the best time to accomplish anything without fuss during Ramadan. In the meantime, I must cover my rear. The PRM still have one or two influential friends. And I need to know more about Mardam's death."

Footsteps crunched on the gravel and climbed the steps onto the veranda.

The Syrian officer called in Arabic: "*Ya,* Ahmed! Go to the back! Don't touch anything. Keep the woman with you." He went to meet them in the kitchen and told them Maître Mardam was dead. He said he was going to lock the woman in the pantry until his men got here to take a statement from her; then he would let her go.

She wailed and protested, but soon a door slammed, a key turned, and her cries subsided.

The officer went on: "I will drive back to the office and send the duty squad. You will stay here, Ahmed, until they arrive. Detain anyone who comes. Walk around the outside of the house. Do not touch anything."

A few moments later I heard him speaking French again. "When are you going to Latakia?"

"Early tomorrow morning," Julien replied.

Their voices were moving along the veranda.

135

"Have you booked a taxi?"

"No; I'll drive myself. I've been asked to take a car back—the Rover belonging to Amery, the director of . . ."

Their footsteps crunched onto the gravel and faded away. Soon all I could hear was Ahmed's slow tread on the path around the house and an occasional moan from the woman in the pantry.

I mopped the sweat from around my eyes and put my jacket on.

Gently, I moved the tiles, opened the trapdoor, and poked the light stepladder down into the box room, lowering it the last yard or so with my feet. I climbed down, closing the trapdoor, put the ladder back where I had found it, and wiped its side rails with a duster. Then I wrapped a handkerchief around my right hand and went over to the door. As I did so, I heard footsteps crossing the kitchen. They came along the hall. I picked up a cut-glass vase with a nicely weighted base and stood behind the door.

The woman heard or sensed the footsteps, too, and whined: "Let me out."

Ahmed's voice told her to shut up or she would be kept there all day. With that, he walked back to the kitchen. She moaned softly. I put down my glassware, turned the door handle slowly, opened the door an inch—and froze. He was coming back, more quietly this time.

He passed my door and went on to the study. I looked out up the hall after him. He was a plumpish man, with dark curly hair, wearing khaki trousers and a cream shirt.

He put a handkerchief around his right hand—he'd seen too many B pictures, too—and turned the handle of the study door. He opened the door cautiously as if he expected Mardam to shout at him. There was no shout, so he went in and half closed the door behind him. I could see the way his mind was working even through the thickness of the wood. Wealthy lawyers generally have well-upholstered wallets; on dead lawyers such luxuries are wasted . . .

I went after him as fast, but as quietly, as I could. I put a hand around the edge of the door, pulled the key out of the inside keyhole, slammed the door, put the key in my side of the lock, and turned. He cried out in alarm. I stood well to the side, in case he had a gun and tried to shoot me through the door, and quickly wiped the door handle and key. Then I ran down the hall, across the kitchen, and out the back door.

I had left the key in the study door so as to provide Ahmed with some time-wasting entertainment. I was hoping he would search for a piece of wire, then ease the key around until he could push it out and pull it under the door, if it didn't get stuck, into the study. He wouldn't want to shoot the door open, if he had a gun, or raise a shutter and smash a way out through a mosquito screen: he'd have too many awkward questions to answer. If he could get away with it, he wouldn't even mention me. But I kept on running. I didn't want to meet the other men the officer was sending.

Fifty or sixty yards from the house, at the end of the garden farthest from the avenue, I was halted by a tall barbed-wire fence. It was that or a tête-à-tête with the Sûreté, so I went over it and only cut one gash in my trouser leg and one across the back of my hand. There was a pistachio plantation on the other side, then a tempting lane that led back to the avenue; but they would expect me to take that, if Ahmed talked and they came looking for me, so I plodded on across another plantation and only then followed a dusty cactus-lined path that led toward the city.

17

There were no letters or messages for me at the hotel, but my fans hadn't neglected me. My suitcase had been searched. Nothing was missing, and the searcher had rearranged my things conscientiously—but he had overlooked two carefully placed hairs.

I showered, changed, and asked the telephonist for Julien and McGlint. They were both out. I wasn't heartbroken. I was more interested than ever in Blane, and Aleppo's leading authorities on that subject were Walid and Salwa. I gave the telephonist Walid's number, hoping my vanishing act had not annoyed him.

Salwa answered. "Thank God. We were getting worried. Will you be back soon? We are holding lunch for you. It's *sfiha** and it can't wait too long."

"It smells wonderful. I'm on my way."

The whole family was at lunch. It was my first meeting with Walid's shy smiling wife, Jamila. Before letting me eat, Salwa put a dressing on my hand and tried to talk me into a tetanus jab.

Over coffee, when we were alone, Walid said: "That powder you had was heroin. I saw the analyst this morning. There was a little left so I flushed it down the toilet, the safest place for it. I've handled dangerous things in my time, but never heroin."

"Would Blane handle it?"

My question surprised him. "I don't think so. Is that why you followed Blane to the Beyt el-Basha—because you think he is in drug traffic?"

* A variety of *lahme b'ajeen* (see p. 91).

"I followed him because I'm a journalist. I'm hoping to get a story out of his kidnapping."

Walid grinned—toothily, unpleasantly. "You are a lucky sort of journalist. Wherever you go, things happen. In a paper I received from Beirut this morning I read that an English businessman was killed there. The Sûreté questioned a friend of his named Ray Alan. Do you think Blane knows something about the murder?"

"I can't decide. I need to know more about him."

"Naturally." He sounded ironical but seemed more relaxed now. "Blane is restless and vain. He likes action and intrigue and is eager to be thought important. He has a great hunger for money—but, like most ex-officers, he expects to get it easily, without really having to work for it or run serious risks. I can't imagine him facing the risks involved in murder or drug smuggling." He jerked his big chin toward the dressing on my hand. "What risks were you taking when you cut your hand?"

I told him about my visit to Mardam's house.

"My God!" he said. "That officer must have been Major Yazid of the Sûreté. I was planning to do something . . . Now I shall do it earlier. I am grateful to you. But I must ask you to stay here, and not use the telephone, for a few hours. Have a siesta, take tea, and, if you wish, watch television. The house is yours. If all goes well you can have another talk with Blane this evening."

"In that case I'll be a willing prisoner."

"Prisoner? Guest!" He smiled, but to himself, not to me.

So I dozed for an hour or so, read the headlines of the Syrian papers, and drank the tea and sampled the books that one of Walid's sons brought me. Then the boy brought in a portable TV set and obliged me to watch an Italian Western. It was some time before the baddies all bit the dust; but they did, eventually, and we celebrated their downfall with Coca-Cola. Then I went down to the second floor, to a little reception room with a good view of the courtyard. The mad painter who designs sunsets in Syria had packed up for the day. I leaned out of the window, watching the stars come out.

The sweet scent of Turkish tobacco crept up behind me and Salwa's voice said: "I suppose you think Walid is crazy."

She was pale, and her pallor was accentuated by lipstick and the midnight-blue dress she was wearing—a tight, sleeveless dress fastened below the left shoulder by a gold brooch in the form of the Ottoman seal. She pecked at her cigarette and sent up untidy blobs of smoke that made her blink. She came and stood beside me and looked out over the dark courtyard.

"No," I said. "But why take such a risk when the Sûreté were going to get Blane out of the Beyt el-Basha tonight, anyway?"

She sipped a toothful of smoke out of her cigarette and blew it away as if it had been annoying her. "It was your news about the Sûreté that spurred him to act. He loves a race; and he enjoys mystifying people."

"He's certainly good at it. I'm right in the dark." She didn't offer to enlighten me, so I said: "That's a lovely brooch."

"It's been in the family two hundred years. It's my private talisman. I wear it when I'm in need of reassurance."

"And you smoke a cigarette."

She smiled. "Keeping the smoke out of my eyes prevents me from worrying about more complicated things."

"Such as Walid's plans for the welfare or otherwise of Blane?"

"You must not put it like that. He's not going to shoot Blane. Walid is a businessman. He was offered a satisfactory sum to forget the past and give Blane some protection in Aleppo. That is one reason for his wanting to rescue Blane. He will be able to claim a bonus. Blane will not know that the Sûreté were going to rescue him anyhow, though I imagine he would prefer not to talk to them."

"Why?"

She coughed and killed her cigarette. "The Sûreté can complicate life for anyone, and they would not find it hard to embarrass Colonel Blane. They need only ask him how he plans to get his money out of Syria."

"There's another question they might ask," I said, "and it could explain Walid's eagerness to keep Blane out of their hands. Where did he get his money in the first place? Blane told me he made it playing cards and transporting merchandise for local businessmen; but that kind of money wouldn't buy much real estate. On the other hand, if the merchandise he transported was something like hashish . . ."

"From the Kurd Dagh and the Jebel Alawi, during the boom after the Six-Day War, when prices were at their highest . . ."

We looked at each other. I gripped the edge of the open window tight while she decided how much to tell me.

Hashish has been cultivated in Lebanon and Syria since chapter one of history. But the men who grow it rarely smoke it. They are proud of the reputation of their produce but despise those who use it. Their traditional market is Egypt. The re-emergence of Israel cut the direct land route to Egypt and the Lebanese growers' syndicate promoted a new one through Jordan to the Gulf of Aqaba and Sinai, where Bedouins smuggled it across the desert to Suez, Ismailia, and Port Said. The Six-Day War, in which Israel captured the Sinai peninsula, killed this trade. Regular shipping services from Lebanon to Egypt were already watched by the Egyptian narcotics bureau. Hashish rotted in Lebanon while hashish prices soared in Egypt.

Salwa resumed softly: "The pipeline company Blane worked for had a ship on—what do you call it?—charter? It brought material from a depot and workshops they had in Alexandria. It took hashish back. Blane organized that part. Walid's men contacted growers in northern and western Syria and saw that the hashish they brought in to Jisr esh Shughur, Haffé, and other collection points was transported to the coast. Now congratulate me on my taste in uncles and . . . the sort of man I fall in love with."

"The drug runner is an honorable man compared with the

141

characters in Russia and the West who've been stuffing the Near East with armaments during the last twenty years."

"You don't make me feel any prouder. Not that I'm in love with Blane any more. What I have just told you should convince you of that: that was why I told you. You thought I did love him still, didn't you?"

"I was afraid you might."

"Afraid?" Her eyes, dark pools of longing, shone up at me.

"I didn't want you to get hurt." I took one of her hands. "I suspect Blane's going to grab his money and run when Walid releases him."

Her hand gripped mine tightly. "Never let Walid know that I told you about the hashish. Promise!"

I promised.

She said: "Walid owes to you the certainty that Blane is in the Beyt el-Basha, yet he behaves as if you are not trustworthy."

"He's not even told me how he's going to rescue Blane."

"The rescue will be play-acting, really, though Blane will not know. Walid warned the PRM that the Sûreté are planning a raid. They were grateful, and as they have finished with Blane, they agreed to let Walid stage an apparent rescue. When Walid and his men arrive, the guards will yield to them and Blane will be taken out the back way, over those garage roofs you crawled on."

"Then Walid's not running any real risk?"

"The Sûreté may arrive sooner than he expects. And there's a Palestinian group interested in Blane."

"Why?"

"I don't know. I think they want to question him. Walid hesitated when he learned that Palestinians are involved. But he wants to have Blane in his debt, so . . ."

She turned away from the window and sat in an armchair. I sat at a right angle to her and let my eyes enjoy the graceful flow of her arms and legs.

"This is a dismal little room," she said. Her big brooding eyes inventoried distastefully the tired armchairs and low table, rejects from other rooms. "It's where Walid parks visitors who are not important enough to be received upstairs. Why did you come here?"

"I like the view over the yard."

"You hope to see Blane, to talk to him?"

"There are one or two things I'd like to ask him."

She shook her head. "He will tell you nothing. And I doubt whether Walid will allow you to talk to him. He is angry because you asked one of his men about some wheels. The man told him. He thinks you may be investigating something which may incriminate Blane—and perhaps himself. He cannot believe that a simple journalist would take the risks you have taken. Here, journalists write only what someone important wants them to write."

A car drove into the courtyard below and braked sharply. We both ran to the window. Another car followed it. At once heavy wooden doors creaked shut and bolts clattered.

Blane was the first person I recognized down in the yard. He was watching two of Walid's men lift a body out of the back seat of one of the cars. The headlights of the other car had been kept on to give them light, and in the low shallow beam Blane looked tense and pale. There was a sneer on his face that didn't fit my memory of him. He needed a shave badly and his hair was disheveled. His suit was about right for a church bazaar.

He started when he saw me. "Good Lord! I thought you were pushing up thistles. I was sure you'd had it when they caught you." His gaze snaked about the yard. "Was it you who told Walid I was there?"

"Yes."

"Good of you. I had my doubts about him, but in the end . . . Thanks."

Walid had been weaving about in the background issuing orders. When he saw me with Blane he hurried over to us. He looked Blane over coolly.

"That was a very pretty job," Blane said in Arabic. "I thank you."

"I am always glad to help an old acquaintance," Walid said.

They shook hands, sizing each other up like a couple of heavyweights.

Walid turned to me and pointed to the body his men were carrying to the house. "That is an Englishman they captured in the Beyt el-Basha."

"The bastard," Blane put in. "He was helping those thugs interrogate me. He was there when Walid's men arrived, so I told them to grab him. He tried to escape as we went over that roof at the back. I tripped him and he fell into the alley."

Walid said to me: "I have sent one of my men for a doctor I know who will take him to his clinic. We shall say we found him in the street. Please go into the house and ask Salwa to give him first aid. You would be kind to stay with him until the doctor arrives. Nobody in the house understands English."

It was politer than putting a gun in my back. I wondered if they had had time to go through the injured man's pockets and decided they hadn't. I turned away.

"See you later," Blane said.

They walked off toward Walid's office, which was over one of the warehouses. I went into the house and up the stairs. A leathery little man wearing a sweat-stained headcloth, an army shirt, dusty black trousers, and a few days' growth of gray bristle appeared out of the darkness and sauntered upstairs, too, keeping a few steps behind me.

Salwa had seen them carrying someone in and was already guiding them into a spare bedroom. It contained a single bed with a naked mattress on it, a bedside table, a chair, and a carved cedarwood chest. They were telling Salwa what had happened, contradicting one another excitedly, as they laid the injured man on the bed. She took a blanket out of the chest and

144

put it over him, and then stood by the bed holding his wrist. Walid's men lowered their voices and went out.

Salwa said: "I saw Blane. He seems older . . . Do you know this man?"

"Slightly. His name is Pete McGlint. He's a mining engineer."

There was a little blood in one of McGlint's ears and his face was flushed. His eyes flickered open and focused on Salwa.

"His pulse is slow," Salwa said. "I hope the doctor hurries. Go to the café, please, and ask them for a jug of ice. We must keep his head cool. I'll get some towels."

The little man in the headcloth was leaning against the wall just outside the bedroom door. He looked as tough as a gnarled old olive root. He raised his head and clicked his teeth at me. I ignored him and began to walk around him to go downstairs. A thin knife appeared in his hand. He pointed it at my appendicitis scar and showed every willingness to make a new one.

"You stay here," he said.

Salwa came out of the bedroom and gasped.

"Are you mad, Abu-Ali?" she cried. "Get away from here—quickly." She put a hand on my arm.

"Walid said this man stay here," he replied, poking his knife at me.

"Walid made a mistake. This man is our friend and guest. He is now going to get some ice from the café."

Abu-Ali clicked his teeth again. "Walid said he stay here."

She was angry now and gripped my arm tightly. "Very well, Abu-Ali. I shall go for the ice myself. Then I shall tell Walid you insulted me. You remember what happened to that Egyptian who spoke to me improperly, don't you?"

He licked his cracked lips and whined a couple of bars, but his knife didn't waver. His small sand-colored eyes watched me warily.

"Wait for me in the bedroom—and don't take risks," she told me. She went downstairs.

I turned back to the bedroom and locked the door. McGlint groaned and muttered something. His eyes were closed. Gently I inspected his jacket pockets. In an inside pocket I found his wallet and a notebook. The wallet contained the usual things—driving permit, Lebanese residence card, a photo or two, money—and I put it back. The notebook was a jumbled anthology of names, addresses, jottings, and reminders. On a page near the beginning was written in a hurried pencil scrawl: *Seacity.*

McGlint's eyes were open again, and watching me.

He murmured: "Och, ma head!"

"The doctor's on his way. You're going to be all right."

"Where am I?"

"In Walid's house."

"Who's Walid? A pal o' Blane's?"

"Yes."

"Ye'll be stayin' around, Alan? To see I get fair play? Blane looks a vindictive sod. And Arabs can be rough when a man's doon."

I quoted the Arab proverb: "When a camel falls, every man's knife hacks at it."

"Aye." He moved, as if to sit up, but pain pinned him down. His tough, lined face now looked weak and worried.

"Who saw that Blane got fair play when your friends had him in the Beyt el-Basha?"

"Nobody laid a finger on him. Those boys are not gangsters. They've an ideal in their heads."

"Who was the idealist that shot Arnold?"

He closed his eyes. "Ask your pal Blane."

"You told me you saw Blane with someone who was no friend of Arnold's a few days before Arnold was killed. Who was that?"

"The man ye found in Arnold's study. Hamam."

"Was Blane with Hamam in Arnold's study?"

"How the hell would I know? Ask Blane."

"I will. Well, if that's all you can tell me, I'll be going."

He forced his eyes open and peered around the room. "I had a tip-off about Blane. He'd been askin' questions about Arnold and the company—what we produce, our concession areas . . . I saw him wi' Hamam. Then Arnold and Hamam were killed. And I learned that Blane wa' comin' to Aleppo. I've good contacts here, so I came too."

"And arranged for the PRM to kidnap him?"

"No. But when ye told me he'd been taken into the suq, I got to thinkin' about it an' made a few inquiries. Ma contacts led me to the PRM."

"Why were they interested in him?"

He blinked at me. "A Palestinian group asked them to grab him. The Palestinians sent a man to question him."

"What about?"

"They wouldna tell me. I'd say they wanted to know what he's up to. The Arabs have no cause to trust wanderin' English officers. Somethin' wa' said about drugs, but I couldna hear the details." He groaned and shut his eyes again. "I asked them to question him about Arnold's murder and his interest in the company, but then his pals barged in. I'll say one thing for him: he doesna scare easy. Not that they put any real pressure on. They're not thugs, those boys. I suppose you bloody hacks call them Reds. Anybody with an ideal is a Red to the press lords."

The light went out; but lights still shone in Walid's office.

"Thanks," McGlint said. "That light wa' botherin' me."

"What's the City in the Sea?"

He sighed. "If I'd worked that oot I wouldna be here noo."

"Where did you first hear of it?"

He moaned. "Ma head! Why should I tell you?"

"So that I stay around. Remember Blane and his pals?"

"Aye. Ye're a'richt, I guess. I saw it in a personal file of Arnold's. *Seacity.* Arnold never mentioned it, so I didn't."

"Did Denbor know what it meant?"

"I tried it on him but he didna react."

"And Blane?"

"I never asked him."

147

Someone was knocking on the door.

"Hold this jug," Salwa's voice said in Arabic. "Don't spill it. The lights have fused. That would happen when the doctor's coming."

"That sounds like the wee lassie," McGlint said. "Let her in."

I put his notebook in my pocket and opened the door. Salwa had a lot of towels in one hand and a big flashlight in the other. She seemed to be shining the light more than was necessary in Abu-Ali's eyes. He stood there blinking, holding a copper jug. I couldn't see his knife.

"An ideal," McGlint said. "How can folk live withoot an ideal? Like beasts in a jungle . . ."

I stepped into the corridor. Salwa gave me the flashlight.

"It was I who pulled the fuse out," she said in French.

I moved aside to let her pass, and as she took her first step forward, I swung around and hit Abu-Ali on the side of the head with the flashlight. As he fell I relieved him of the jug and passed it to Salwa. We were as slick as a trio of acrobats; but Abu-Ali spoiled the act by getting the knife into his hand and rearing like a cobra. I kept the light in his eyes, put my heel in his face, and then stamped on his wrist, hoping he wouldn't cut my foot off.

"Poor Abu-Ali," Salwa said.

"His mother should have taught him not to play with knives."

His fingers appeared to have gone dead. I kicked the knife clear and dragged him into the bedroom. McGlint's eyes were shut again. I balanced the flashlight on a chair, opened the cedarwood chest, and pulled out two blankets. With Salwa's help, I put Abu-Ali in the chest, laid the two blankets on top of him, shut the lid, and turned the key.

Salwa said: "I went to Walid's office but I didn't go in. They were arguing." She made an ice pack for McGlint's head. "Blane will leave for Latakia tonight. The atmosphere is not good. Walid is agitated. It will be better if you keep out of sight for a day or two. I will telephone you at your hotel."

She finished with McGlint and we walked out of the room. The house was still. We stood in the corridor, listening.

"Go quickly," she said. "Seeing Blane again has made Walid hard and bitter. I will talk sense into him. In a day or two—"

"I still have a few things to discuss with Blane," I said. "If I don't see him again in Aleppo, I may follow him to the coast."

Suddenly she was trembling. "Then I may not see you again?"

"I'll be back."

"Forget Blane. Don't go after him. He's trouble."

"I must."

"No, no . . ." She put her arms around my neck and pulled my head down. We were linked in a long, futile kiss.

At last I said: "Goodbye."

The pale blur of her face receded a little. "You were right," she murmured. "The girls in our family don't have . . ." Her voice failed her.

"We'll meet again. Don't forget to let Abu-Ali out of his box."

Halfway down the stairs, I paused. She hadn't moved. She was sobbing there, quietly, in the dark.

18

I fumbled along the black hallway, opened the door slowly, and blinked at the brightly moonlit yard. The two cars glittered like Soviet generals. The coffee shop's loudspeakers were gurgling rapturously.

I walked along the dark side of the yard toward the arched porte cochere. I was nearly there when a car door slammed. An engine started and headlights came to life. One of the cars began to move, its headlight beams raking the yard. I pressed myself into the shadow of a doorway.

The car—a big old Ford—poked its nose under the porte cochere and stopped. The driver got out, called someone, and walked to the big wooden doors across the street end of the arch. A man came out of a doorway near mine. He seemed to be a guard or watchman. He said: "I'll shut them for you." I didn't like that.

I watched them slide open a bolt the size of a polo stick. They had the headlights on them. I was behind the headlights and could have danced a Highland fling without their seeing me. The driver was Habib, the man who brought me here when the hospitality ran out at the House of the Pasha. As they pulled open the creaking wooden doors, I got into the back of the Ford. I closed the door gently and lay on the floor. It was gritty and smelled of dead feet.

Half a minute later, Habib got in and drove off. Just outside the porte cochere he heard my door rattle. He leaned back, opened it a little, and slammed it.

We kettledrummed over cobblestones, turned onto a smoother street and zigzagged around the edge of the suq. The car was suddenly aglow with the lights of a bright avenue.

Harsh mercury lamps flashed by for a minute or two. Then we turned right, into a dim side street. Habib parked the car, switched off the engine, locked up, and walked away.

I waited until I could hear no footsteps and raised my head. There was no sign of Habib or anyone else. I got out and walked toward the avenue—the way Habib had gone.

A new hotel glowed on the corner. Much of its ground floor was a European-style coffee lounge, with big tinted windows, red and blue armchairs, low tables of black glass and stainless steel, and a bright tiled bar. Through one of the windows I saw Habib sitting on the edge of an armchair. He glanced at his watch, checked it with the bar clock, and lit a cigarette.

The coffee lounge shared a wall of untinted glass with the hotel lobby; and on the other side of the lobby were two telephone booths. I went into the hotel and shut myself in one of the booths. I picked up the receiver but kept my finger on the button. I watched Habib and wondered what he was doing there and what business it was of mine. He was dressed like a London-Irish apprentice celebrating St. Patrick's day: green suit, yellow shirt, green-and-gold tie. He had had a shave recently.

A plump man went into the booth beside mine. A waiter took an order from Habib. An army officer approached the booths, saw they were occupied, and marched up and down in front of them. Habib leaned back, watching his cigarette smoke. The army officer noticed my finger on the button and stared at me. I moved it, put a coin in the box, and dialed the number of my hotel.

The usual girl answered. She never seemed to have any time off. I asked her if there were any letters or messages for me.

"No letters," she said, "but one telephone message. From a lady. She asked that you call her."

"What's her name?"

"I don't know. But she told me her number. Would you like to know it?"

"That might be useful."

151

She gave it to me, adding: "Ask for room 43."

The plump man came out of the next booth and the officer dashed into it, scowling at me. I put another coin in the slot and dialed again.

A man said briskly: "Hotel Nablus."

"Room 43, please."

A buzz. A girl's voice said: *"Naam?"*

"Anna?"

She asked in Arabic: "Who's speaking?"

"The secretary of the AAAA."

"The what?" In English.

"The Association of Abandoned Admirers of Anna."

"How kind of you to remember me! But who abandoned whom?"

"I ran into a little trouble."

"Are you sure you weren't looking for it?"

"No comment."

"Did Salwa console you satisfactorily?"

"Not as satisfactorily as you might have done."

"How can you know what I might do?"

"Even journalists dream."

"We did not come here to dream, Mr. Alan."

"But something was said about the citadel by moonlight."

"It is too late. I have to return to Beirut."

"When can I see you?"

"I said I have to return to Beirut. Very soon. I shall be busy until I leave Aleppo."

"Don't you want to know about my activities?"

"I have heard something about them. Now, perhaps, you will agree that you were on the wrong track?"

"Perhaps. But I'd like to tell you—"

"In Beirut, if you wish. In the meantime, our mutual friend—the one in whose house we met—would like to know if you are continuing or discontinuing the inquiry."

"Continuing."

"Good. Then he suggests that you concentrate on your

French acquaintance. We have sufficient information now about the Englishman you traveled with, and a source close to him is keeping us up to date, though we don't really consider him important. But we know very little about the Frenchman's activities. Can our Beirut friend rely on you to concentrate on this subject now?"

"What a waste!"

"What do you mean?"

"Those eyes and that smile—on a computer. But you don't always talk like that."

"Not always." Her voice softened. "But you've been so exasperating."

"I didn't really fall for Salwa. How could I, having met you?"

"Please . . ."

"Tell me you'll relax a little the next time we meet."

"I'll try."

"Will it be so difficult?"

"No, unfortunately. I must ring off now. You are getting that look in your eyes again."

"Aren't these videophones wonderful?"

"So you'll study the French subject?"

"I'm getting out my Larousse now. Shall I leave Aleppo when he does?"

"When is he leaving?"

"Tomorrow or the day after."

She hesitated. "That will probably be your best course. Stay close to him. I'll tell our friend. Goodbye. Take care."

"What time does your plane leave?"

The line was dead.

Habib was sipping an orange-colored drink and watching television. I left the telephone booth and walked out of the hotel. Because of its tinted windows, the coffee lounge looked darker from outside than from the hotel lobby, but I could still see Habib. The word NABLUS was painted on the window I was looking through. I gaped up at the elongated Arabic script of

153

the blue neon sign over the hotel entrance: HOTEL NABLUS. I wondered how much new heads cost. I needed one.

There was little traffic along the avenue now, but the sidewalks were crowded with strollers, mostly men, enjoying the cool night air. I strolled along with them, past the end of the side street where Habib had parked the car, then back again. Habib was looking at his watch. I sauntered slowly on, past the hotel entrance, twenty yards beyond it, and back.

Habib had moved. He was sitting at one of the low tables near the entrance, clapping for a waiter. Opposite him sat a striking dark-haired girl. Her profile was familiar. I turned back just beyond the side street and looked again. It was Anna.

Shielded by the crowd, I ambled back and forth, loitered and waited. They drank coffee. Anna did most of the talking. At last, Habib paid the bill and they stood up. I went quickly to the car, got into the back, and lay on the fetid floor again.

I was expecting Habib to drive Anna to the airport; but when, after five minutes, he came to the car, he was alone. He drove off at once, humming contentedly. Two left turns took us back to the avenue. More mercury lamps flashed by. Then we left the avenue for good and sped through a dimly lit suburb. I hoped we weren't going to pick up a load of morphine on the Turkish frontier. I sat up a little in search of a bearing. There were no street lights now. Moonlit treetops moved by.

Habib slowed down and turned sharply onto an earth track. Acrid dust seeped into the car. I breathed slowly through my mouth so as not to sneeze. Another sharp turn, and the car thumped over a few ruts that almost broke my hip. We halted. Habib put the hand brake on and got out, leaving the engine running. He walked to the front of the car, as if inspecting the track ahead, and then returned and took something out of the trunk. I heard a scrape of metal.

He laid whatever it was on the ground a few yards away, came back to the car, and opened his door. But he didn't get in. I realized suddenly that the car was tilting downhill. He released the hand brake and stood back, slamming the door. The car began to move forward. He was ditching it.

I sat up, not minding if he saw me now, and looked ahead. There was a ravine where the track ought to have been.

The car was gathering speed. I opened the nearest door and jumped out. I landed in a clump of thistles and fell sideways.

I saw the Ford hurtling down a slope. The front grille took a bite at a boulder, silver arcs were spat out from the windshield, and the back wheels left the ground. For a second or two the car stood on its nose. Then it flopped over and slid on, upside down, making a noise like a shipyard, into a black gash. There was an instant of silence before the final thunderous crash. Dust billowed up into the moonlight.

Stones stirred behind me. I sat up. Habib was coming over—warily, like a mutual-fund salesman. He had a gun in his hand.

He asked: *"Min ente?"**

"Habib!" I exclaimed. *"El-hamdulillah!"*†

I stood up. I hoped he didn't know my relations with Walid were strained.

He laughed tensely. "I thought you were a jinn. You gave me a shock. Why were you in the car?"

"I've been staying in Walid's house. He and his niece have been very kind to me. This evening I wished to get some clothes from my hotel."

"Walid told you to come with me in the car?" He sounded unconvinced.

"I sat in the car and waited. I must have fallen asleep. I'm still weak from those drugs the PRM gave me. When I awoke, the car seemed to be driving itself, so I jumped out."

He put his gun away and we shook hands.

"Two more seconds and you would have been killed," he said.

* Who are you?
† God be praised!

155

He picked up a collapsible bicycle—this would be what he took from the trunk of the Ford—and shone its light on me while I plucked fragments of thistle from my hide. Then we walked along the track to the highway, Habib pushing the bicycle.

"Whose was the car?" I asked.

"A friend's. It was getting tired. He does a lot of long-distance runs. He wants its number for a new car—you understand?"

I did. Putting old numbers on new, generally smuggled, cars is almost a Mideast tradition.

When we reached the highway he sat on the little bicycle. He said: "This isn't strong enough for two, so I must leave you now. I'm sorry, but someone is waiting for me."

Anna, I told myself. I turned my face from him lest the moonlight betray the bitterness I felt.

"And I have a long drive early in the morning. There's a big café down the road. If you wish, I'll telephone Walid from there."

Almost sullenly, I asked: "How far is it?"

"The time to smoke a cigarette." This is a unit of measure Syrians use to cover five minutes or half an hour, five hundred yards or two miles. I said: "Never mind. The walk and the night air will do me good. I'll have a drink there and call a taxi. I don't want to delay you or be a nuisance to Walid."

"It's very near. And you can't get lost. This is the main road into Aleppo from Jisr esh Shughur and Latakia."

We shook hands and he pedaled off toward Aleppo.

There was the usual crisp breeze that blows over the Syrian steppe at night in the early summer. The sky was a flawless black-and-silver brocade. But all my mind really saw was a captivating Anna and a captivated Habib. *I have a long drive early in the morning.* Was he driving her to Beirut?

I heard an engine straining behind me and leaped over the low wall of an olive grove. Two light army trucks sped past, moaning the peculiar lament of Russian-built military vehicles.

Their occupants would have been intrigued by the sight of a solitary Westerner so far from a bar at that hour.

A little later a powerful headlight beam began boring through the night from the direction of Aleppo. I hid behind a contorted olive tree, wondering if Habib had telephoned Walid after all. A big car came along the road, not very fast. It looked gray in the moonlight, then olive-green. It had a V-shaped dent in its rear left door. Through the window above the dent I saw a profile that looked like Blane's.

I walked on. A quarter of a mile down the road, shielded by walls and trees, an open-air cabaret was beating out a Western pop song. As I went in, the lights were dimmed and the orchestra switched to a Turkish tango. I fumbled my way to the bar, shook off a desperate-looking Egyptian girl, ordered an arak, and watched the action. There wasn't much, and the script was an old one. The usual officers and foppish youths were being milked of their or their fathers' money by the usual sycophants and cola-sipping hostesses. On the dim little dance floor, one couple was performing something like a tango and three others were shuffling cozily.

The lights came up again and the musicians mopped their brows and lit cigarettes. I found a telephone, dialed the number of my hotel, and asked the girl for Julien Montrand. She sounded as if she had her head in a beehive. So did Julien.

"I've been worried about you," he said. "Where 'ave you been? What is this buzzing? Are you in a sawmill?"

"It must be the line." With so many officers coming here, it would have more taps in it than the public baths. "I'm speaking from the Badr cabaret."

"Where is that?"

"Just outside Aleppo on the road to Jisr esh Shughur."

"Ah! I've 'eard of it. If it weren't so late I'd join you."

"I'd like you to join me, anyhow. I want to get to Latakia fairly quickly. When are you going?"

"Tomorrow morning, early. But 'ow do you know my intentions?"

157

"Bazaar gossip. Aleppo's like that. I was hoping you might go tonight. I'd have liked to travel with you. I could take turns driving. I'm hot stuff on a Rover—provided it's got all four wheels, of course."

"You are positively telepathic. But is it so important to go to Latakia at once?"

"I think so . . . for all friends of Mr. Blane's."

"Is Blane with you?"

"No. He's on his way to Latakia, though."

He thought it over. "Blane's affairs are no business of mine, though I admit that I am a little curious about 'is—and your—recent adventures. When will you return to the hotel?"

"I'd rather not come. Someone unfriendly may be looking for me there. So if you could bring my suitcase with you—"

"I 'ave not yet said that I will drive you to Latakia tonight, let alone act as your valet. But I suppose that someone must rescue you."

"France will be proud of you, Julien."

"You will 'ave to wait one hour at least. The car is some distance away, and I must pack, make a few telephone calls, and . . . Where will you be?"

"I'd better wait here. I want bright lights and people around me."

"I 'ope the cabaret girls fleece you," he said.

19

The body and front wheels of the Rover were the same red as the wheels I had seen in Walid's yard. The back wheels were blue.

"Better blue wheels than none," Julien said. He drove fast, with neat, precise movements. We seemed to have the whole moonlit steppe to ourselves. "I got them from a scrapyard. Fortunately, an English diplomat's son got 'igh on 'ashish during the last university vacation and drove 'is father's Rover into a bus. But for 'im . . ." He shrugged. "That's the trouble with these obscure makes of car. Now, if it was a well-known make, like a Renault . . ."

"Did you discover who took the wheels?"

"I asked the police if they 'ad found them. They said no. Me, I do not discover things. I am a businessman." He added mockingly: "You seem to be the special investigator. You should 'ave tracked them down."

"I did."

"It would be useful to know who took them. The information would point to the identity of Arnold's assassins."

"Not necessarily," I said, to get him arguing.

"The wheels were stolen to keep Arnold in Alep while 'is apartment was searched. The men who searched it killed 'im. Therefore, the wheel thieves are linked with the assassins."

"It's possible."

We sat in silence while Idlib, a sleeping market town, flashed by. Then Julien asked quietly: "Did you really trace the wheels?"

"Yes. But you're not interested. You're a businessman."

He groaned. "What is upsetting you?"

"Nothing. But if you're going to shoot me that businessman line, I'm going to sling it back. I didn't invite you out tonight merely to see Syria by moonlight."

"*Merde!* I 'ad the impression I was doing you a favor."

"I was hoping you'd want to do yourself a favor by comparing notes with me."

"Give me a sample of your notes. The wheels, for example."

"I saw them this morning in a garage behind a café owned by a man named Walid."

"*Chapeau!*" He raised an imaginary hat. "You 'ave done well!"

"I had to do something to save my face, with you running around telling Sûreté officers how stupid I am."

Julien whistled. "I did say something like that to Major Yazid, but only to protect you. *Mon vieux*, I 'ave underrated you. So it was you up in the roof chez Mardam?"

"That was termites you heard."

"I didn't 'ear anything. But when Yazid went back to the 'ouse this afternoon, 'e saw a stepladder that was not there this morning. And 'is men found footprints in the roof space. Then 'is driver confessed—after a short beating—that three men surprised 'im and locked 'im in Maître Mardam's study. Yazid told me all this on the telephone this evening."

The highway rose out of the plain, curving and climbing through olive groves and vineyards. Julien's big face looked relaxed in the moonlight. He went on: "Now I understand 'ow you knew that I was going to Latakia and taking this car. You 'eard me tell Yazid. Why were you there?"

"You haven't told me why you've got this car."

He laughed. "There is no mystery about that. A friend in the British consulate asked me to drive it back to Beirut. Maybe they did not know that McGlint was going to be in Alep."

I whistled a few bars of "Colonel Bogey." Julien looked at me.

"You can do better than that," I said.

He drove on in silence. A twinkle of lights on a blue-gray

160

hillside, the howl of a dog in an orchard, and we were past Eriha. The road swung westward and upward to skirt the Jebel Zawiya. The moon hung ahead of us like an overripe apricot.

At last Julien said: "You 'ave not been wasting your time in Alep. Do you know now why Arnold was killed?"

"I've met an occasional whiff of dope along the trail. Could Arnold have become involved in a dope racket? This car might have hidden compartments for smuggling the stuff."

"A little primitive. And 'ow would I fit in?"

"You might be either Arnold's associate or some kind of investigator trying to break up the racket. A lot of Frenchmen are unhappy about France being a major heroin producer. Maybe you're a Sdec correspondent." (Resident agents of the Sdec are referred to as *correspondants.*)

"You really think Arnold was in a dope racket?"

"No."

We surged over the shoulder of the mountain and a vast dark valley opened before us. The road dipped sharply.

Julien asked: "Your interest in Arnold's death—is it mainly journalistic?"

"I may write something about it one day. But I have a personal interest in seeing justice done. The Lebanese Sûreté have me on their list of suspects."

"Frankly," Julien said, "I 'ave not wished to discuss Arnold's affairs with you, and I still 'esitate. It is not simply that you are a journalist, though that is bad enough; but you seem, in your writing, to enjoy embarrassing officialdom."

"Ordinarily, I'd say that the oftener officialdom is embarrassed the better for society's health. But I'd rather be a bad journalist than a bad friend. Was Arnold or his company involved in something that might embarrass officialdom if the news got around?"

"Yes."

"What brand of officialdom are we talking about, by the way? British? Lebanese?"

He shrugged. "Western; European . . . Take your pick."

161

"European? Not Research Service Three of the European Community?"

"What do you know about it?"

"Not much. Just that it's an old-fashioned intelligence service in modern dress. Service Three A gathers intelligence, I believe, and Service Three B is the security branch."

He glanced at me. "Were you sneering when you said 'old-fashioned'?"

"I don't think so. If we're not yet civilized enough to abolish our armed forces and intelligence and diplomatic services, I suppose the next best thing is to pool them. That should limit the damage they do and save a lot of money. But I've heard that Service Three is a rather toothless hound."

"It's 'ad a difficult commencement. Both the British Foreign Office and the Quai d'Orsay despise it—as they despise everything new. But the service is proving itself, especially in the economic sphere. It's good for the French, the English, and the Germans to be cooperating at last instead of stabbing each other in the back."

"And you think Arnold was involved in it?"

"Arnold was very enthusiastic for the European movement and 'e 'ad been in the service for more than a year. I believe that 'e 'ad experience of secret work before that, no doubt for the English intelligence."

I laughed. "Arnold was also a great legpuller. The one thing he couldn't do was keep a secret. If he had been any kind of spy he'd have been shot within a week."

Julien caressed the steering wheel. It looked like a toy beneath his big hands. I waited. At last he said: "Reach down with your left 'and. Find the 'andle that controls the position of your seat. Give it three turns. Now press it upward."

A shallow drawer slid out from beneath my seat. The map-reading light showed me a black short-muzzled .38 automatic, two small boxes of ammunition, a canvas shoulder holster, a ring of skeleton keys, a wad of hundred-dollar bills, two small bottles, a pair of tiny headphones, a packet of coin-sized telephone bugs, and a tin of Balkan Sobranie pipe tobacco.

"Shut it," Julien said. The drawer fastened with a click, leaving no outward sign of its existence. "That is to show you that I am not the victim of a legpull."

"Lots of people have secret compartments in their cars for keys and valuables."

We were running into mist now in the valley bottom.

"There are two fog lights on the car," Julien said. "But neither is of any use in fog. One takes infrared photos, the other ordinary color photos."

He dimmed the headlights and drove at walking pace for the next half mile. Then the road began to rise and we left the mist.

"All right," I said. "I suppose the radio can transmit as well as receive?"

He nodded. "Direct and 'igh-speed tape. The micro is 'ere, in the center of the 'andlebars."

He depressed the steering-wheel hub slightly and gave it a quarter turn with his thumb. Then he pressed a button on the radio.

"Cute," I said. "Broadcast while you drive. Less chance of being pinpointed. Hey! I hope you're not recording me."

He played with a couple of buttons and the radio exclaimed: "Hey! I hope you're not recording me."

The road plunged beneath another blanket of mist. Slowly, the Rover crossed the Orontes bridge at Jisr esh Shughur and nosed its way up the dark main street of the little town.

Julien said: "I'm telling you more than I should, but we 'ave known each other for many years and I do not wish you to think that I am seeking a personal advantage from Arnold's death. Arnold and me, we 'ad a sort of pact. When I first came to the Levant, France was still recovering from the war. The Arab rulers thought that she was finished and that England would be the dominant power in the Near East. So they put on

163

a show of being anti-French and pro-British. Of course, few Englishmen were so stupid as to be taken in by this—few outside the Foreign Office, anyway—and Arnold was not deluded for a moment. Always 'e remained faithful to 'is French friends, and to me 'e was very 'elpful when I commenced in business. Very soon the Arabs saw that America and Russia were the only powers that mattered and dropped their pretense of anglophilia. Then, as French economic strength revived, the early postwar position was reversed: the Arabs now professed to be pro-French and anti-British—and it was my turn to 'elp Arnold occasionally."

We were out of the mist suddenly and climbing the ridge that dominates Jisr esh Shughur. A pack of snarling pye-dogs ran toward us. Julien accelerated noisily and hooted, and they fled.

"About eight months ago," he went on, "Arnold told me that 'e was working with Service Three and invited me to cooperate. I began passing them occasional items of economic intelligence, and later I accepted a sort of protective role in Arnold's group."

He paused. I wondered if Arnold had really recruited him for the new European service or, without his knowing it, for the SIS. We had Americans on our books who thought they were working for the CIA. To get him talking again, I said: "You were the group's security man?"

"Something like that. Now you will understand why I went to Alep to collect this car. I was asked to do so by the Beirut coordinator of the service. Most of the gadgets in the car are well concealed, but if it was left in a garage for long, they might be discovered. We may 'ave to arrange for it to be stolen and set on fire."

"What a waste of good tobacco!"

"Comment?"

"I was thinking of the Balkan Sobranie. Pity your security was having a night off when Arnold was killed."

He groaned. "As it 'appened, two of our men followed you and Arnold back from La Sirène."

"In a blue Opel?"

"Yes. They are trainees. They 'ad an exercise that night—"

"They needed it. They were terrible."

"Well, as part of their exercise I told them to cast a protective eye on you and Arnold. I was surprised when you told me that Arnold was returning so soon. I 'ad almost a presentiment that 'e might run into trouble: 'is office 'ad been searched and 'e seemed uneasy. Our men parked in a side street near Arnold's place. They 'eard nothing, but one of them—the other 'ad gone to do pipi—says that 'e saw two men, one 'elping the other, come out of the building and go to a car in another side street: it 'ad a driver in it, and drove off at once. It would 'ave been impossible to follow them inconspicuously so late at night, and 'e 'ad no reason to do so. They waited another twenty minutes. All was quiet, so they went 'ome."

"Could your watchdog identify the men who left the building?"

"No."

"Is he sure there were only two of them?"

"Yes; but 'e says that soon after they were driven off another car moved away in the same direction. It 'ad been parked nearby and someone could 'ave got into it without 'im noticing. There are a lot of cars in Beirut. 'E says the driver's 'ead was muffled in a *kufiya*. But now I 'ave the right to ask you a few things. Why were you in Mardam's 'ouse?"

I told him as much of my story as I thought was good for him. Soon we were climbing to the Bdama pass. Black woods straggled up the slope on our right toward the Turkish frontier, only a few miles away. At the col Julien stopped the car and said: "Your turn to drive." We changed seats, shivering a little in the cool mountain air.

The eastern half of the sky was a pink spray of dappled clouds and tendrils of sunlight. Beyond the col, darkness lin-

gered like sludge after a flood; but within minutes the dawn
had flushed it away and the sky took on the luster of a pearl.
The road climbed down into a green gorge, crisscrossing a
stream that in winter would be a torrent.

Julien dozed. The stream flowed into a river—the Nahr el-
Kebir—and the road followed its left bank for a while. I slowed
down to edge past a flock of thick-tailed sheep that two shep-
herds were ushering toward Latakia. Their dogs barked at us.
Julien stirred and frowned at the sheep.

"Why," he asked suddenly, "are you so keen to rush after
Blane? Do you 'ope to corner 'im and burn matches under 'is
toes until 'e tells you—what? Who killed Arnold?"

"I'd like to know where he goes on the coast and who he
meets there. When he was a prisoner in the Beyt el-Basha he
asked me to tell his lawyer to 'warn our friend on the coast if
there's any delay.' I've an idea whoever he's meeting will be
coming from Beirut to help him transfer his money out of
Syria."

"Money? 'As 'e so much?"

"He invested the proceeds of his hashish smuggling in real
estate, the value of which has soared in the last three years.
Now he's sold everything, so he should have quite a pile in Syrian pounds. Unfortunately for him, the Syrian lira's not con-
vertible. He has more sense than to buy dollars or marks on the
black market and try to smuggle them out: that way, he could
lose the lot. So he needs an influential local ally, a well-placed
Syrian or Lebanese official or businessman. In return, he may
have helped his local ally in some small way—such as snooping
into Arnold's affairs. He may have helped whoever searched
Arnold's apartment. They'd need someone able to winnow
swiftly through Arnold's files."

The river valley swung off in a meander, so the road took a
shortcut over a low hill. On top of the hill we met a breeze that
had the tang of the sea in it.

Julien said: "You 'ave no proof that Blane was ever in Arnold's apartment. But if 'e was, what would 'e be looking for?"

"Something his pals could turn into money. Let's imagine that, while looking for copper or mushrooms one day, Arnold's company discovered uranium or some other valuable mineral not covered by its concession agreement. Arnold would consult the British embassy and be advised to say nothing: he wouldn't get a concession from the officers now running Syria—and he might well provoke an international wrangle. So he'd bury the discovery in his files . . . unless the mineral was important enough to tempt him to extract it without a concession. Whatever he did, this being the Levant, news of the discovery would be bound to leak out."

We were down in the coastal plain now. The river, lined with tall reeds, swung in from the north and the road crossed to its right bank. The sky was a pale turquoise blue with a few feathery cirrus strands high over the Turkish mountains. I felt suddenly lightheaded with fatigue and the exhilaration of the sea air.

"Not bad," Julien said. "The main facts may well be as you 'ave guessed."

That hurt. "Deduced," I said.

A big truck growled by, forcing me to swing the Rover onto the unpaved shoulder of the highway. Julien read the garland of Arabic script along its side while I clung hazily to the wheel and yawned.

"Levant Mining & Chemicals," he said. "They 'ave a copper mine near 'ere. The concentrate is shipped from Latakia. Their chrome ores, though, go from Tripoli."

"And their yawnanium?"

"Better ask Blane if you catch 'im."

I was driving, lightheaded as a cockatoo, toward a bright cubist mural of flat roofs and chunky minarets and, beyond, a palette of all the blues in the sea. It was not yet 6 a.m., but squat peasants in jagged black pants were already scrabbling in orchards and gardens, and the road was suddenly punctuated with old trucks, carts, and spindly donkeys. I yawned cavernously.

Julien said: "You're tired. You need a good strong coffee. You know Latakia, don't you? Down there to the seafront . . ."

In a hotel near the port we found a day waiter who had just come on duty, and ordered two breakfasts. He took our suitcases and led us to a cloakroom where we could wash and shave. I said I was expecting to meet a friend in the hotel—an Englishman who was traveling in a Green Flag taxi. I asked if he had arrived.

"He gone," the waiter said. "He just gone. With his madame."

I was too tired to leap in the air. I asked him what the Englishman looked like.

"I not see him. I see the back of the taxi as it go away. One green taxi with Lebanese number."

"That could be it. Who served him?"

"Emil, the night waiter. He gone now. It was Emil tell me he one Englishman."

"Did he say what the lady was like?"

"Helwa. Very nice."

I gave him five liras and said slowly: "If it was my friend he probably telephoned to other friends of mine at Baniyas or Tartus to leave a message for me. I suppose he expects to see me there. Can you find out what number he called? Emil may have made a note of it. If not, the exchange will tell you. You can say you are checking the bill."

Julien already had his shirt off and was imitating a water buffalo. When the waiter had gone he stopped gurgling and said: "You are wasting your time. Still, it would be interesting to know the identity of 'is little friend."

"It may be Salwa."

"The niece of Walid? But you said that she 'ates 'im now."

"Hate is the obverse of love, not its opposite. Something flips the emotions, and one replaces the other."

His big spaniel eyes gazed at me over a mask of lather. "You 'ave been doing some research." He thought about it, then raised a soapy eyebrow. "So that was 'ow you passed your time chez Walid: a cozy little affair with Salwa . . ."

"We held hands a couple of times."

"*Espèce de libertin!* And then you walked out on 'er. As a reaction she may 'ave fallen back into Blane's arms." Beneath the flippant tone there was concern in his voice.

The waiter came back with a carbon copy of Blane's bill. There were two items on it.

Julien read the Arabic scrawl: "*Three breakfasts*—why three? Oh, the driver, I suppose—and *telephone Tartus.*"

The waiter gave me another scrap of paper with Arabic numerals on it. "This is the number he ring in Tartus. Emil write it in the book we keep to check telephone bills."

I thanked him and gave him five more liras. "That must have been my friend. I'll telephone after breakfast for his message." On the way to the dining room I looked up the number in the telephone directory. There aren't that many numbers in Tartus. It belonged to a lawyer.

Over breakfast I said: "I must go to Tartus this morning."

Julien sighed. "In my Rover, I suppose."

"In Arnold's Rover. I owe it to Arnold to follow the Blane lead through. I'll be back before evening."

He shook his head. "You won't. You will be floating on the edge of some quiet little cove with a knife in your back and the shrimps nibbling out your eyes."

"I've told you what I think. I'm not going to challenge Blane to shoot it out in the main street of Tartus. This isn't the last reel of a horse opera. I simply want to know who meets him."

He shrugged. "In the 'ope of learning something interesting, I should be willing to run the risk of your collecting a 'ole in your 'ide. It is the car that worries me. It would be bad if the Syrians got 'old of it. If only you could guarantee to destroy it before you are destroyed yourself, everything would be perfect."

"Why not come along? You can watch over it from a café."

"It is not possible. I 'ave people to see 'ere. *Voyons:* if you

169

take the car and something goes wrong, I must dissociate my-self from you at once by announcing that you stole it. You un-derstand what that means? Whoever there is to mourn you will suffer the added shock of being told that you died a thief."

"There's nobody to mourn me."

He looked at me uneasily. "You 'ave a lonely sort of life."

"All journalists are lonely. Hundreds of acquaintances but no real friends. That's why they confide in the public."

Julien finished his coffee, wiped his lips carefully, and stood up. "There is something that I must remove from the car be-fore you take it. Wait 'ere—I do not wish to be seen 'anding it over to you."

He was back in a couple of minutes. He gave me the keys and we walked to the french window that opened into the hotel garden. He seemed ill at ease. He clasped my hand briefly.

He said: "I won't come out. Be prudent. *A ce soir . . .*"

The morning was as gay as a new print dress. The Mediter-ranean was regulation travel-poster blue and the sky was cloudless. A big chameleon, out on a limb of bougainvillea be-side the french window, watched a fly with one eye and me with the other, and hurriedly turned a darker shade of green.

"Don't worry," I told it and Julien. "It's going to be a won-derful day."

I'll never learn to keep my big mouth shut.

20

The coastal highway had recently been widened and resurfaced, and I made good time. As far as Baniyas the road follows the base of the foothills, two to five miles inland; but from there the coastal plain is narrower and you rarely lose sight of the sea.

I parked beside a high blank wall on the outskirts of Tartus. I waited until I was sure nobody was paying me any attention and opened the secret drawer beneath the seat. I pulled my left arm out of my jacket, strapped the canvas shoulder holster under my armpit, and slipped my jacket on again. Then I picked up the black .38 automatic. It was held down in the drawer by a strong spring clip that clicked back loudly as I removed it. I put the gun in the holster and pushed the drawer shut. I got out of the car, locked it, put on a pair of those dark mirror-glasses that make everything look like Liverpool, and set off down the main street in search of the lawyer's office and a café or barbershop from which to observe it.

As I walked away, something slapped me on the back and I was all but stunned by the roar of an explosion. The road sparkled with glass dice. Fragments of metal fell like shrapnel in an air raid. A woman was screaming. I looked back, and my heart went cold.

The Rover was on fire. Flames and white phosphorous smoke were billowing through where the windows had been and through a hole in the roof. A woman was running away from the car, but a man and two boys were approaching, chattering eagerly.

I turned away, feeling sick, and walked like an old man into an alley on the right. "A Lebanese number," somebody shouted; then: "Where's the driver?"

I stumbled over a rut in the unpaved surface. Why had he done it? Julien, of course. Who else? To make sure the car was destroyed, to avoid its falling into Syrian hands, the loyal part of me said quickly. But need he have cut it quite so fine? I had got to Tartus in a little under an hour. Normally you allowed just over an hour for the trip. He had obviously used a one-hour delay mechanism. I should still have been driving, seven or eight miles north of Tartus, when the car blew up, had not the Syrian Public Works Department improved the road.

The alley had been curving to the left and now brought me to the seafront. Graceful two-masted schooners with prows like swordfish swayed lazily in the little harbor. Two miles offshore, to the southwest, the island of Ruad glowed in the sun: a compact town of fishermen, sponge divers, and boat builders squatting on a rock in the sea.

I came to a paved road again and crossed it to lean against a rust-pitted railing and look down at the sea. A boy standing just below me on a rock jabbed a trident into the water and brought up a flailing octopus. I walked on toward the crumbling Crusader cathedral and, beyond it, the commercial center, where merchants, lawyers, and smugglers have their offices. I watched a whorl of gulls swirling over an incoming fishing boat and tried to stop thinking about Julien. And then, from one second to the next, I stopped thinking about Julien.

A tall fair man wearing dark glasses but otherwise looking as British as a double-decker bus emerged from a side street fifty yards away and strolled over to the seafront railing. He'd had a spring-cleaning recently. He was wearing light-gray trousers and a navy-blue blazer with metal buttons, and carrying a handsome brown briefcase. He walked like a middle-age civil servant on vacation—calm, confident, reposed. I watched him blankly, remembering I was tired, wishing I were a civil servant on vacation, even if it meant living in a desirable residence exactly like fifty thousand other desirable residences in the sort of suburb good ants go to when they die.

He stood comfortably by the rail looking out toward Ruad. I crossed over to the side street he had just come from and watched him from an archway. Two Arabs passed him and said: "Hello, mister! Cigarette, mister?" He replied gravely: *"Naharkon saïd,"* and gave them a cigarette each.

I told myself I wasn't going to follow Blane. All I wanted to know was who met him at the lawyer's office. If I hurried, I might still reach the lawyer's place before whoever it was returned to Beirut, if it was someone from Beirut. To hell with Blane.

Blane set off toward the port. I followed him.

He gazed around him as he walked—the contented tourist drinking in the sun and sea air, enjoying the play of light on the blue water and tawny stones. Was it an act? Twice he glanced back toward Ruad. He paused for a moment where I had stood to watch the boy with the trident. I couldn't see the boy from my side of the road but I heard him trying to sell Blane an octopus. Blane resumed his stroll, unhurried, at peace with the world.

The seafront road swung left to serve the low somnolent port buildings. Blane sauntered straight on, up a lane that rose gently beside the harbor toward the twelfth-century castle built by the Templars to defend it. There were few passers-by here and I had to fall back. Soon he halted in the middle of the lane and gazed intently at the castle. It was a good tourist act—a little too good. Either he was here to meet someone or he had left the crowded streets of the town to see if he was being followed. I expected him to swing around after a few seconds.

There was a warehouse on my right with a shutter halfway down over its entrance. Sensing that Blane was about to turn, I ducked under the shutter. There was a smell of tar and cord and oil; there were coils of rope, cans of paint, nets, oars, tarpaulins. A smartly dressed young man emerged from a lane of shelves. It was my turn to put on a tourist act. I took off my dark glasses, blinked at him, and asked if he spoke English.

"*Shwoye,*" he said. "A little."

"I'm sorry to trouble you. I've just remembered that I must telephone someone. I was hoping you might let me use your phone."

I was expecting him to say they didn't have one. I hadn't seen any wires.

He said: "*Et-talafon? Maaloum*—of course. Come." He led me to the back of the building, to a tiny office, to a dusty desk. On a shelf beside the desk was a pale-blue telephone with a mouthpiece shaped like a shell—the sort of thing they used to make for filmstars' bathrooms.

I knew only one number in Tartus, and when the operator awoke I asked for it. This was one of those moments when life is an escalator you can't step off. The instrument of Fate stood beside me and gave me a cigarette, a beautiful Turkish contraband job with red and silver writing on it.

There was a colored portrait of the Aga Khan, head of the Ismaili sect, on the wall.

I asked: "Are you an Ismaili?"

He tossed his head back contemptuously. "My father is. But I say: 'What the Aga Khan do for us?' The Ismailis send the Aga Khan jewels and gold. So he build hotels and villas in Europe. He give banquets for rich Europeans—not for poor Ismailis."

Inside the telephone a voice said: "*Naam?*"

I asked it for the lawyer—in English, trying to sound crisp and officer-like. If the lawyer's English wasn't too good, one English-speaking voice would sound very much like another on the wire. After all, I told myself, he hasn't seen or heard much of Blane. If he has seen him, you nit, another part of me said. What if Blane is just whiling away the time, waiting for his appointment? I shrugged. Fate hadn't organized this for nothing.

The lawyer came on the line.

"Blane speaking," I said, over the top of the mouthpiece. To test his English, I asked: "Can you hear me clearly?"

"Not very clear, but I understand. Can I help you, Colonel?"

His English was good, too good. I kept the cigarette in my mouth to muffle my voice. "Is our friend still in town?"

"Our friend? I do not understand."

"The one I saw this morning," I said desperately.

"One? This morning?"

I looked beseechingly at the Aga Khan. This was it: all or nothing. "Do you remember seeing me this morning?"

A slight gasp. "Of course." He sounded offended.

"Then you remember our friend? The other person? I don't want to mention his name. I am in a public place."

"Ah. I understand. I was bewildered. Yes; but why?"

"I wish to ask him something. Do you know where he is now?"

"On his way back to Beirut. He left almost at once."

"Well, I'll write to him, then."

"Yes." He didn't volunteer the address. Why should he? Blane would know it.

Quickly I said: "I'm never quite sure of the exact spelling of the address. Could you give it to me, please?"

"I will ask my secretary to address an envelope for you on the Arabic typewriter. Then you can be sure it is correct. If you call in the office in five or ten minutes she will give it to you. Well, goodbye, Colonel."

I pulled a face at the Aga Khan. Fate? Phooey. I put down the receiver and thanked the young man. He pushed the shutter up a little so that I didn't have to stoop, and stood beneath it watching me walk away toward the castle.

Blane had vanished.

I put my sunglasses on again and walked slowly to where I'd seen him last. On the left of the lane, overlooking the northern end of the little harbor, was the jagged stump of a circular watchtower. Beside it I could now see a path leading toward the harbor basin. I looked back down the lane. A Syrian wearing a Western jacket and pants but muffled in a white headcloth was sitting on a rock near the warehouse, watching me. I stared

175

at the ruined tower for his benefit, for half a minute, and ambled along the path. It sloped down to a flight of ten or twelve eroded steps that followed the curve of the tower wall. Lizards scattered as I went down.

At the bottom, an arched doorway yawned in the base of the tower. The path continued, down five or six more steps, to a leprous stone jetty. I stood on the top step looking into the shallow prism-clear water, thinking about the Crusader knights and masons who had hewn a kingdom out of the hard Syrian rock and then fled before a resurgent Islam whose resurgence they had themselves provoked. Some of the last of them had sailed from this harbor—perhaps from this very corner of it, now silted up and abandoned.

Footsteps crunched behind me.

A voice asked: "Is it me you're looking for?"

Blane was standing in front of the arched doorway at the foot of the watchtower, his left hand gripping the briefcase, his right hand in his blazer pocket. There was nothing of the carefree tourist about him now. He looked tough and angry.

"Hello," I said. "For the moment, I'd forgotten about you. I was thinking of the Crusaders clanking down here in their armor with the Moslems breathing down their necks."

"If that's the mood you're in, you should be over there." He nodded toward the big square keep a hundred yards along the shore. "There you can see the postern the last Templar garrison jumped from into a waiting boat." He turned his head slightly, as if listening for something. I heard the mew of a seabird and a fishing boat chugging in the distance.

I asked: "Are you about to jump into a waiting boat?"

"Is that any business of yours?"

"It might be. I was hoping to have a chat with you before you leave Syria. About Arnold Amery's murder."

He looked surprised. "Well, that's . . . unexpected, to say the least. What about Amery?"

"Before I left Beirut—I didn't tell you this the other eve-

176

ning—I interviewed a gentleman named Hamam. So did the Lebanese Sûreté. He admitted having helped Arnold's murderer."

"That was smart, tracing him. What else did he say?"

"He made a wild accusation against a European businessman. Someone quite respectable: someone like yourself. Then I started moving in business circles myself. I got on the track of a businessman who had some interests in common with Arnold's killer, who had been seen with Hamam, and who seemed in a hurry to cash his chips and get out of the Levant."

"Don't be misled by coincidence. I know nothing of the interests of whoever killed Amery; but I may have been seen talking to Hamam, and I am cashing my chips and moving out. If I never see the bloody country again, it'll be too soon. But that doesn't make me an associate of—of a murderer."

"Of course not. You're an officer and a gentleman, not a dope smuggler and a burglar. You are also, I've heard, an affectionate father."

"Who the devil's been gossiping to you about . . . that?"

"Salwa told me—with something like admiration."

He was silent for a moment. Then he said softly: "I mentioned coincidence. It can play nasty tricks on a man. Twenty years ago I got married. I married the one girl in a million I ought not to have married. She had a rare— But the details don't matter. My wife died in childbirth, leaving me with a baby daughter. She's nineteen now; and she has the mind of a child of six. I've got to be sure there'll always be funds to provide her with a home and care. I wouldn't want her dumped in a National Health Service snakepit. She's a lovely girl—the fruit of a coincidence. Coincidences like that can drive a man to extremes."

"Even to the extreme of killing a better man than himself?"

"I didn't kill Amery," he snarled. "Anyway, Amery was nothing to get pious about. He was your friend—fair enough, but don't make a saint of him. This is the Levant, the world's oldest marketplace, where everything and everybody has a

177

price tag. Amery was no exception. I suppose you know about that new mineral his firm found. But did you know he was exporting it without telling the Syrian government? They'd flog it and fiddle it as fast as anyone, no doubt; but, after all, it's in their back yard."

"Are you sure that story wasn't fed to you by the people who persuaded you to help them search Arnold's apartment? They had to tell you something to overcome whatever scruples you might——"

"I've done nothing illegal. A man I know intends to buy from the Syrian authorities the right to do openly what your friend Amery has been doing secretly. He is applying for the appropriate permits and will pay the appropriate baksheesh to whoever happens to be governing Syria at the end of each financial year. The law is on his side. And so far as I'm concerned, everything's clean and——"

"And there's not even a drop of blood on your sleeve. That's an advantage of using a firearm."

He trembled with anger, but he kept his right hand in his blazer pocket. "Don't be a bloody idiot! Even if I were the type to shoot a man down in his own home, would I be likely to jeopardize everything I was working for by committing a murder? Murderers aren't just criminals, they're fools. That's why they should be hanged. Criminality can be cured; stupidity can't."

"Everything you stood to gain would have been jeopardized if Arnold had not been shot. It was you who bonked me on the head, wasn't it? Arnold must have seen you hit me. Even if you'd got out of the apartment, he would have traced you; and Hamam would have talked. So Arnold had to be——"

"You don't even know I was in the flat with Hamam. And Hamam's dead——or so I've heard. You can't prove a thing."

"If you put it like that, I don't have to."

His lips puckered. "And who cares? Why don't you go home, if you've got a home, and write about the Crusades?"

"I'd prefer to write a series entitled *Who Killed Arnold Amery?*——though, naturally, I'd have to mention you in it.

178

Within a week, all Fleet Street and a good many American and Continental papers would be on your track to fill in the gaps in my story. Your photo would be in fifty papers. Your private life would be dissected, your every move reported."

"You swine," he said. "You filthy keyhole-peeping swine. What do you want? I suppose you've fixed your price."

"I have. My price is information. I know most of the story and I'll fill in the gaps without your help if I must. If, by chance, you didn't shoot Arnold, it's in your own interest to help me. In return, when I publish my account—"

"Ah! Softening-up tactics. Let's have a look at your gaps."

"Was it you who batted me on the head in Arnold's study?"

"Clubbed, old boy. With a golf club. You're lucky I didn't know you then as well as I do now: I'd have clubbed a lot harder."

"Who was the third person, besides Hamam and yourself, in—"

"Of course—the Third Man! I might have guessed. There's always got to be a Third Man. Makes intriguing headlines, I suppose. Well, if you know so much, you tell me who—" He glanced at the sea and smiled.

A motor purred behind me. I turned. A fast launch with a glittering white wake was curving in toward the old stone jetty. Blane shouted a staccato Arabic phrase. When I looked back at him, he had moved away from the arched doorway. He still had his hand in his blazer pocket, but now it was pointing something at me.

Someone appeared down the twist of stone steps beside the tower—a stocky, brown-faced Syrian with a white *kufiya* concealing most of his head. He nodded to Blane and looked at me like a stranger, but when our eyes met I recognized him: Habib, the man who had nearly dumped me in the ravine with the Ford. His expression told me he would have liked to run through that scene again. I glanced back toward the launch. It had passed out of sight, but I could hear it chattering to itself impatiently. Its wake was lashing the little jetty.

179

"Let's get this over with quickly and cleanly," Blane said. "No fuss, mess, or melodrama. Go into the tower. When you get in there, stay put. Above all, don't turn."

I took my sunglasses off and put them in my breast pocket. I wondered how long it would take me to get the gun out of the holster under my left armpit. Too long. Blane looked taut and grim. Habib watched blankly, standing behind Blane at the bottom of the steps, tossing two or three pebbles up in his left hand and catching them and tossing them again. His right hand hung loosely at his side.

"What's that you've got in your pocket?" I asked Blane. "I hope it's not a pipe. That gag went out with Professor Moriarty."

"Move," he snapped. "And raise your hands."

He took the gun out of his pocket—a small revolver with white grips and a silvery barrel. It looked like the sort of thing Santa Claus brings with your first cowboy suit, but I didn't want to argue with it.

I raised my hands a little and walked toward the archway. It was dim in there. Once inside, I might leap to the right, get out my gun, and if I didn't fall down a well shaft, we should see what we should see. I halted under the arch and blinked hard to get used to the shadows beyond. Blane came a couple of paces nearer.

"Go on in," he said. "Farther! And don't turn."

"Don't you know that a second murder just makes doubly sure the killer gets caught?"

"Why should you worry? Anyway, if you're sensible, we'll only tap you on the head. Go on! Forward."

I took a slow step forward onto the rubble-strewn floor of the tower. Another step, and I tensed to spring. A step more . . .

A gun went off.

21

I stood there, paralyzed, telling myself he'd missed me and waiting for him to try again. I couldn't have moved if he'd offered me an oil well and a troupe of belly dancers. Someone drew in a breath that sounded as though it was both achievement and agony. Something metallic fell behind me. That released me.

I turned. Blane was sinking forward on his knees, gasping, pressing both hands against his chest. His slim briefcase twisted like a weathervane at the end of a short chain fastened to his left wrist. His gun lay glittering in the dust. Slowly, he put one hand forward, onto the ground, as if to crawl; but his arm trembled and gave at the elbow, and he lay down, still clutching his chest, sobbing gently.

Habib was putting something in his back pocket. He looked at me, deadpan, and said: "This is one more time I rescue you. You run too many risks. Maybe the next time I will not be there—unless you make me your bodyguard."

"I thought you were Blane's bodyguard when you arrived."

He sneered at Blane, who was trying to crawl again. "So did he. Walid told me to follow him in Tartus, to see nobody harm him. He arranged that with Walid. But I could not let him shoot you. Walid will understand that."

"He wouldn't have shot me. He was going to tap me on the head."

Habib stared at me in amazement. "He was going to shoot you. I saw him pointing the gun."

"Blane arranged with Walid for you to protect him. But someone else decided he must die. So you followed him here not to protect him, as he thought, but to kill him."

181

He tapped his head. *"Ente majnoun.* I save your life and you call me a killer. I am going now. If the police discover him and catch me, I'll tell them I shot him to save you. And you'll tell the same story. *Tayyib?"* He patted his gun pocket.

"Okay. Maybe you're right—maybe he would have shot me."

He shook his head, as if puzzled, wrapped the *kufiya* over his mouth and nose, and ran up the steps.

Blane was trying to reach his gun. I kicked it into the tower and rolled him over to lean his head and shoulders against a block of stone in the shade inside the archway. I opened his blazer and shirt and found a bullet wound just below his right shoulder. There wasn't much blood until he opened his mouth to say something: in a few seconds his chin and shirtfront were a slimy red mess.

"Thanks," he whispered. "I heard what you said. I wasn't going to shoot you. I'm not a killer . . . but I'd've shot that swine then if I'd reached . . . gun." He groaned.

"Do you mind if I leave you like this while I run for a doctor?"

"Too late," he whispered. "Do something for me. Important. Take my briefcase. Walid may come for it."

"Where must I take it?"

"Ruad. Boat down there, waiting. It take you to Ruad. My fiancée there. Give her my briefcase. Only her. Not Walid. You promise?" He spat out more blood as if impatient to be rid of it.

"I promise."

"All I have—money, everything—in here. You give it to my fiancée. Tell her half for her, half for my daughter. She must help my daughter. Lovely, lovely kid. All alone now. She must help her. Half each." He closed his eyes.

"I'll do that," I said. "I'll tell her. But you must tell me something in exchange."

He opened his eyes, blinked to shut out the bright gay sky beyond the archway, then groaned and closed them again.

I said slowly: "Tell me who killed Arnold Amery."

He whispered: "Forgive me."

"But who shot him? Was it you? It doesn't matter now. I'll still go to Ruad for you. I wouldn't want your daughter to suffer. But I must know who killed Arnold."

His eyelids trembled, but he couldn't open them. "My fault. I'm to blame." More blood slid down his chin. "Tell my fiancée that. Tell her I told you. You must tell her. No secrets. All straight. Then she help my girl. Cathie. Little Cathie."

"What's your fiancée's name?" I asked; but it was too late. There were suddenly tears seeping under his eyelids, a paroxysm in his throat, more blood, and his head swiveled slowly toward the light. I listened for his breathing and felt for a pulse beat, but there was nothing. I was alone now.

I disengaged his hand from the silver chain attached to the briefcase and fastened the loop around my own wrist. The briefcase felt tightly packed. I tucked it under my arm and backed slowly away from the tower. Lizards skittered over the sunbaked rocks and steps. I looked for the last time at Blane. His eyes had opened and he seemed to be watching me. I turned and walked down the five or six steps that led onto the ancient jetty.

The launch was waiting about thirty yards down the cove, its motor purring softly. I waved, and when the boatman saw me he got alongside the stone carcass of another medieval pier. I ran to it: I couldn't get there fast enough, bounding like a schoolboy along the ribbon of damp shingle at the water's edge—back to the world of the living.

"*Ahlan wa sahlan!*"* the boatman cried as I leaped aboard. He was a little man, as brown and as bald as an acorn, with dark eyes and a bushy black mustache. "You understand Arabic?"

"A little," I said.

"The water at the tower jetty is too shallow," he said. "No-

* Welcome!

183

body goes there now. I told your lady that. But she said that if I went near it you would hear the motor and come. She said you'd be carrying that case."

I stood beside him as he steered us gently out of the cove, watching the truncated tower shrink into a backdrop of ramparts and hills. The sea beyond the harbor basin was as smooth as a *Times* editorial; but, like a *Times* editorial, the Mediterranean sometimes pounces just as it's lulling you to sleep, so I sat down. Our wake traced a neat arc as the boat swung southwestward.

"Your lady will be waiting," he said. "She is fragrant and beautiful, like rose petals in a fountain. She gleams like these diamonds we are plowing up out of the blue plain of the sea. I am a poet—I see beauty and meaning in every stone—and when she approached I turned my eyes away lest they be dazzled." He paused, then asked: "How can a man not be a poet in so wonderful a world?"

Minarets and flat-roofed houses emerged from the sea. Basking schooners nodded sleepily in a blue harbor. A white dome bloomed like a rose in a thicket of masts and old walls. A wooden windmill with eight canvas sails was tilting at a listless breeze.

"There are no trees or gardens in Ruad," the boatman said. "Just houses and mosques and ruins and rock. Just the city and the sea."

"The City in the Sea," I said. I saw Arnold, pale and apprehensive, and Ondine, backing away, puzzled.

"That was what the old Phoenician name meant," the boatman said. "They shortened the name to Arvad. The Greeks made it Aradus and the Arabs Ruad. Three thousand years ago Ruad dominated all this coast. There is an Englishman here interested in archaeology. Often I take him out in my boat and he dives with a glass over his face. On the sea bottom he finds ancient pottery."

"Is his name Manning?" I asked. Arnold was saying: *I don't think there's anyone in the Levant I trusted more* . . .

184

The boatman looked surprised. "Yes. Do you know him?"

"He is the friend of a friend of mine. Can you take me to his house?"

"Of course. And your lady?"

"Is she anywhere near Mr. Manning's house?"

"No. Look! You can see the yacht now. She is there, on the yacht. It is in the cove beyond the main harbor. The cove is as good as the harbor except when the northwest wind blows. The Englishman's house is on the other side of the island. I will take you there first, if you wish, and then come back and tell your lady where you are."

"Thank you. Tell her I'll be with her in half an hour."

A big schooner was leaving the harbor, gliding toward us like a gull. I heard a shout. The boatman grinned, waved, and swung us to the left, across its bows. The schooner slashed through our wake, its two tall masts raking the sky. We scudded around the east coast of the island and pulled into a deserted stretch of shore littered with remains of the cyclopean wall with which the Phoenicians surrounded Ruad.

I asked him how much I owed him for the trip. He said: "Nothing. Your lady paid me half the price before I left. She will pay me the other half when I return. That is Sayed Manning's house."

He pointed to a neat stone house, twenty yards from the water's edge. It had a flat roof, like all the others, and a big veranda, with a low wall and semicircular arches around it.

We shook hands, and hugging Blane's briefcase, I jumped onto a short jetty made of blocks of stone that had once formed part of the Phoenician wall. A dinghy was beached beside it. The launch sped off at once, trailing a tiny rainbow. I turned and began plodding across the hot hard beach.

"This is strange," a man's voice said. "Your father's in some passion that works him strongly."

A girl replied: "Never till this day . . ."

I realized suddenly they were speaking English and stopped. The voices were coming from Manning's veranda. Like the rest of the house, and the neighboring houses, it was built on top of a step of rock that rose abruptly seven or eight feet above the beach. An older man broke into the conversation. I resumed my plod. "Our revels now are ended!" he exclaimed.

A dozen steps led up to a gate in the veranda wall. As I put my foot on the bottom step, a man looked over the gate. He had a tanned oval face with calm brown eyes and a mop of steel-gray hair. When he'd had a haircut he was probably quite handsome.

"Hello," he said. "I thought I heard a motorboat."

Somewhere behind him, the older voice declared: "We are such stuff as dreams are made on, and our little life is rounded with a sleep."

I could play that game too. "Sir, I am vexed," I said. "Bear with my weakness; my old brain is troubled. Be not disturbed with my infirmity." The voice in the background said it all with me.

The gray-haired man laughed. "If you be pleased," he said, "retire into my cell and there repose."

He opened the gate and went back into the shade of the veranda. When I got up there, he was switching off a tape recorder. "It's just right for Ruad," he said. "This is Prospero's island to perfection. He's set all his spirits free, of course: they make up most of the male inhabitants. The women are a sort of mass-Miranda. The only doubtful character is me: I can't decide whether I'm Prospero or Caliban."

I took my sunglasses off and peered about me. The context sounded wrong, but I asked: "Are you Dick Manning?"

He closed the tape recorder and came toward me, holding out a long, slim hand. He was a big man, with powerful arms and shoulders, and moved with an easy boyish lope. He was wearing a yellow shirt, blue shorts, and leather sandals.

"Of course," he said. "And you're Ray Alan, aren't you? I've been expecting you."

22

Manning turned to a small refrigerator in a corner of the veranda. "Take a pew," he said. "What'll it be? Coke or a can o' beer? No arak, I'm afraid. Deference to Moslem susceptibilities and all that, even though the locals mop it up like sponges in their own homes. Beer comes in with the canned vegetables, so it's kosher as far as the boatmen are concerned."

"Beer, please."

"I don't observe Ramadan so you can stay for lunch. I used to observe it—I thought the smell of cooking might torment the neighbors. But then their cooking aromas tormented me. I found I was the only mug on the island keeping the fast."

He gave me a cold pewter tankard and served himself its twin. I sat in a white cane armchair and put Blane's briefcase on the floor beside it.

"I'd like to stay but I've another call to make. And I've got to get back to—" I stopped. To where? To Latakia? I thought of Julien again.

Manning flopped into an armchair beside the tape recorder and raised his tankard. "Another call? In Ruad? But forgive me. People who live alone are apt to get nosy. Have a thing." He held out a blue jar with hieroglyphics on it that looked as if it had once contained Cleopatra's face cream. It was full of cigarettes. "Take no notice of the pot. Twelfth-dynasty bazaar trash. Found it at the bottom of the old harbor. But the tobacco's Turkish."

"Thanks, but I'm off cigarettes."

He lit one for himself and went on: "Arnold told me on the phone that you'd be coming to see me. He rang from Aleppo.

Eight or nine days ago, I suppose, but it seems like yesterday. I can't get used to the idea that he's dead."

"You're on the telephone here?"

"No. Arnold called me at the lab. We used to ring each other from time to time, to keep in touch. He didn't go into details, but I gathered he was grooming you for stardom, more or less. Going to make you his personal assistant and trouble-shooter. What are your plans now?"

"I'll hang on for a while. McGlint's asked me to help with a few things."

"McGlint? Is he sitting in Arnold's chair now?"

"For the time being."

"Then heaven help LMC! McGlint's sound enough in his own field, but he hasn't the— But tell me about Arnold. Do the police know who killed him?"

"I doubt it." I hesitated. "You'll think me very rude, but I've had a few unpleasant surprises lately. Could you show me something to confirm that you really are Dick Manning?"

He sighed. "That, I suppose, is what comes of reading too much John Buchan in one's youth."

He got up, pushed through a bead curtain, and came back with a passport. The passport photo was of the usual escaped maniac, but the description tallied. *Profession: Geochemist,* it said.

"You're an archaeologist, too, I believe."

"Only on a humble amateur level."

"You mentioned a lab. Is that a company lab?"

"Not an LMC lab. It belongs to a local company I have an interest in. We—but didn't Arnold tell you about it?"

"Not in any detail."

He looked down into his tankard and swished the beer around. "There's nothing you can tell me, I suppose, that would amount to a sort of last message from him? No, that's ridiculous."

"There is one thing. He wanted me to ask you about something a Beirut journalist told him. He mentioned it during din-

188

ner and said he'd written a memo about it. The journalist claimed to have got onto something startling that could land you—and, perhaps, the company—in trouble if it were publicized."

"Did the journalist say what it was?"

"He told Arnold the essentials."

"And what were they?"

"Arnold didn't have time to tell me. He was going to give me the memo the next morning and send me to see you about it. That was to have been my first errand. He said it was important. But, for him, the next morning didn't come."

"Who has the memo now?"

"McGlint, I suppose."

"Hell! What's the journalist's name?"

"I don't know. It will be in the memo, I suppose."

He frowned. "What am I supposed to do?"

"It would help if you gave me your side of the story. Then we can decide what to do about the journalist—ignore him or buy him."

"But my side of which story? Lebanese journalists have vivid imaginations. I've no idea what the man may have said about me."

"I gathered from Arnold that the story had a factual basis. He wouldn't have been worried, otherwise."

He ran a hand through his thick hair. "Then it must have been about the Tartus company, I suppose. But I can't say much about that or I'll be in the soup. It's supposed to be frightfully hush-hush."

"Never mind, then. No doubt I'll read the story in the Beirut papers next week."

"You must keep it out of the papers—at almost any cost."

"I can't if I don't know what I'm keeping out."

He groaned. "Understand my position. I'm bound by . . . and you are, after all, a journalist."

"I was. Now I'm looking after LMC's interests. As Arnold said, when he offered me a job, ex-poachers make the best

189

gamekeepers. He couldn't exactly proclaim me his personal security officer, but . . ."

"I see. Promise me, then, that you'll never publish a word of what I tell you—in my lifetime, anyhow." He laughed briefly. "You can immortalize me in your memoirs, if you like."

I promised.

"Well, as you know, I'm a geochemist. I worked for Arnold for two years and before that for Iraq Petroleum. I came to live here because—well, if you want the full story, my wife left me. Just like that. Very sensible of her, really—we hadn't an interest in common—but it gave me a bit of a jolt. I had enough to retire on so I came here. I had to have blue water and green mountains to rest my eyes on after years of looking at deserts and Iraqi mud; and Ruad has always fascinated me. I rented this house, and the very first morning, when I saw the sun rise over the mountains on the mainland, I knew I'd never want to live anywhere else. Look at that view!"

He killed his cigarette. "The only drawback is that living alone makes you so talkative when you get a visitor that you quickly drive him away."

"I'm still here."

"Well, I bought the house, added this veranda and a bathroom, and got hooked on local history. I dug and poked about wherever I could, here and on the mainland, and one day, north of Tartus, I discovered a deposit of an industrially useful form of hydrated magnesium silicate. Do you know what I mean? One form of it is meerschaum. I told the three brothers who owned the land, and we formed a company to exploit the deposit. I'm the managing director. Arnold gave us a lot of help—even supplied equipment and an experienced foreman. A few months later I hit what ought to have been the jackpot. How's your chemistry."

"Not so hot. I haven't done any since I was sixteen."

"Good Lord!" He looked shocked. "Well, you must at least have heard of zirconium. Its oxide and certain compounds such as calcium zirconate are used for making refractory ceramics

190

for high-temperature crucibles and furnace linings. In nature, zirconium is rare and consequently valuable. Not far from the magnesium silicate, I found a deposit of one of the rarest zirconium compounds. I asked Arnold to make a few marketing inquiries, expecting to sell the stuff to firms that produce refractory ceramics, and a week or two later he hove to with a character named Denbor in tow. Head of economic intelligence or something at the embassy. D'you know him?"

"We've met. We're not exactly bosom pals."

"I thought him a bit of a twerp myself. He'd never heard of Ugarit. Imagine! Holds down an embassy job and doesn't even know where the world's first alphabet took shape. Mind you, his chemistry's all right."

That was my cue to pull my socks up. I said: "If I'd known you were interested in Ugarit, I'd have brought you a copy of a piece I wrote about it for *Outlook.*"

He beamed. "Ah, you wrote that, did you? I read it. Good show." He got up and took two more cans of beer out of the refrigerator and refilled our tankards. "Well, to come back to the seamy side of life, Denbor told me that my zirconium discovery had lit a gleam in the eyes of the U.K. Defense Ministry. Remember your promise never to publish any of this."

I nodded.

"The zirconium compound I discovered is required for the manufacture of a light alloy used in intermediate-range ballistic missiles. I agreed to sell it to a British firm engaged in defense work. They paid our local company a fair price, of course, but for security reasons we pretended it was a less important mineral. As an added precaution, everything we produced was marketed through Cyprus, through a subsidiary of LMC that has its own plant and jetty there. The stuff isn't bulky and went out in shipments of magnesium silicate."

"Who were all these precautions supposed to fool? The Russians?"

"If the Russians had learned about the deposit they would no doubt have made trouble for us here. But there were other

191

considerations. According to Denbor, the people concerned at the Defense Ministry were anxious to keep the Foreign Office in the dark—partly for security reasons, partly because they thought the FO might veto the whole shebang. You know how scared the FO is of the Arabs. It would put its entire female staff up for auction in Mecca tomorrow if it thought that would win it six months of Arab goodwill."

"But isn't Denbor an FO man?"

"On the surface. But his allegiance is obviously to the Defense Ministry. There are Defense and Intelligence chaps in most embassies, disguised as diplomats, as you may know. The regular dips look down on them, but they can't give the game away. To come back to our precautions, though: we had also to keep the Syrian authorities ignorant of what we were doing. That may sound rather unethical . . ."

He paused, as if waiting for me to contradict him. I didn't.

He went on: "But there's no Syrian law against exporting zirconium. I'd agree that's rather a lawyer's quibble—but, after all, if we'd brought in the Syrian authorities, what would have happened? You know as well as I do. Our little company would have been expropriated in favor of a new outfit composed of influential army officers and their relatives, and I'd have been got rid of. Well, I didn't want to be got rid of; and by staying, I was able to see that the local people concerned received a fair deal."

"But in the Levant secrets die young. I first heard the phrase 'City in the Sea' from a singer in a Beirut restaurant."

"Good Lord!"

"She had heard McGlint trying it on Denbor. He had come across Seacity in a personal file of Arnold's and was eager to know what it meant."

"It was a sort of code name and security alarm. The idea was that if anyone who was not in the secret read it in a confidential file and—like McGlint—used it or asked about it, he'd attract our attention. And if he succeeded in opening Arnold's or

Denbor's safe, he'd find a completely misleading file on an imaginary tourist project named Seacity."

"Are you still exporting your zirconium compound?"

"No. We had a scare. A local tax man began taking an interest in us. We pay our taxes, of course, so I thought he simply wanted baksheesh. But one day he brought in his cousin, a major who turned out to be connected with Syrian Intelligence. We decided to discontinue production for a while. That was four months ago."

"And since then there've been no other developments?"

"No."

"But from what Arnold told me, I understood that the journalist who went to see him had dug up something new—something Arnold didn't know about."

"That's impossible." His steady brown eyes watched me carefully, with a hint of distaste. "Arnold knew everything—in much greater detail than I've been able to tell you."

We looked at each other and wondered. I heard the sea murmuring to itself and, distantly, the stutter of a launch.

"Another visitor?" Manning said.

We went to the veranda wall. A launch was approaching slowly. The passenger sitting under its awning was Julien.

"D'you know him?" Manning asked.

"I thought I knew him well until this morning. Now I'm trying to get used to the idea that he may have tried to kill me." I told him quickly about the explosion in Arnold's car.

"Lord!" Manning gripped my arm. "He mustn't find you here. Wait in my study until I find out what he wants."

"I've no need to run away. I'd like to ask him—"

"Please! You say he tried to blow you to bits. I can't risk having unpleasantness here or attracting attention. And, whatever he wants, he'll talk more freely if he thinks I'm alone."

"All right. It's your house."

He hurried me toward a french window. I parted the bead curtain that hung over it. Inside was a dim room with bookshelves, leather armchairs, a tiled floor, and a Kurdish rug. I stepped through the curtain.

A flame flashed in my head. The rug was suddenly a black well shaft and I was falling down it. Falling, falling—faster, faster, faster. Increase in velocity of a falling halfwit: thirty-two feet per second per second. They did at least succeed in driving that into my skull before I left school. I could still feel the hole they drove it through.

23

I was lying at the bottom of a blue cliff. I tried to move my arms but nothing happened. I didn't seem to have arms any more. I tried to move my legs, but all they did was creak. I could wiggle my feet, though. That was something. I'd have congratulated myself but my tongue felt about six inches thick and was so heavy I couldn't have lapped up an arak.

My eyes were misty, but I could see something flying over my face, circling slowly like a vulture, nearer and nearer. I tried to blow it away but couldn't. It landed on my chin. A big fly. I jerked my head back. Something hurt.

I blinked my eyes clear. The cliff was made of light-blue tiles. A white door came into focus; then pipes and a washbasin . . . I was in a bathroom, lying on the floor, wrapped in a rug. I rolled over a couple of times, my head throbbing, and worked my arms free. They were a little numb, but the same has been said of my skull and I make out. I struggled out of the rug. It looked like the one I had seen in Manning's study.

I stood up, leaning against the washbasin while ants scurried about in my arms and legs. Someone had stuffed a sponge into my mouth. I pulled it out, rinsed my mouth, and washed my face and the bruise on the back of my head. I drank some water, used the toilet, flushed it without thinking, and stood beside it—feeling sick, waiting for the door to burst open—as the water crashed and gurgled.

I remembered the gun I had taken from Arnold's Rover. It looked different now, but I didn't mind: it was a gun. I sat on the toilet lid, covering the door with it.

Nobody burst in. The house was silent. I put the gun down, wet my head again, and decided I felt better.

Gun in hand, I tried the bathroom door. It was locked and there was no key in sight. I put my gun to the keyhole, pointing it toward the lock mechanism, and pulled the trigger.

Nothing happened.

I tried again, with the safety catch off. This time there was a noise like the Ramadan cannon. I tugged at the door. It yielded.

I looked out into the corridor. Five yards away, Julien stood, his big face grim and pale. He was pointing a Lüger at me.

It was beginning to look like the last reel of a horse opera, after all. We stood there pointing our artillery at each other, waiting for someone to start something.

Julien said: "You make a lot of noise when you go to the bathroom. Why the shooting?"

"Somebody pushed ahead of me in the queue."

He lowered his Lüger. "May I look in there?"

I nodded and put the little revolver in a pocket.

He walked into the bathroom, studied the door and lock, and asked: "Somebody locked you in 'ere?"

"How did you guess?"

He stared at the rug. "Did you bring this in 'ere?"

"It brought me. I was rolled up in it."

He gaped at me. "You measure one meter eighty-five or more; you are in good condition and armed with a pistol. Yet you let people roll you in a rug! Why is your 'air wet?"

"Today's Monday. I wash my hair every Monday."

He walked around me, looking at my head. I watched him in the mirror. He touched the back of my head. I yelped.

"You could 'ave locked yourself in the bathroom," he said, "and 'it yourself on the 'ead."

"Why would I do that?"

"Because you 'eard me arrive and didn't 'ave time to get away. That's what the Syrian police will think."

"Why should the police—"

"Viens."

I followed him out of the bathroom, along the corridor, to Manning's study. Manning was lying, face downward, on the tiled floor, like a starfish, his arms and legs spread out.

Julien asked: "Was 'e like this when you saw 'im last?"

"No. He was standing on the veranda watching your launch approach. He asked me to wait in the study. I was hit on the head as I came through the curtain and woke up in the bathroom."

We bent over Manning and rolled him onto his back. He had been shot in the chest at very close range: the mess just beneath his heart looked like a contact wound.

"Manning 'it you," Julien said. "You fell but you were not out. You were able to grab your gun. When 'e leaned over you to 'it you again, you shot 'im. You can plead self-defense."

"There was somebody in here, waiting with a gun in his hand. Waiting for Manning—he wasn't interested in me. When I came through the curtain, he just hit me with the gun. Manning heard me fall, I suppose, and rushed in—straight into the waiting gun barrel. The murderer dragged me, on the rug, into the bathroom and locked me in—a convenient fall guy."

"Show me your gun."

I showed it to him. He held out a hand. I shook my head—and felt a jab of pain.

"What is the matter?" Julien asked.

"I'm in a mistrustful mood. I've had a rough morning."

"Ne fais pas le con." He put his Lüger on a chair. "Open your gun."

I broke the revolver open. He looked closely at the chambers and sniffed them. He frowned, his dark eyes searching my face uneasily.

"Three shots 'ave been fired. All three fairly recently. A gun of this caliber could 'ave killed Manning. The police are going to love it."

I blinked at Julien. "I'm asleep. It must be the knock I got. This is a revolver. The gun I brought with me was an automatic. The killer must have taken it and left me this."

"You'll 'ave fun trying to prove that."

"You can help. I took it from the Rover—from the secret drawer you showed me. You can confirm—"

He started. "You can't tell the police that. You would 'ave me arrested. They would say that Arnold was a spy and me 'is associate."

"So let's forget I had this gun."

I wiped it carefully and put it on the floor beside Manning. Then we rolled Manning back onto his chest and arranged his legs and arms the way they were before we moved him.

Julien picked up the Lüger again. He said: "There is still one thing wrong with your story. Where is the Rover?"

"In the main street of Tartus."

"You 'ad no trouble with it?"

"No. Why?"

"That is what is wrong with your story. If you 'ad really taken the pistol from that secret drawer, the car would 'ave exploded one minute later. If one removes the pistol one must give the clip 'olding it one complete turn. Otherwise, a spring will pull it down, actuating a one-minute fuse which will set off a small explosive charge beside the fuel tank."

"What's the point of that?"

"To destroy the car if it is in danger of falling into the wrong 'ands; or to destroy the wrong 'ands if they find the drawer."

"Why didn't you warn me?"

"I did not imagine that you might want to play cowboy. Anyway, you did not take the pistol, or you would 'ave been—"

"I did take it." My voice trembled. The relief of knowing he had not tried to kill me had snapped the tension in me and left me almost breathless. I sat on the edge of a chair and told him what had happened.

He looked at me wryly. "Now I know why you were so mistrustful over the pistol. You suspected me of arranging the explosion?"

"Of course not. Well, not for more than a few seconds . . ."

He threw his hands up in a mock-theatrical gesture and walked out onto the veranda. I followed him. Broken glass crunched under my feet near the french window.

"Quel ami! To suspect me of . . ." He took two cans of beer out of the refrigerator, punctured them, and handed me one. "I ought not to drink with you, but I need something." We drank from the cans.

I looked at Manning's view. A fat buttock of cloud sat on Mount Lebanon now. The westerly breeze had freshened and sharp-ridged wavelets were chasing each other over the sea.

"Didn't you see Manning from the launch?" I asked.

"I saw someone. When I came 'ere and found nobody, and saw the window-door locked, I was surprised. I knocked and waited and turned to go. Then I saw that briefcase on the floor, and two tankards with beer in them, still cool. I looked through the window, and when my eyes became used to the obscurity in there, I saw a body on the floor. So I broke the window with a tankard and went in." He finished his beer. "What were you doing 'ere?"

"In Tartus I learned that Blane was intending to come here to meet somebody. I decided to come, too. A boatman I hired told me about an Englishman who lived on Ruad. I remembered Arnold's mentioning Manning and thought it might be interesting to meet him. I didn't intend to stay more than a quarter of an hour or so—but, of course, I didn't expect to be bashed on the head. Now, tell me why you're here."

"My agent in Tartus told me something interesting. 'E's my agent for sales of agricultural machines but also 'e informs me about local affairs. I called 'im on the telephone from Latakia, and after talking business I mentioned Blane and asked 'im to keep 'is eyes and ears open. 'E knows everybody. 'E told me that a yacht belonging to a rich Lebanese, Edmond Assury, was anchored off Ruad, and that a Beirut lawyer connected with Assury was in Tartus, apparently waiting to meet someone. I 'ired a car and came to Tartus. My agent told me that Blane 'ad met the Beirut lawyer and then gone in the direction of the port—on foot. There seemed a possibility that Blane was going aboard Assury's yacht and I thought that it might be interesting to discover what was 'appening. Also, I was amused by the thought of surprising you: I guessed you would 'ave followed Blane."

"But why did you come here instead of going to the yacht?"

"I 'ad established a connection between Blane and Assury. I wanted to see if there was a connection between Blane or Assury and Manning. In view of Manning's past links with Arnold's firm, that would open interesting lines of thought. I know Manning slightly—I 'ave met 'im in Beirut—and I assumed that you would be concentrating on the yacht." He looked at his watch. "Let us look around the 'ouse. Then we must decide what to do."

I took Blane's briefcase in with me. While Julien locked the french window, I went over to Manning's desk. From the middle of the desk a small rectangle of blue-and-white card beckoned me. *Superfine Talcum Powder,* it said, in English and Greek; *Made in Cyprus.* I had seen a similar scrap of card on Arnold's desk, after his murder, and another on the desk of a dead Aleppo lawyer.

I told Julien.

He said: "This seems almost to be somebody's *carte de visite.*"

"Or their trademark. In Arnold's bathroom I found the type of carton this was cut from. It contained heroin."

He slapped me on the shoulder. *"Mon vieux,* which would you prefer: the *Légion d'Honneur* or a life subscription to *Le Canard?"*

"Le Canard. Why?"

"I've been looking for a lead like this for eight months. I'm one of those Frenchmen you mentioned who are un'appy about the Marseille drug traffic. I let Arnold persuade me to join the European Service Three because I thought it might give me an opportunity to gather some information about 'eroin. The rest, to me, was of minor importance. I 'elped on an economic inquiry. I 'elped, as you will 'ave guessed, with the security side of what they called Operation Seacity."

"Manning's undercover mineral exports?"

"Manning's and Arnold's. Arnold was in it, too. I 'elped with one or two other matters. But I 'ad no enthusiasm. My 'ope was to uncover a drug traffic. And all the time, per'aps, I was 'elping to cover one! *Les salauds!* I've told you too much—but to 'ell with security! From now on we are looking for cartons and 'eroin. You look in the desk. I will try the bathroom."

The only thing of interest I found in the desk was a .32 automatic. It was loaded and had not been fired recently. I put it in my shoulder holster.

Julien returned from the bathroom and said: "Nothing."

We looked quickly through a small filing cabinet and behind several shelves of books, and went on to Manning's bedroom, spare room, dining room, and kitchen. From the kitchen, stairs led down to a cellar. There, beneath a plastic dust cover, we found a crate containing scores of flattened-out blue-and-white cartons, labeled in English and Greek: *Superfine Talcum Powder, Made in Cyprus.*

"They are new!" Julien exclaimed. I opened one out and tucked in the tabs, top and bottom, to make a little cardboard box that would hold about a quarter of a kilo of talc . . . or heroin. "But where did 'e fill them? Not 'ere. *Quel salaud!*"

"He told me he had a laboratory on the mainland. It belongs to the Tartus mining company he ran. But if you go there, take some law with you."

"We must call in the law now. I've finished covering up for Manning. I don't care if all the Near East knows about 'im."

"Give me ten minutes to get away."

His mouth sagged. "Why? You do not risk being accused. I will say that I found you unconscious."

201

"If they learn I was present when Arnold was shot and when Hamam was poisoned, and if that Aleppo Sûreté officer finds my fingerprints in Mardam's house, they may doubt your word. And I still want to know who's on board that yacht."

"You are taking a risk. All right: I will not mention you. I will dazzle them with talk of drug smuggling. I will say that I 'eard a rumor about Manning in Beirut."

"Leave Arnold out of it. He wasn't in Manning's dope trade."

He shrugged.

"I'm sure of it. The night he was killed he told me he'd learned something startling about Manning from a Lebanese journalist. He wanted me to help him get to the bottom of it. Arnold didn't have time to tell me any details, but the journalist must have stumbled onto this heroin racket."

We covered the crate and went back to the study. I picked up Blane's briefcase.

Julien said: "That is a nice briefcase. I do not remember seeing—"

"It was a present from Blane."

He smiled indulgently and shook his head. "I brought your suitcase from Latakia. It's in my agent's office in Tartus." He told me how to find the office and added: "If you are not in a 'urry to return to Beirut, we will 'ave dinner together in Tartus tonight. There's a good little restaurant by the port. *D'accord?*"

"*D'accord.* Unless I'm invited to dinner aboard the yacht."

"If you are," he said solemnly, "keep a life jacket 'andy."

24

From Manning's house I picked my way northward through a chaos of narrow alleys and passageways. The island seemed deserted, as if all life had been crushed by the hot sun and the fatigue of Ramadan. But as I came at last to the little bay at the northeastern end of the island, a boy emerged from a hut and asked me for baksheesh. A yacht, a gleaming white ninety-footer, swayed drowsily in the cove in front of us.

I gave the boy a few coins and said: "I need a boat."

He waded to a dinghy and rowed it to a stepping-stone landing stage. I got in. He rowed well and we approached the yacht silently. Its name was *My Harem*. Voices met us: a girl's and a man's.

As we drew alongside, the girl was saying: "There is no sense in dramatizing. Let us part friends, and without pretending that we were ever more than casual friends."

"Casual!" the man exclaimed. "That's most cruel of you, Anna."

"Let's be realistic, Denny. You like me as a girlfriend, but you would not really want to marry me, even if your wife agreed to a divorce tomorrow. I might damage your career. The Foreign Office would not like you to have a Polish wife. And you love your career, your work, more than you can love any person."

"How little you know me."

I cleared my throat loudly. Nobody reacted. The glare of the yacht's white hull was dazzling. I took the dark glasses out of my breast pocket.

"So we just walk out of each other's life," Denbor was saying, "and you chuck yourself away on that nitwitted journalist?"

"If you wish to put it like that," Anna said. Both lenses were cracked. I made as if to throw them in the sea, which was clearly the island's rubbish dump, but the boy grabbed them and put them on, grinning. "You have many qualities that I admire, but I never pretended to be in love with you."

"And you think you're in love with—with this . . ."

I cleared my throat again as if I had a fishbone in it. Nobody minded.

"Sometimes I think so. Not always. But—"

"Seriously, Anna, what kind of life could he offer you?"

"I don't know. It's crazy, I agree; but . . . Please go now, Denny. Let's not part bickering. Go and have tea with that nice American economist. The Foreign Office would approve of her."

I shouted: "Press!"

Their heads appeared at an open window. Anna had shed her dark wig and makeup. Her hair was a golden glow again; but her face was solemn. Denbor was frowning.

A fair man wearing a white naval-style cap, a white jacket over a horizontally striped tee-shirt, and white ducks emerged from a stairway near the stern. He nodded as if he recognized me. I gave the boy some money and climbed aboard.

The fair man said: "*Ahlan wa sahlan!* You no remember me?"

I looked hard at the plump face, the hazel eyes, the long lashes. I caught a breath of perfume. "I remember you well, Jemal. *Kif halek?*"*

"*El-hamdulillah!*"†

I shook his clinging hand and asked: "Is Edmond Bey aboard?"

He tossed his head back, clicking his tongue.

Anna came out, followed by Denbor. Jemal turned away and

* How are you?
† God be praised!

told the boy in the boat to wait. Anna said nothing. She stood gripping the rail, staring at me, her hair rippling in the breeze and sunlight—a vision in blue and gold, like the first time I saw her.

Denbor hesitated, then came toward me as if this had been just another social call. He said tightly: "Anna was on the point of throwing me out. And I must get back to Beirut fairly soon. So I hope you won't think me rude if I dash away."

I remembered what Manning had told me about Denbor. It was Denbor who should be handling the Manning problem and coping with the police, not Julien. Denbor would be great at hushing things up.

I said: "I have a message for you. I met Dick Manning on my way here. He'd like you to call on him urgently. He says something important, something very serious has happened."

Denbor blinked. "How extraordinary! How did he know I was here?"

"It's a small island."

"Evidently. Well, I'd better go and see him. Thank you." He turned to Anna. "Goodbye, Anna. God bless you. If ever you change your mind about anything . . . send me word."

She let go of the rail, took both his hands, and kissed him on the cheek. "Goodbye, Denny."

He turned away quickly, stepped down into the little boat, and sat facing the island. With swift clean strokes the boy rowed him away. He didn't look back.

Anna watched in silence. At last she said: "I hate saying goodbye. It's an amputation—of part of one's life." She looked at me again. "It's hot out here. Let's go inside."

She led me past the gleaming clinical galley to a gay lounge with curtains that sang of blue seas, golden islands, white sails, and bright-red fish. There were scarlet divans port and starboard, sea-blue armchairs fore and aft, radio, television, tape recorder, a small bar, a cinnamon carpet, and—in an austere gold frame—a *Cap d'Antibes* by Monet that was probably worth more than the yacht.

She turned just inside the doorway and put her hand on my arm. Her mouth was taut but there was wonderment in her eyes. She said: "Thank you for coming. I don't know how you managed it, but thank you." Then she went to the divan on the side facing the island and knelt on it, watching the dinghy through the open window. I leaned Blane's briefcase against an armchair and sat on the divan beside her, watching the light curl and ripple over her hair. Her pale-blue dress made her eyes seem darker than they were. It was short, sleeveless, and buttoned all the way down the front—the sort of dress that shows you too much of its owner for your peace of mind and generates a terrifying kind of magnetism between your fingers and the buttons.

She swiveled around to face me and sat on her ankles, showing me some exquisite suntan. She said: "You don't like Denny much, do you? He is a much nicer person than his formal public manner might make you think—kind, discreet, dependable . . . And I liked his rectitude—does that sound old-fashioned?—and his consideration and correctness, especially with regard to me. Most of the men you meet in Beirut undress you, mentally, every time you cross a room."

"Speak for yourself. They don't do that to me."

She smiled at last. "You don't undress me; you devour me."

"I used to work for the *Good Food Guide*."

She looked at the carpet. "There is something I must tell you, and I may not have much time. Last night, in the car with Colonel Blane, I realized suddenly that I might leave Syria without seeing you again. I realized, too, how much I wanted to see you—to explain what I was doing, to ask you not to despise me for it. I prayed that we might meet again before the yacht sailed. When I saw you in the launch, coming from Tartus, I was afraid for a moment: I thought you were a hallucination."

"I've been called a lot of things, but never that. How did you see me in the launch?"

"With the binoculars." They were slung over the back of a chair. "I was expecting Blane. It was I who sent the launch for him. When I saw you in it, I guessed that he had been delayed and that you were coming either to bring me a message from him or to tell me what a low-down adventuress I am. When the boatman told me that you had gone first to visit someone else, I judged that nothing extraordinary had happened and that you were not even angry with me. If you had been angry, you would have come straight here."

"You sound disappointed."

She bit her lip. "I should have liked you to be angry on learning that I may marry Blane."

"Would it make any difference if I were?"

"It might. If you really wanted it to." She caught sight of Blane's briefcase, stared at it for a few seconds, and looked at me uneasily. "That looks like Blane's. Did he give it to you to bring? I hope . . ."

"He couldn't get away as soon as he expected; and he was scared Walid might make a grab for the briefcase. So he asked me to bring it to you. I haven't looked, but I gather it contains money."

"It should. One hundred thousand dollars in hundreds, and checks for eighty thousand dollars and two hundred thousand sterling. Twenty thousand dollars are mine immediately, and I shall receive ten thousand sterling if I get him safely to Cyprus. But if I accompany him to Cyprus, he will expect me to marry him. So I could forgo the sterling . . ."

"My paper's thinking of sending me to Cairo. We have a three-room apartment there for whoever is our correspondent. Fourth floor, no elevator, a rowdy café downstairs, anti-foreign demonstrations whenever the government has a scandal to cover up, but lots of sport chasing cockroaches in the kitchen. You'd love it."

"You ought to be a salesman. Why go to Cairo? Why not stay in Cyprus while you write your masterpiece? All journalists wish to become writers, don't they?"

"Bar talk. All clowns want to play Hamlet. Why not just annex Blane's briefcase and raise anchor?"

"That's not my way of doing things—or yours."

"Wow! I'm still a sufficiently junior Levantine to consider that a compliment. I ought to kiss you."

I put a hand on one of her cool smooth knees and our heads drifted together. I pecked at her lips and drew back.

"Blane," I said. "I've got to know about Blane. A girl like you doesn't marry a man she doesn't love—even for a lot more dollars than Blane is offering."

"Please don't say things like that. You'll make me cry for lost illusions; and you'll make me think you don't know much about girls. Love is a luxury not everyone can afford. A girl will do a lot of demeaning things to buy security and a reliable passport if she's more or less stateless in a city like Beirut."

"Your arrangement with Blane is just a business deal?"

"Yes."

"You agreed to help him get his money out of Syria?"

She nodded. "It's as simple as that."

"There's more to it than that, surely. There must be. Why did he pick on you? You've lived in the Levant long enough to know the ropes, but so have a great many other people."

"That is not very flattering."

"Okay—so you have big blue eyes. He was probably captivated by them the moment he first saw you in Salem's office." She frowned. "Salem would be the lawyer who looked after Blane's loot. Because your English is so good, Salem probably asked you to handle Blane's affairs on his behalf." She nodded. "You didn't know Blane had enriched himself smuggling hashish. All you saw was a decent-looking fellow—Salwa told me he could charm women—who was selling some property and might be swindled if someone didn't keep an eye open on his behalf. Blane feared that, too, and realized you'd make a perfect ally."

She said: "You're right—but don't exaggerate the captivation. One reason Blane would like me to marry him is so that I cannot give evidence that might incriminate him if he has embarrassments later with the British authorities."

"But you're not going to marry him."

She whispered: "No."

I took one of her hands and gripped it tight. This wasn't the comeback she was expecting, but I'd shirked telling her long enough. "He's dead. He was shot in Tartus by one of Walid's men. Before he died he asked me to give you his briefcase. Half its contents are for you and half for his daughter."

She dug her nails into my hand and bit her lip. Soon tears came. I let her cry on my shoulder and tried for a minute to ignore what the fragrance and contours of her body were doing to my senses. But only for a minute. Then I put two fingers under her chin and raised it until her lips were level with mine. They parted slightly and the tears stopped. I gaped at her with the feeling that I was onto the biggest discovery since Newton and the apple. What every young man should know: how to avoid getting your neck wet.

Her lips tasted of salt, her tongue of wild strawberries.

At last she said: "You are not very good at breaking news, darling. I'm not a subeditor." She sighed. "Poor Blane. You say he smuggled hashish, but a life is a life: one can't just write it off. Perhaps he would have made amends. We must get the money to his daughter. We are in this together, now, aren't we?"

I heard a launch approaching and looked through the window. There were two men in it, one in uniform. They looked at the yacht, but the launch chugged on past it.

"We must move from here," I said. "When Blane's body is found, the police may get the idea that the murderer escaped by sea. If they trace the boatman who brought me to Ruad, I'll be their top suspect. You'd better tell Jemal to weigh anchor."

"You tell him while I prepare lunch. He dislikes taking orders from me. Tell him to sail for Cyprus, as planned."

"Did he know that Blane was to be the passenger?"

"No; only that it was an Englishman."

I found Jemal and a lean man in a blue sailor suit sitting side by side under an awning at the stern, smoking and sipping coffee. A small radio yapped beside them.

Jemal said: "This is Jamil, the best boat engineer in Lebanon."

I shook hands with Jamil and declined the coffee they offered. "I haven't eaten yet. When will you be ready to set sail?"

"We are ready. Are you the passenger we will take to Cyprus?"

"Yes."

"And the woman?"

"She is coming, too."

Jemal looked doubtful. "Edmond Bey did not tell me that. He said one Englishman. The woman would bring him to us."

"She's going to stay in Cyprus."

He grinned. *"Tayyib.* The time to finish our cigarettes, and we go."

We ate lunch at a hand-carved oak table in a dining room hung with Persian miniatures. We started off with a good sherry, and while we drank it, Anna made an hors d'oeuvre of ham cornets containing salade russe and green olives. The ham and macédoine came out of cans and the mayonnaise from a tube like toothpaste. Preparation time: four minutes. Toss the empty cans and tube out the window. The good life is the simple life.

The refrigerator in the galley contributed a roast duck—stuffed with chestnuts, pine nuts, and sausage meat—and a good Ksara wine. The salad was rather tired; but one must expect to rough it at sea, so we passed uncomplainingly on to the apricot tart and cream.

While Anna was heating the coffee, I asked: "Does one wash the dishes on a yacht or just throw them overboard?"

"The galley cat licks them," she replied, "and there's an electric dishwasher for when she's busy having kittens."

We drank the coffee kneeling side by side on a divan,

watching the Syrian coast recede. Then we put the cups on the floor and lay on the divan. Her tongue still tasted of wild strawberries. She didn't seem to be wearing much under the blue dress. I undid two of its smooth, silvery buttons and tickled her midriff.

"This is a beach dress, really," she said. "I changed just before Denny arrived. I was going for a swim."

My hand explored her warm lithe waist. "You forgot the swimsuit."

"Philistine! It is a rather brief two-piece one. I thought you might like it."

"Thank heaven for Denbor. If he hadn't turned up and you'd displayed yourself in that, the Ruad folk would have lynched you. They're all Moslems—except Manning, of course. Do you know Manning?"

"No. Who is he?"

"An English chemist."

"Why did Denny have to go to his house?"

"They have some business interest in common. Julien's in it, too. They'll be in conference all afternoon—plotting how to make a quick thousand."

"Whereas you can afford to be snooty about such trifles, can't you, darling? You have tens of thousands lying on the floor; and a beautiful blonde to help you count them and serve your lunch."

"Sure. A dead man's thousands, a dead man's blonde, and a dead man's lunch. Nice work, grave-robbing."

She pushed away from me, shocked and angry, and sat up. "Do you have to say things like that?"

"Sorry. It had to come out. I'll feel better for it."

"I shall not."

I sat up, too, and swung my feet to the floor. I said: "I never got top marks for tact. I'd better change the subject. How did Denbor come to be on Ruad?"

She refastened her buttons and ignored me for what seemed a long time. Then, in a strained voice, she said: "He told me

211

that he had discovered that I obtained a Cyprus visa recently. Michaelides, the man who issues them, pulled his leg about it and asked if we were planning to elope. The next day he learned—it is part of his job—of the transfer to Cyprus of a large amount in sterling and dollars for collection by a British subject. The transfer was made by Salem. Denny knew that I was in northern Syria, and that I worked with Salem, and some instinct told him that I might go on to Cyprus. He went down to the harbor in Beirut, to the quay where Edmond Bey normally keeps this yacht, and Jemal told him that he was preparing to leave for Ruad. When Denny saw the yacht sail from Beirut yesterday afternoon, he set off too by car—partly, he said, out of curiosity, partly in the hope of persuading me to stay."

"How did Assury know when to send you the yacht?"

"I telephoned him yesterday from Aleppo."

"After Walid had told you he was all set to rescue Blane? You had a lot of confidence in him."

"You despise me for having dealings with Walid, don't you?"

"No. I didn't dislike Walid. And I knew you were in cahoots with him when he told me what he did when he heard that Blane might be in the House of the Pasha. That had been my theory and I'd mentioned it only to you. So Walid must have heard it from you—which meant you were interested in Blane, perhaps on Assury's behalf. After that, when you tried to discourage me from taking an interest in Blane, you merely spurred me on."

"I deceived you," she said dejectedly. "I had not realized how much you meant to me."

"I'll get over it. I always do. But what about Assury? He's not going to be happy when he learns you've sailed out on him. Aren't you afraid he may send a couple of gorillas after you to teach you he's not to be made a monkey of?"

She shook her head, but her eyes were uneasy.

I asked: "What was in all this for Assury?"

"Not very much. A percentage of the proceeds of the sale of

212

Blane's property; another percentage for getting Blane's Syrian money into dollars and sterling. As you've guessed, Salem looked after Blane's property, but Salem is part of Edmond Bey's empire. Edmond was well disposed toward Blane personally: the English officer-diplomat type, with its rituals and pretensions, amuses him. And he knew something of Blane's past, including the hashish smuggling with Walid. Edmond has a percentage of a lot of things."

"He wanted a percentage of Levant Mining & Chemicals—Arnold Amery's company—didn't he?"

She shrugged. "Perhaps."

"What did he think Arnold was up to?"

She hesitated. But at last she said: "He thought that Amery was exporting something from Syria without a permit—smuggling it out, in other words. An important mineral, perhaps."

"Who gave him that idea?"

"That Lebanese journalist who was killed. His brother-in-law, a clerk working for LMC, had discovered that certain cargoes sent to Cyprus were treated differently from other shipments. Edmond Bey had inquiries made to check the story, but didn't learn much. Then the journalist was murdered."

"Who killed him?"

"My information is that it was a Palestinian group: he had stumbled onto some of their secret operations. But Edmond believed—well, he had had the journalist followed and learned that he had been to see Amery. Two of Edmond's men questioned him and he admitted that he was trying to blackmail Amery. When he was killed Edmond assumed that Amery had hired the killers, and took his death as confirmation that Amery had something to hide."

"But Assury still needed documentary evidence before he could cash in on the journalist's story. He'd sent Hamam to raid Arnold's office and Hamam had brought back junk. So he persuaded someone with a better knowledge of English to help Hamam search Arnold's apartment—someone called Blane. He could threaten Blane with the exposure of his hashish

213

of the guilt—and asking you, in exchange, to take over his burden: his daughter."

She sighed. "What can I say if you turn even Blane's confession against me? Wouldn't it be simpler and more logical to believe Blane?"

"He was dying and desperate. He'd already admitted having hit me on the head with a golf club. He couldn't have both struck me, in the doorway, and shot Arnold from behind the curtain. And Hamam was flat out on the carpet: he couldn't have shot a crap."

"They may have had a third person with them and he hit you."

"Two men, one helping the other, were seen leaving the building and getting into a car. They would be Blane and Hamam. So there were only two of them actually searching the apartment. That makes sense. More than two would get in each other's way; and Assury would want to limit the number of people in the know. But there would be a third person acting as a lookout—sitting in another car, his or her head muffled in a *kufiya*. It would be someone who knew Arnold by sight, someone Blane thought he could trust. But whoever it was had probably learned that Arnold was back in Beirut; and he or she wanted Arnold killed for a reason Blane and Assury didn't know about. Killing him while Blane was in his apartment would be smart since it would oblige Assury to persuade the Sûreté not to investigate the murder too zealously; and it would put Blane on a leash. So when the lookout saw Arnold and me get out of our taxi, she rushed up to the apartment, warned Blane—it was too late to warn Hamam—and hid behind the curtain. After shooting Arnold she dashed down to her car again."

Anna picked up a big white handbag with a long shoulder strap that was leaning against the divan and put a hand in it. Something clicked. My heart kicked me in the chest. I raised my hands, ready to grab her. She came up with a handkerchief the size of a bus ticket.

216

She dabbed her eyes. "I'm willing to make allowances, even now. Amery was your friend. I understand how you feel. As you said, we're . . . we're lonely people . . . and friendship is precious." She looked beyond me and blinked, as if holding back tears, and dabbed again. Then she leaned toward me. "Look in my eyes and tell me whether you believe me. I did not know Amery, except by sight. And I did not kill him."

I looked into her eyes and then at the shining metal button at the top of her dress. It was slightly convex and showed me my own reflection, a window somewhere behind me, and, silhouetted against it, a distorted human figure that was slowly looming larger.

I reached into my jacket and grabbed the automatic in the holster under my left armpit. I looked at her eyes again.

"I believe you, angel," I said.

I pulled the gun out, swiveled around, and fired.

Habib was standing three or four paces behind me, his right hand grasping a wrench. He cried out and clasped his right shoulder. The wrench thudded onto the carpet.

My right forearm was suddenly paralyzed by what felt like a bullet. I dropped the automatic and looked at my arm. Anna had hit me, just above the wrist, with a little gun of her own.

She smiled tautly. "Handbags are a match for shoulder holsters any day." She stood up and kicked my defeated artillery toward Habib. She told him in Arabic: "I will fix your shoulder. Take his gun and cover him with it. But don't shoot him unless he attacks either of us."

Whimpering, Habib picked up the gun with his left hand and glared at me through tears of pain. The gun trembled as he turned it on me.

"Careful, Habib!" Anna said. "There has been enough killing."

"I'm not going to kill him," Habib said. "I'm going to give him something—something he will always remember me by.

I'm going to shoot a bullet up his thigh. It won't kill him. But it will make him scream like—"

"No! This is Edmond Bey's yacht. There must be no trouble on it."

She tugged at the bloodstained right sleeve of his jacket. He bellowed and the gun wavered. More gently, she opened his jacket and shirt and helped him take them off, covering me with her gun while Habib pulled his left arm clear. Then she put her gun on the other divan, drew up a chair for him, and went through a door behind the bar that led to the galley.

She called: "Watch him, Habib!"

He sat down and watched me. His face was sallow and sweaty, but his eyes were clear now and his left hand was steady. He would have loved me to start something.

I said in Arabic: "I'm sorry about this, Habib. But you shouldn't have come up behind me. I thought we were friends."

He swore at me.

I watched the blood trickling down his arm. "Your shoulder looks bad. We must get you to a doctor."

Anna came back, carrying a glass and a first-aid box. "I'll soon clean up your arm. Drink this."

He drank whatever was in the glass.

"Cleaning it isn't enough," I said in my slow Arabic. "The bone will be splintered. He must have it fixed and the bullet removed quickly or he may lose the use of his arm. A shoulder wound is bad."

"I don't need your advice," Anna said.

Habib winced and swore as she mopped up the blood and put a dressing on the wound. I rubbed my forearm, just above the wrist, where Anna had hit it. It was coming to life again and hurting.

"You certainly know where to hit," I said in English.

"I have some knowledge of anatomy," she said primly.

"Your anatomy's wonderful."

"What is he saying?" Habib asked. He didn't understand English.

"I'm worried about your shoulder," I told him. "We must return to land. There's a hospital in Tripoli. If we go all the way to Cyprus before seeing a doctor, your shoulder will be paralyzed."

"He is talking nonsense, trying to confuse us," Anna said. She was bandaging Habib now.

"We won't reach Cyprus until tomorrow morning; and the only good hospital for bone surgery is in Nicosia, a long drive from the coast. Do you know Cyprus roads? The journey will be agonizing for Habib—if he's still conscious."

He flashed Anna an anxious glance.

She said: "He's trying to frighten you. He's hoping—"

A bell rang.

Anna looked at her watch. "That's an alarm clock," she told Habib. "I set it to remind myself that I have a radio call to make. I must send a report to Edmond Bey. Watch this man— but don't listen to him. Remember how cunning the English are."

She pinned his bandage and hurried away. Habib leaned toward me, pointing the gun at my stomach.

"I'd forgotten the radio," I said. "We could call for help for you. There may be a ship nearby with a doctor on board."

He sneered at me. "You think you can scare me?"

I shrugged. "Please yourself. It's your shoulder. You have a lot of faith in Anna. It's quite charming. You're the only Arab I've ever met who takes orders from a woman."

He raised the gun as if to hit me with it, then brought it down quickly and pointed it at me again. "I'll remember you said that. I work for Edmond Bey. He told me to be Anna's bodyguard."

"Edmond Bey didn't tell you to shoot Blane and Manning."

"My God! You are in love with trouble."

I heard Anna talking into the radio. She was speaking English but the pulse and throb of sea and engines muffled her words.

"And you have eloped with trouble, Habib. Do you really know where this woman is taking you? You don't even know who she's working for."

"She works for Edmond Bey, too. She's talking to him now."

Anna seemed to be signing off, but her voice was indistinct. I said: "Edmond Bey doesn't speak Hebrew."

He jerked back in his chair and winced. "My shoulder! You are a devil. She's talking English. She always talks English with Edmond Bey."

"She's talking Hebrew. Now do you understand who she really works for?"

Anna came back into the lounge. She looked tense but reassured. She told Habib: "I've sent a message to Edmond Bey, and I reported that we have an injured man aboard. I didn't mention your name, of course. Beirut will try to contact a ship in these waters with a doctor on board. I'll call back in twenty minutes."

I said: "Have you ever seen a public hanging, Habib? In the center of Damascus or Baghdad? Soldiers, cheering crowds, jeering children, and the condemned man with several bones broken and a placard round his neck saying A TRAITOR TO THE ARABS . . ."

"Devil!" he shouted. "Quiet!"

"Are you mad?" Anna asked me angrily. "Are you trying to provoke him to shoot you?"

"I want him to know the truth about what you've both been doing—and who you're really working for."

"He knows." Her eyes were worried. "We've been on a special mission. It's over now. It was . . . secret—but in a noble cause. Habib knows everything, but he's not going to tell the story to a headline-hungry journalist."

"Don't tell me any secrets, Habib," I said. "Just tell me who you think you're working for."

220

He looked at Anna, frowning.

"All right, Habib. Tell him." She glared at me defiantly.

He said: "Anna is an agent of the American Narcotics Bureau. She has credentials in Arabic and English. I have seen them. She knew me because we both work for Edmond Bey, and she recruited me to help her. She persuaded Edmond Bey to let me be her bodyguard so that we could work together. The bureau sent me a message saying that if this operation was a success I would go to America for training and be made an agent."

"Did the Narcotics Bureau pay you?"

"Yes, of course. They—"

"That's enough!" Anna snapped.

I said: "Your mission was to smash Manning's heroin network by killing him and his kingpins in Aleppo and Beirut?"

Habib's mouth tightened.

I went on: "Manning's raw material, morphine base, would come from Turkey. Several drug routes pass through or near Aleppo—one from the northwest via Meidan Ekbes or Kilis, one from Gaziantep and the north, another from the northeast through Jerablus. The Aleppo lawyer, Mardam, probably organized that side. I can understand your wanting to shoot him—though he saved you the trouble by having a heart attack when you pulled a gun on him. But why did you kill Arnold Amery? Because you'd heard a rumor that his firm was smuggling something out of Syria?"

"It was more than a rumor," Anna said.

"So, as he and Manning were friends and business associates, you assumed Arnold was organizing Manning's drug exports. Near each of your victims you left a piece of blue card cut from the talc cartons in which Manning packed his heroin. Your idea would be to warn other members of the network that they would meet the same fate if they tried to revive it. Fair enough—I'm against the heroin trade, too—but you blundered badly when you killed Arnold. And why shoot Blane?"

"Partly to save you," Habib replied. "You won't believe me,

but it doesn't matter. Anna had said that you must not be harmed. I thought he was going to hurt you badly, maybe kill you. Anyway, he knew too much. And he was a dope smuggler: that was how he got the money to buy property in Syria."

"I was against killing," Anna said, "until I understood what the heroin racketeers are doing. They're like the Nazis— they've declared war on humanity and especially on youth. And, like the Nazis, they must be crushed physically. You can't reason with thugs."

"But be sure you're not crushing innocent bystanders."

She said: "The lives of innocent people were endangered every time the Allies bombed Berlin and Hamburg. But if risks like that had not been taken, the Nazis might still be in power."

"True." I smiled at Habib. "We seem to be in agreement now. So let's lick our wounds, shake hands, and have a coffee."

Habib clicked his tongue. "No. You are like Blane—worse than Blane. You know more about us than he did."

I looked at Anna. Her eyes avoided mine. She said nothing.

"You've helped me twice, Habib. Once in Aleppo; again this morning by the old watchtower. I repay my debts. You can count on me to keep quiet—"

"We can't take the risk. You think we committed two, three—I don't know how many—murders. Wherever we go, one word from you and we'll be arrested."

"Can't the Narcotics Bureau protect you?"

He hesitated. "A little. They might protect whoever killed Manning; but not a person who killed someone innocent by mistake."

I nodded. "I've heard that secret services abandon agents who make mistakes." I looked at Anna again. She stared out to sea. "And you, Habib, are in big trouble. You're not even on the Narcotics Bureau's payroll. The narcs don't hire gunmen to shoot people. They collect evidence, lay it before the local police, and prod and chivy them until they take action. I doubt if the U.S. narcs have ever even heard of Manning. His heroin was going to Cyprus and then, I'd guess, to Israel, not America."

"He's setting a trap for you, Habib," Anna said. "He's trying to entangle you in lies."

It was hard work in Arabic, but I plodded on. "The Israelis are worried about a flood of cheap dope that, they say, an Arab extremist organization is funneling into the country. Their anti-narcotics people wouldn't get any help from the Lebanese or Syrian police, so they'd have to use their own agents to track Manning down. And then, so as not to expose their agents, they'd hire a local gunman to shoot Manning and his friends. They'd want a good reliable gunman, of course, not some hopped-up punk, so the agent who hired him would show him forged Narcotics Bureau credentials and even give him a hope of a job in the bureau if—"

"*Ya, Anna!*" he cried. His face was livid. His left hand was trembling again. "He's a devil, I know; but what he says is true. I've felt there was something—"

"You're tired, Habib." She smiled uneasily. Carefully I slid my wristwatch over my hand and clenched a fist around it. The steel wristband fitted snugly over my fingers like a knuckle-duster. "You're wounded," Anna was saying, "and you've lost blood. Can't you understand that he's lying to you all the time in order to worry and weaken you?"

He said softly: "Until a minute ago, Anna, I was in love with you. I'm glad of that. Only a man who has loved knows how to hate."

He pointed the gun at her.

I had been poised to spring for the last five minutes, but I muffed it. My right arm had a crick where Anna had hit it, and I put my foot on a coffee cup. I landed short of Habib's gun-holding left hand and stood for a moment, half crouched, in front of him. We eyed each other like matador and bull. The automatic wavered and I hit him in the face with my armored left fist. Snarling, his eyes watering, he swung the gun around, toward me. With my right hand, I chopped at the critical point just above his left wrist. The blow hurt my forearm as much as his, but he lost his grip on the gun. It slipped, and he grabbed and caught it by the barrel. I kicked it out of his hand and clipped him on the side of the jaw with my knuckle-duster. He blinked and looked unhappy. What he now needed was a poke in the face from my right fist, but he had a hard face and I had a rubbery right wrist. I picked up the wrench he had dropped, and as he sprang from his chair in pursuit of the gun, I tapped him on the side of the head, just behind the ear. Not too hard—you have to be careful when you hit someone on the head with a wrench—but hard enough. He dropped.

Anna had been standing only a few feet away, wide-eyed and rigid, watching the semifinal to see whom her match would be against. Now she backed toward the divan, where her little gun lay. I strode after her, raising the wrench.

"Don't touch it, Anna. Don't force me to break your arm."

"Would you?"

"Rather than let you shoot me."

"I would never shoot you."

"Not while you could pay Habib to do it, anyway."

"Please believe me, darling."

"Belief is something I'm all out of."

"Take the gun."

I picked it up, sniffed it, and threw it out a window. I retrieved the automatic and put it in my shoulder holster. I searched Habib, found the gun he had taken from me in Manning's house, and threw that out. Then I sat on the divan, checked that there was no more hardware in Anna's handbag, and tried to breathe normally again. I felt like the morning after my ninetieth birthday.

In a pocket of the huge handbag I found a cigarette lighter. But there were no cigarettes and I'd never seen Anna smoking. I squeezed the trigger and the lighter snapped open. There was no flame, but something beeped in one of Habib's pockets. I squeezed twice. Two beeps.

"So that was how you called him."

"He was my bodyguard. Our arrangement was that if I called him he should come at once, prepared for the worst. That was why he was carrying the wrench. I would not have let him hurt you. I wanted to give you a shock, to slow you down and give myself time to think. You were driving me desperate with your silly accusations. But I didn't want you harmed: Habib told you that himself."

I put the beeper back in her bag and searched Habib for his receiver. It, too, looked like a lighter. I put it in my pocket and sat down again.

"Will you call me sometime?"

She nodded. Then, cautiously, she came over and sat beside me. I kept a firm grip on the wrench.

I said: "It's time we sorted out this mess. And it's your turn to talk."

"The only serious mess is the . . . misunderstanding between us. The rest is secondary. We'll soon tidy it up." She put her forehead against my cheek.

I clung to my wrench. "You've a lot of explaining to do."

"So have you. Why did you turn Habib against me? He might have hurt me."

"He might have hurt my head. Your friends seem to have a thing about my head."

"Perhaps they're jealous, darling. It's stuffed with nonsense, but it's a reasonably decorative head." She kissed my cheek lightly and forced herself to laugh. "Edmond Bey was rather taken with it."

"Did he know about the heroin racket?"

"No. But can't we forget that now?" She nestled against me.

I transferred the wrench to my left hand and put my right arm around her. "I suppose you persuaded him to approach me and—"

225

"He didn't need much persuading. I wondered if you knew anything about the heroin. But Edmond was worried by your tracing Hamam and wanted to know what Hamam had told you. An obvious way of satisfying our curiosity was to make an alliance with you."

She kissed me again, and this time I kissed her back. Blane's ghost was exorcised now. I let go of the wrench and soon had both arms around her. We keeled over onto the divan, away from the wrench—I had that much mind left, though it was evaporating fast—and she arranged herself hospitably.

I undid her top button—the helpful shiny button that had shown me Habib. I undid another and the bra of her blue bikini surged into view like a blossoming orchid. Another button and another. My hand explored her waist again and the contour of her hips, and just as I was losing all sense of reality Habib moaned and I wondered if the object of the entertainment was to give him time to recover his wits and test some more steel on my skull.

I rolled away from her a little and said, for no reason at all: *"Shall I compare thee to a summer's day?"* My mind added: *"Thou art more lovely but more treacherous."*

She smiled. *"Sometime too hot the eye of heaven shines, and often is his gold complexion dimmed.* My father taught me that. He used to say there must be good in the Russians because they're fond of Shakespeare."

"Are you working for the Russians?"

"No. I know too much about them to do that. Did you mean what you said about our . . . our climbing rainbows together?"

"Yes; but that was a long time ago. I'd be scared now."

"Scared?"

"Scared that halfway up the first rainbow we'd meet a man with a wrench."

"The wrench business is over. You know that, really, don't you? And you know that you love me."

"I'm crazy about you. The stress is on *crazy.*"

Habib groaned.

226

I sat up and looked at him. "Habib's going to be back in the wrench business soon if we don't tie him up."

She said: "I gave him a double dose of tranquillizer."

I turned to her. She still lay there, delight made flesh, wanting me now—unless she was a superb actress . . .

I sighed. They only issue you with one head. I reached for the wrench on the divan and walked over to Habib. He was twitching a little, but still unconscious. It was a stage Anna's friends had to go through, like measles or acne.

I poked around the galley in search of cord or wire, but all I found was kitchen string. I went back to the lounge. Anna was kneeling on the divan watching the sea slide past. The lounge looked gaudy now. Only Anna's subtle luminosity saved it from tawdriness. And she, I told myself sourly, was just possibly the most meretricious object in it. Or, another voice inside me whispered, the bravest as well as the most beautiful girl I'd ever met. I shook my head. Wondering about Anna was turning me into a debating society.

She smiled teasingly. "Can't you relax? You have the only gun."

She's playing for time, ape, said the anti-Anna speaker. Can't you see that? Force the pace. Put some pressure on.

I stood by Habib again and said: "I think we ought to take him to the hospital in Tripoli."

"He is not seriously hurt."

"He needs a doctor. And then he ought to have a chat with the Sûreté."

She sprang off the divan. "Are you mad? He'll drag me into it. And Edmond Bey. And your friend Amery. Amery is dead; but do you want the whole world to know that he was associated with Manning in a dope racket?"

"Arnold wasn't in a—"

"You believe he was innocent, but who else will? The newspapers would make a sensation of Habib's story."

Go on. Step it up. "There'll be a sensation building up already over the murder of Blane and Manning. And someone's going to remember that this yacht was off Ruad when they were shot. The crew are going to be asked who came aboard. The sooner Habib's delivered to the Sûreté, the sooner we'll be in the clear."

Her contempt was withering. "Throw Habib to the wolves, then! My name will be dragged through the mud, and so will Amery's. And Blane's daughter won't get her money. But why should you care? The important thing is that you won't be inconvenienced, and that you'll have a nice comfortable smug self-satisfied feeling. How badly I misjudged you!"

I turned toward the door.

She called after me: "Ray!" It was the first time I'd heard her pronounce my name. I stopped. "Don't go! Don't wreck everything! We had a glimpse of happiness together. Doesn't that mean anything to you?"

The debate was still raging in my head. I had to find a quiet corner, away from Anna's magic, and let them argue it out. And I needed some rope.

I walked on to the door and opened it. It was one of the hardest things I ever did.

26

My head was throbbing where two acquaintances had tried their strength on it. My right forearm ached. Sun flashes on the sea hurt my eyes. Jemal's radio was singing like Donald Duck's nephews. Amidships, Habib was cursing me. A yacht is a great place for togetherness.

Habib was locked in a cabin. Jemal and another man had helped me get him there. I told them he had tried to kill me and hijack the yacht. He came to life while we were tying him up and, taking a biased view of the situation, kicked Jemal in the stomach.

"I never liked him," Jemal said, when he got his wind back. "He's never been aboard before. Was the woman helping him?"

"Probably. But I'm not sure. I need to think about it."

So I sat under the awning near the stern, sorting out thoughts as tangled and slippery as spaghetti. Jemal was on the sundeck above the lounge doing something with an instrument that measured crosswinds. He told one of the crew to bring me an arak.

When the arak arrived, I added water from an earthenware pot and sipped it. It was tepid and tasted like kerosene. This wasn't my day.

Out of an eye-corner I saw Jemal crouch suddenly. I watched him. He was peering alertly over the side as if he had a line down there and a big fish was following it. I saw him pick up a fishing rod and lower it over the edge of the sundeck. He waited a moment, then yelled savagely and lashed at something.

There was a cry followed by a splash. I leaped to my feet. "The woman!" Jemal shouted.

A blue crater was already swallowing her up. It flashed away, its rim closing in on her with an eruption of foam. I threw a life preserver after it, tore off my jacket and shoulder holster, and unzipped my pants. Jemal was imploring me to stay put and shouting to Jamil to stop the yacht. I dived overboard.

The sea was cool blue silence and invigoration. Life was suddenly clear and simple. My mind called to Anna as I swam, telling her I was coming and would find her and take her to Cyprus and never walk out on her again. I knew I would find her. It couldn't happen any other way.

I swam to where I thought she ought to be and discovered I hadn't yet reached the life preserver. The yacht had been moving fast. When I got to the life preserver I rested on it and called her name. There was nothing to guide me. Even the yacht's wake had vanished. Every wave looked like every other wave. I swam on, pushing the life preserver, and called again.

I sensed the throb of a powerful engine behind me and looked back, expecting to see the yacht returning. In its place I saw a submarine. The yacht was streaking away at top speed.

Submarines are designed for dwarfs. This one was British-built and had an inch more headroom than most, but I still banged my head on a girder within a minute of being hauled aboard. The girder had something chalked on it in Hebrew.

I asked the sailor accompanying me: "Does that mean 'Mind your head'?"

He grinned. "Yes. You speak Hebrew?"

"Only when I bang my head."

He led me to a cramped cabin where a keen-eyed young man wearing a white shirt and white slacks stood beside a tiny desk wrestling with the Sunday *Times*. A handsome black-and-white Persian cat watched him dubiously.

"Lieutenant Moss," the sailor told me.

The floor was damp in patches. Someone else with wet feet had been in there recently.

"Welcome aboard," the lieutenant said. We shook hands. "We don't see many hitchhikers on this run."

"I didn't expect to get a lift so soon. I was looking for a friend—a girl who fell or jumped from a yacht I was on. I was worried about her until I saw your submarine. Then I guessed you might have picked her up."

"You know what sailors are."

"Can you tell me if she's safe?" I began shivering.

"What's her name?"

"Anna."

"Yes, she's all right. A little damp, but she won't have shrunk. May I know your name?"

"Alan. Ray Alan." My teeth were chattering now.

He turned to my escort. "Dov, take Mr. Alan for a mug of tea and a hot shower. When he's comfortable, bring him back here."

As I left the cabin, something buzzed. Then the light wavered and the floor seemed to tilt. I clung to the door, wondering whether I was fainting or Moss was pulling something.

"Don't worry," he said. "It's our private earthquake. We're submerging."

A cook gave me scalding dark tea laced with Rishon brandy. Then I had a scalding dark shower in a cubicle the size of a broom closet for thin brooms. I dried myself with a towel Dov had given me and found dry underwear and a pair of white shorts hanging on a hook. Hoping they weren't the captain's, I put them on. Dov reappeared, gave me a pair of tight sneakers, and ushered me back to Moss's cubbyhole.

Anna was there, dressed like Moss, except that her shirt and slacks bulged mutinously in defiance of naval constraints. Her hair had vanished beneath a lofty turban. Moss was sitting behind the desk and she beside it, looking at a big charcoal sketch of a Syrian schooner. She glanced at me coldly.

I smiled weakly. "Hello. It's nice to see you again. You had me worried."

She didn't smile. "I had myself worried. I was beginning to wonder if I'd get here alive."

"Sit down, Mr. Alan," Moss said. There was just room for the three of us and the cat, so long as the cat didn't have kittens. Moss rolled up the sketch and opened a notebook. He asked Anna: "Did you suffer any ill treatment?"

"Not until I was diving overboard," she said. "Then someone hit me with a stick. It was agony."

I said: "That was Jemal with a fishing rod."

Moss made a note.

Anna asked me: "Did you put him up to it?"

"Of course not. I didn't know you were planning to go for a swim."

"I wouldn't have been able to swim if he'd landed a proper blow. Luckily my handbag took most of it." I suppose I blinked. "It was strapped on my back," she explained. "It's a special waterproof bag intended for emergencies."

Moss spoke again, like a war-crimes prosecutor. "Were you subjected to threats or moral pressure?"

"I spent an anxious five minutes while Mr. Alan incited Habib to turn against me."

"I had to throw him off balance somehow, so that I could jump him. He was pointing a gun at me. He would have loved to shoot me and toss me overboard. He knew I could tie him to the murder of Blane and Manning, and he may have been jealous: he said he was in love with you."

Moss raised half an eyebrow and scribbled something.

Anna said quickly: "Mr. Alan guessed that I was working for Israel and told Habib. I was scared he might tell the yacht crew. He also said that he wanted to return to land and hand Habib to the Sûreté. I'd have been arrested, too, of course."

"I was only trying to scare you and provoke you to do or say something that would tell me who you were really working for."

232

"You certainly succeeded."

"If I hadn't put pressure on, you'd have stayed on the yacht and gone to Cyprus?"

"Of course. There's a man from the . . . from our anti-narcotics service waiting in Famagusta now to debrief me."

Moss and I looked at each other as blankly as we could; but there was a twinkle in his eyes and I suppose there was one in mine. Anna glared at me.

I said: "But you knew before leaving Ruad that this submarine would be within call if an emergency developed?"

Moss put in: "You mustn't ask questions like that, Mr. Alan. You'll have us all keelhauled or spliced at the main brace or something."

"May I just think aloud, then? I suppose you were reporting to the sub when you made that radio call you set the alarm for? Then, while Jemal and I were locking Habib up, you got on the radio again and called for help. You must be a pretty important agent for your service to have a submarine standing by for you."

Anna glanced at Moss. "It's the operation that was important, not me. I'm not a professional agent. It just happens that my mother was Jewish and I dislike the traditional division of labor whereby the Jews produce twice as much literature, music, and science as most other peoples and receive three times as many knocks. And I loathe dope traffickers. So when I was approached by—"

Moss cleared his throat. "I'm only a simple jack-tar. I don't know all the ins and outs of this affair. But I imagine there are—well—security aspects: things that ought not to be published just yet. Don't think me discourteous, Mr. Alan, but I would like to get my report—and Anna's—back to Jerusalem before our cabinet ministers read the story in the papers. I've no doubt you'd be willing to promise not to publish anything for a week or two . . ."

"Of course."

He smiled. "But what journalist worth his salt ever let a

promise come between himself and a good story? Journalists are, after all, human."

"That's big of you."

Anna said: "I have heard other theories. But I'm not worried about Mr. Alan. If he blows us, we blow him. He works for the SIS."

Moss's face registered exaggerated surprise, then relief. "Not the old Antelligence Serveece? How jolly! That entitles you to honorary membership in the mess and a ration of tobacco, whiskey, and invisible ink. Why didn't you drop a hint?"

"I couldn't. It's not true."

Anna laughed. "I asked headquarters for guidance on Mr. Alan when he appeared on the scene. Their reply said that he used to work for a supposedly Arab radio station run by the SIS. He joined the station full of patriotic and social-democratic zeal, eager to demonstrate the enlightenment of post-imperialist Britain. He was no doubt shocked to find that his job entailed political mischief-making, supporting military dictatorships and feudal deadbeats, and sniping at reform movements."

"Poor boy," Moss murmured. "One's heart bleeds."

"One day," Anna continued, "a directive came from London ordering the station to pander less to the extreme Arab nationalists and to urge the Arabs to be realistic about Israel. He wrote a commentary in accordance with the new line and— after approval by the station's director, also an Englishman and an SIS appointee—it was broadcast. But most of the station's Arab employees didn't know who their real bosses were, and the extremists among them protested and demanded a head. The director, whose main interests were alcohol and the wife of one of his engineers, asked Mr. Alan to address a meeting of the senior Arab staff and explain the commentary as a personal initiative—in short, to cover up for the service. Naïvely, Mr. Alan did as he was asked; and of course, the Arab ultras were convinced that he was a traitor to the cause they thought the radio station was serving. So, a little later, he left the station, no doubt for another glorious assignment. Do you get extra pay in the SIS if you're a masochist?"

"No," I said; "but promotion comes faster. Most of your story is accurate. Who were the sources? I left the SIS in due course, so I'm not going to run telling tales."

"One was an Arab—"

Moss groaned loudly. "Did you ever read George Crabbe? Late eighteenth century, and quite modern. For example, he wrote:

> *"Secrets with girls, like loaded guns with boys,*
> *Are never valued till they make a noise."*

"An Arab who has since been murdered," Anna said. "He was one of those who saw your director and was assured that your head would fall. Actually, he was a moderate, working with Israel."

"So you left the SIS," Moss said. "Who d'you work for now?"

"*Outlook*," Anna answered for me. "Behind which—surprise!—there is a distinct whiff of SIS."

"If there were," I said, "I wouldn't be on the payroll. You don't know how vindictive the SIS can be. After I resigned, it wouldn't even give me the National Insurance cards I needed to get a job in England. I had a hard time in the breadline of freelance journalism until a friend helped me land a job with *Outlook*."

The telephone rang. Moss answered it, listened respectfully, and told us: "The captain. He wants to know how you both are and hopes you'll have dinner with him."

We said we were fine and would be delighted.

Moss translated that into Hebrew and hung up.

I asked him: "What are your plans for me?"

"Don't put it like that," he said. "We haven't made anyone walk the plank for over a year. Well, we thought you might like to see Haifa. Lovely town, built on a hillside around a bay. In

Haifa you could rest from journalistic labors for a few days while we get our reports in. And two or three people there may want to talk to you: colleagues of Anna's—and, no doubt, her husband."

He caught me. I glanced in dismay at Anna. He grinned.

"Sea urchin!" she cried, punching his arm.

"If she's got one, I was about to add. You intellectuals are too quick on the uptake for us horny-handed sailors. Which reminds me"—he looked at his watch—"that I have some horny-handed duties to perform. Will you excuse me?"

When he had gone, Anna leaned forward and looked at me intently. "Now I think of it, why were you in the water?"

"I was looking for you."

"To drag me back to the yacht and lock me up for the Sûreté?"

"No. To take you to Cyprus or wherever else you might want to go rainbow hunting. It may sound improbable, but it's true."

"You'd have taken me to Cyprus even though you thought I killed Amery?"

"I thought that for a while after talking to Blane. When I got to know you better, I realized that shooting someone from behind a curtain wasn't your style. But I wanted to ruffle you, to make you tell me what you knew. It was Habib who shot Arnold, wasn't it?"

"Yes; but I sent Habib up to the apartment. He was the driver of the car Blane and Hamam used. I was sitting in another car. When I recognized Amery I signaled Habib—with the beeper—and he went upstairs, immobilizing the lift to delay you. He warned Blane and hid behind the curtain. Blane knew that Habib was under my orders and considered me partly responsible for Amery's death. That, no doubt, is why he talked the way he did when he was dying. I've got the money and checks he left, by the way. I packed them in my bag before I dived overboard. I'll see that his daughter is provided for. I have her address."

"How did you get to the submarine so quickly? I didn't see you in the sea at all."

"I was picked up by a minnow. It's a sort of baby submarine piloted by one man, with space and air supply for a passenger. It can't go deep but it's useful for . . ." She looked at the door. "Oh! Don't repeat that or Moss will have a fit. Now will you believe that I'm not a professional agent? I'm glad the operation is over and I can soon forget about lies, deception, security . . . I'm sorry about Amery, but the case against him was strong. Manning's heroin was smuggled to Israel via Cyprus, in talcum-powder cartons hidden in slabs of cattle cake shipped by Amery's firm."

"Where was the cattle cake made?"

"In a Levant Mining & Chemicals factory in Tartus."

"Manning could have organized that without Arnold knowing."

"Perhaps. But we had no reason to assume that Amery was not involved. We knew why Manning had gone into the heroin business. He and Amery had been exporting a rare mineral illegally. An Arab extremist group got to know about it and blackmailed LMC. The company had to pay: the alternative would have been a ruinous scandal. Then the Arabs tightened the screw and forced Manning to collaborate with them in what they called Operation Frost, the smuggling of large quantities of heroin to Israel. We learned of this partly through Palestinian informants. In normal circumstances, Manning and Amery would have been taken to court and given a fair trial. But we were working in countries hostile to Israel: we had to be police, jury, judge, and executioner. Can you understand that?"

"Yes."

"Go and see a treatment center for heroin addicts one day. When you've seen children who are hooked—kids who will rob their parents in order to give money to the pushers—you'll understand the need for what we did."

I said: "There's something I don't understand about Habib.

237

Was it he who left the strip of blue-and-white card on Arnold's desk?"

"Yes."

"Why did he tape Blane's visiting card to it?"

She gasped. "Lord! Did he?"

"That's why I became interested in Blane. I'm not Sherlock Holmes."

"Perhaps he hoped that the heroin traffickers would liquidate Blane. He didn't like Blane; and he was a little jealous, I imagine. I had to beam a flash of charm Habib's way, from time to time, to keep him cooperative, and I suppose he overestimated its significance—and resented my occasional meetings with Blane. Oh, the fool! That would explain why the Palestinians interrogated Blane in Aleppo. Blane told me about that in the car. He didn't know about the heroin traffic and was baffled when they accused him of being a British intelligence officer helping the Jews track down a dope ring. After he had convinced them that this was not so, they told him that they had learned from a contact in the Lebanese Sûreté that he might be connected with the killing of Arnold Amery. I suppose that the Sûreté found the card but could not decide what to make of it."

Moss came back. "I've good news for you, Mr. Alan," he said. "You're going to breathe real air again soon. We've arranged for a helicopter to collect you at twenty-two fifteen. It will take you to a fast and reasonably waterproof corvette that will be in Haifa tomorrow morning. And the service is free. How's that for the welfare state? The chopper's crew are on a training exercise, actually, and will be delighted to have a real body to play with. But for you, they'd be hoisting a sack of oranges."

I asked: "Is Anna coming, too?"

"No. She has some homework to do—a long essay to write. And it's so unusual for us to have a woman aboard that we're going to make the most of her. You know: blarney her into darning socks and baking jam tarts. Also, confidentially, the op isn't completely over. We're keeping an eye on a schooner we think is carrying a load of heroin for transfer at sea to a cargo boat."

"I'd like to know more about that. Can't I stay with you?"

"My dear chap, we'd love to have you. But there's not so much as a vacant mousehole aboard. And we can't give you a hammock on the deck—you'd get wet."

Anna asked: "Where are you going to put me?"

"The captain is giving you his cabin and taking my bunk; and I'm moving to the bunk of a fellow on night duty who reeks of black tobacco. So those tarts had better be good."

After that, Anna and I were never alone. We had dinner with the captain, Moss, and two other officers, and then listened to two of Moss's records: an old pop song about a yellow submarine and a Mozart symphony. The submarine surfaced at five past ten, and while Moss was talking on the telephone, I asked Anna if she expected to arrive in Haifa while I was there.

She said: "No."

"Can you give me an address in Israel where I can—"

"No. I don't know what I'm going to do now. My life was in Beirut, but . . ."

"Will you look me up in Cyprus—or at least write?"

She nodded. I told her my address.

Moss hung up and said: "We've got the chopper on our screen."

He led me to the bottom of the conning tower, where I banged my head again. Two men strapped a harness on me.

I shook hands with the captain, Moss, the harness men, and finally Anna. She held my hand tightly and I kissed her on the cheek. She looked pale—or maybe it was the subdued yellow light.

They didn't talk the helicopter down or flash any lights. It was all done by electronics. A buzzer told us the chopper was precisely overhead. When it was at the right height, the guidance panel beeped. Two rings behind my shoulders were

239

clipped to a double thread of gossamer hanging out of the sky.

"I hope you've warned them I'm not a sack of oranges," I said, but nobody heard.

Dimly I saw Anna again—pallid, holding a handkerchief to her face as if already mourning me. Even Moss looked funereal. The captain saluted gravely.

The conning-tower officer pressed a switch and the beep changed its frequency. The submarine and dark sea sank beneath me as if someone had pulled the plug out of the Mediterranean. Fifty seconds later I was aboard the helicopter and only darkness lay below us.

The officer I shared a cabin with on the corvette spoke good English with a vaguely Dutch accent. He gave me a beer and asked after Moss. They had been on a course together.

"Moss used to be in the English Navy," he said. "He's got that English vay of talking—you know? But, deep down, he's serious; and quite an artist. Vonderful deft, especially vith chalk and charcoal. Ships and gulls and girls. Especially girls. And he knows how to pick them . . . I still remember a girl I saw him vith in Cyprus last year. A blonde, she vas, but not the flashy kind. Cool and cultured. So beautiful you'd hardly believe it possible. Not a day passes but I think of her—and I'm married vith two children."

"What was her name?"

His eyebrows wrinkled. "I can see her now. If I vas Moss I could draw her for you. He introduced us and she smiled at me. But her name? Sally or Penny or . . ." He shrugged.

"Was it Anna?"

"Maybe; but I think it vas a more English name. Vy do you ask? You think you know her?"

27

Two Israeli Intelligence officers met the corvette at Haifa, bought me a few clothes and a toothbrush, and accommodated me in the house of an elderly widow who spoke only Hebrew and Lithuanian. They urged me not to write anything about Operation Frost lest I give its organizers clues to the identities of the agents and informants who had frustrated it. If I let them down, they said, they would feel obliged to publish something about the clandestine mineral exports of Levant Mining & Chemicals. I told them I didn't mind about LMC but I didn't want Arnold's memory bespattered. I agreed to sit on the story until I could consult O'Neill.

It was a week before I got back to Cyprus. (The British consul in Haifa took a poor view of drunken journalists who fell off yachts and had to be rescued by foreign corvettes—that was the story I told him, forgetting to mention the submarine and helicopter—and he took his time about issuing me a new passport.) O'Neill grumbled about my "Goodtime-Charleying around the Mediterranean," but he gave me a brandy sour and only docked two days off my leave allocation. He was mollified when London thanked him for the information I had brought back about Operation Frost and the Israelis' counteraction. London added, though, that the journalistic version of my report, which I wrote for *Outlook,* would not be published unless the Arabs or Israelis broke silence: it might harm Levant Mining & Chemicals and arouse Arab suspicion of other British firms in the region.

The Israelis said nothing, and the Syrian and Lebanese authorities had their own reasons for not publicizing Operation Frost. A Syrian paper reported that Manning had shot Blane in a drunken quarrel and then committed suicide with the same gun.

The following November, yielding to political pressure, Levant Mining & Chemicals sold all its interests in Syria relatively cheaply to a Lebano-Syrian consortium of which Edmond Assury was a member. Pete McGlint was appointed chief engineer of the new company. A month later he married Salwa, who now (I have been told) speaks English with a unique Syrian-Scots accent.

After three weeks without news from Anna, I wrote to her, care of the Israeli anti-narcotics service. I received no reply.

In the early autumn I spent a few days' leave in Israel and called on the Israeli narcs. They told me Anna was not on their books and they had no idea where she might be. I walked seven or eight times along the tree-shaded street outside the headquarters of Mossad, the Israeli Intelligence service I thought most likely to employ Anna, and watched its office staff coming and going; but I saw neither Anna nor the two officers who had met me in Haifa.

I put ads in the personal columns of the *Jerusalem Post* and the *International Herald Tribune.* I received replies from an Italian schoolmistress named Anna, an American woman named Anna who had lost her husband in the dimly lit rooftop bar of the Athens Hilton, a private detective, two matrimonial agencies, and eleven assorted clowns, comedians, cranks, and creeps. I kept the two letters signed Anna. They were the only ones I ever received.